BLOOD GAMES

Chicago Heat Series — Book Two

Suite 300 - 990 Fort St
Victoria, BC, Canada, V8V 3K2
www.friesenpress.com

First Edition — 2015

ISBN
978-1-4602-6405-8 (Hardcover)
978-1-4602-6406-5 (Paperback)
978-1-4602-6407-2 (eBook)

1. Fiction, Mystery & Detective

Distributed to the trade by The Ingram Book Company

First and foremost I want to thank Shelley McLellan, my research assistant, medical advisor, travel companion, and best friend since the '70's. These novels are all the better for her help and inspiration.

I must also thank Sylvia Holcomb, whose line-by-line editing of *Ashes*, taught me so much. As a brilliant writer herself, Sylvia inspired me and taught me "less is best."

Thank you to the many friends that have read the book and gave corrections and suggestions, especially a young man named Nicholas Clarke, who also gave me a great many ideas and reminded me that it is old fashioned to use a fax machine. I am, after all, still on the slow road to technology.

I would also like to say working with the editor at Friesen Press has been above and beyond what I thought was possible. She is brilliant and I look forward to a long relationship.

With a special thanks and many hugs to my mother and father who read and loved every story, but more so to my dad, Wayne Stanyer, who found more commas and small word problems even after many edits.

Thank you to my husband Dennis Gramatovich, the inspiration for my novels. And to my daughters, Natasha and Katrina, their help throughout the writing of these novels has kept me on my toes

BLOOD GAMES

Chapter One

The Chicago wind howled from the north, slapping the snow across the open field like a hockey player shooting at the net in a frantic last attempt to score. Detective Dennis Kortovich parked his Crown Victoria away from the howling northern wind, knowing that the vehicle would only give small amount of cover, his partner Chuck O'Brian followed close behind. A police cruiser had already arrived at the scene and two young officers were questioning a young man in a bright, red hooded jacket whom seemed to be freezing in the sub-zero weather. The January day was as cold as a whore's heart and twice as deadly.

"Put that young man in the back of the cruiser," yelled Kortovich shaking his head at the need to state the obvious. "He will be able to answer the questions if he's not half frozen." The wind whipped around Dennis's ankles trying to find entry into his warm boots as he moved around to the south side of the cruiser, to get a full view of the crime scene, knowing what he would find. The markers made it easy to focus on the bodies of a young couple. The male lay a few feet from the female, his body facing toward the young woman. His arms were stretched toward his partner in what looked like an effort to embrace her. She had her arms crossed on her chest, seemingly rejecting him even in death. It was obvious that the killer had posed the couple after he dumped the bodies in the open field.

Dennis looked away from the the frozen couple as a gust of cold wind whistled past his head. The sky was heavy with bleak possibilities of even colder weather coming in from the north. The wind made it difficult to breath; it assaulted Dennis's lungs with its frozen fingers, its grip tight and unforgiving. God, how he hated these freezing Chicago winters, he thought as he moved closer to view the scene. As he stood over the bodies, Dennis began pulling off his winter gloves replacing them with latex. If he had to touch anything he wouldn't compromise the evidence. He pulled his fur-lined hood over his head and bent down over the closest body, the young women. Chuck stood off to the side, his notepad in hand.

"How many of these bodies do we have to find before we get a break?" Dennis said under his breath…his rhetorical question unanswered by Chuck.

Dennis examined the body of the women while Chuck made notes in the familiar black pad. The victim was young, under thirty and pretty, her long dark hair partially covering her face. Her makeup, once artfully done, was now a death mask of horror. The winter coat she wore was twisted around her body and looked as though someone had put it on after her death; the buttons were not in their correct holes, she wore a skirt, her legs a bluish hue from a night spent in the cold field of snow and ice. Her wrists had been bound and taped, marks could be seen where Jack Frost had laid his icy fingers. Her ankles also bore the marks of her assault.

"There's something different about this one." Dennis turned to his partner as he looked up from the victim. "What do you make of it?

Dennis could see a twinge of irritation cross his partner's face when he asked the question. It wasn't that Chuck didn't know the answer. Chuck was a great cop with well-honed observation skills, but Dennis knew Chuck wished he would just tell him what he saw and let him off the hook. Dennis liked to irritate his partner with his Holmes and Watson antics. It made solving crimes a lot more fun when his good-natured partner was put on the spot. Besides, it was a good way of thinking out loud and getting on the same page.... not that they disagreed very often.

"As usual, this isn't where the murders took place; this is just where he dumped the bodies. There are no fluids around the bodies; everything is clean as a whistle." Chuck offered.

"But the victim didn't put the coat on herself. It had to have been put on by her killer. It's the same MO as the others, but it's the first time the killer has gotten sloppy." Chuck said.

"If we're lucky he might be getting cocky. If so, mistakes will be made. There always are, eventually. Maybe we'll get a break and find a print on one of the buttons." Chuck continued fingering the misbuttoned coat as he looked up at Dennis, the look of irritation still evident on his chubby face.

Dennis nodded in agreement. So far the killer hadn't made a mistake. However, whoever was doing these crimes was upping the pace.

He had dumped more bodies over the past few weeks than he had since the crime spree had begun in early November. Once again the victim's throat had been cut clean by a very sharp object. As often as Dennis had seen death over the last twenty years, this was still a chilling and uncomfortable sight. He had seen death in all of its insidious shapes and forms, but death was something that he had yet to make peace with. These murders, however, were more depraved than the other homicides that Dennis and Chuck had dealt with in the past. Most of them had been gang and drug-related, with the occasional spouse offing his or her partner.

"Look at her ankles. It's the same. You can tell by the severe indentations that she was hung by her ankles before she was killed. The killer once again slowly slit her throat and drained all of the blood while she was still alive, bleeding her like cattle at the slaughterhouse." Dennis said, trying to keep the disgust from his voice. "It's the same guy and we still haven't enough clues to even come close to one suspect."

Dennis reached over to the side of her coat to see if anything would be in her pockets that might help with the investigation. He pulled out several gum wrappers and a ticket stub from a movie house. The date on the ticket said it was from the night before. They would follow up later in the day to see if anyone at the theatre remembered the couple. A boot lay a few feet from the body; it had fallen off when the killer had dumped her. Her handbag lay at her side. Dennis touched her frozen face; her skin almost seemed translucent, pale beyond imagination. He didn't have to look at the girl's companion to know that he too had come to the same grisly end.

"The crime scene investigative team will be here in seconds, they can go over the scene for fibers and prints. All of the other victims have been clean. No evidence that can be traced back to a suspect. With all of our victims from out of town, it's impossible to link them to one common suspect." Dennis said as he walked over to the male. "They look like they had one hell of a scare just before their deaths. I'm sure they were aware of what was happening just before he slit their throat. It would be terrifying to come to this kind of an end."

Dennis bent over the young man and continued his summation. "I'm going to assume that they were drugged just before their deaths. The Coroner said all of the other victims but the first had a dose of Halcyon just prior to their murders. It would have knocked them out long enough for our killer to tie them up without a struggle. Still, by the time he slit their throats they would have been fully aware of what was happening to them." Dennis said as he pulled the coat away from the young man's chest, reaching inside the jacket pocket and pulling out a small bag of soil.

"It's the same killer alright. He's left his calling card once again. What the hell is he trying to say by planting a bag of soil on each of the victims? This is one crazy bastard and we had better catch him soon."

Dennis placed the bag of soil back in the victim's pocket while a team of investigators descended on the area. He stood and greeted the senior member of the team, a woman by the name of Corrine Wilson.

Corrine Wilson was a tall brunette with more curves than the Indianapolis 500. She was close to the same age as Dennis, fifty, but her face was holding up well. Strong features with smooth, wrinkle-free skin, made her a shoo-in for a Dove commercial. Corrine's bulky winter coat covered up her abundant chest, an embarrassing distraction for Dennis. He always found himself straining to keep his eyes on her big, baby blues.

"What have you got, Kortovich?" Corrine asked as she drew closer to the scene.

"The same thing we've had for the past four months." Dennis said as he moved closer to Chuck, allowing Corrine to view the two victims now behind them. "More bodies than clues."

Corrine gave Chuck a friendly nod and turned her attention to Dennis. "I'm about as sick of this as you are. It's starting to get embarrassing. My reputation is on the line."

As Corrine moved closer to the male victim the rest of the team started to take photos and scour the scene. She had been recently promoted to head investigator of her forensic team. A bright, energetic woman who had been divorced for almost a year, she had earned Dennis's respect. At almost six feet, Corrine could look a man straight in the eye. It made her seem powerful and in charge of her environment, qualities Dennis liked in a woman. He respected her ability and had enjoyed working with her in the past. But recently he felt as if her energy had taken a strange shift toward him and he still hadn't been able to figure out what was different.

"Look, let me do my job" Corrine said in a serious tone. "It's still early and I'm sure I can get the basics done by the end of the day. If you're up to it, we can meet for a drink and go over the preliminary report. Shelley will need a little more time with the bodies, but I'm sure I can get you photo, print, and fiber reports as well as a toxic screen. The soil analysis shouldn't take all day either. We have all of our resources working 24/7 on this one."

Dennis knew she was right and that everything the department had was being diverted to the multiple bodies that had been turning up all over Chicago.

"Call me as soon as you have anything and I'll see where I'm at then. If we have time for a drink, fine. If not, just scan and send me the report on my cell," Dennis said, noting a strange look crossing his partner's face.

Dennis would have liked to ask Chuck what the look was about, but members of Corrine's team were moving in on the male victim's body. It was time to leave and let the investigators do their stuff. Besides, Dennis was beginning to feel a little warm, even on this subzero winter day. As they moved away from the scene he turned around to take one last look. Corrine was still standing where he had left her, the look on her face intent. Dennis thought maybe a drink would be nice, after all this case had turned into a nightmare and Veronica, his wife, was used to his working around the clock.

Dennis Kortovich was one of Chicago's finest detectives. With nearly twenty years of service, his reputation for detail had made him irreplaceable when securing a crime scene. It was his ability to see the micro and macro of his surroundings that always amazed his partners. Dennis's notes were meticulous and he seldom forgot a conversation or an interrogation. He could recall hundreds of small details of cases long past; an ability many of his colleagues envied. His first partner, now deceased, used to say, "When in doubt, ask Kortovich," knowing that Dennis always had the details and answers well at hand. But lately Dennis felt he was slipping, and this case was beginning to make him doubt his long years of service and the department's recognition for his ability to solve crimes on good solid work and observation skills. He had never been one to hang his reputation on hunches. Give him the facts and only the facts.

"Well what do you think?" Chuck's brisk baritone voice broke into Dennis's thoughts. The strange look was still on Chuck's face.

Dennis decided to ignore the look. Chuck had been his partner for the past four years and Dennis knew when to just leave things alone. Chuck's square face and evenly placed features gave him a familiar look. Everyone felt as if they had met him before, and they had, in the imaginations of their youth. His thick hair hung over bushy brows and full rosy cheeks. Dennis figured that one day, twenty years from now, when Chuck hit seventy, he would look into a mirror and realize that if he ever grew a beard he could pass for Santa Claus. His stocky build and barrel chest would eventually succumb to gravity and become a paunch…definitely a Santa Claus stand-in. Dennis smiled. He really liked the guy. So far Chuck was his favorite partner and as such was a frequent guest at his home. Veronica, Dennis's wife of thirty years also had a soft spot for his chubby partner and thought it was a shame that he was single. An extra plate was always set at the table every second Sunday, with an occasional female guest thrown in for flavor. Veronica hated to see a sweet guy like Chuck stay single and she was determined to find him a good wife.

"What I think," responded a frustrated Dennis, "is

that there are too many bloody bodies and it's starting to make me sick." He removed his latex glove as they moved closer to the Crown Vic.

"These are numbers ten and eleven and the hell of it is, we still haven't a bloody clue what the hell is happening. Who? Why? Not even one suspect. It's now the end of January and we're almost four months into the investigation and we have nothing. Meanwhile the Superintendent and Mayor are having a shit fit." He pulled the front door of the Vic open.

Once in the car Dennis pulled his warm gloves back over his frozen hands before pulling away from the scene of the crime. His foot pushed all the way down on the gas causing the car to veer to the right, just missing the police cruiser with the witness. He had instructed the officers to bring the young man to the station. He and Chuck would need to handle the questioning of the witness themselves. Every 'T' would have to be crossed and every 'I' dotted. There was so much heat coming from above they couldn't afford to miss a beat. Dennis knew that his usual calm was beginning to crumble. This string of murders was just about the biggest and toughest case the city of Chicago had ever seen.

A full task force had been pulled together after the fourth and fifth bodies had been found and it was Dennis who had been put in charge. Six more bodies later and he was feeling like a man going down for the third count in a boxing match, KO'd out cold for the match.

"So, what is it we know so far?" Dennis asked Chuck, wanting a brief overview of all that had happened to date.

"The first body was discovered alone, the next two were a young couple found together; then numbers four and five, all within two weeks. Except for the first, all of the victims were found in pairs." Chuck flipped through his notes as he spoke. "It was early November when the first body was discovered and it is now three-quarters of the way through February and these two make the body-count eleven." He summed up what they both already knew. "Our killer is getting bolder. He is killing at a faster pace. If he starts to get too cocky he may start making mistakes. Till then we are out in the cold." Chuck looked over at Dennis as he continued. "These latest two victims must be a yuppie couple. Their clothes were expensive; matching mohair dress coats. Rolex watches. The male's suit was Armani. Other than the gash across his throat, I'd say he was a real catch." Chuck rolled his eyes and then gave a small laugh. "Neither of them could be over twenty-five and from the looks of them I'd say they have a hefty paycheck in order to afford to dress the way they do. We'll get more information once we run a check on their ID and prints. Before the end of the day we should know everything we can about them."

He slapped his notepad shut.

"There hasn't been any forensic evidence to go on so far and the killer seems to have knowledge of police procedures and the way we collect evidence. He or she has the ability to cut a clean, precise incision along the neck much like a butcher or meat cutter. It's hard to say what kind of knife made these incisions. We'll have to get the M.E. to nail that down. All of our victims are thirty or under. There is also a small bag of soil planted on all of the bodies except the first, an indication that the first killing was done on an impulse while the others may have been planned. All of the victims had the same contents in their stomachs and were killed within hours of their last meal." Chuck finished, without the benefit of his notes. "What do you think the odds are that eleven people could be killed and all of them would have the exact same meal?"

Dennis answered, "Slim, to none. But it seems each of them ate their last meal in their hotel room. I think the killer may have sent them the meal. Either they knew the killer, or it was an unexpected gift from a stranger. Never look a gift horse in the mouth. I'm sure the victims ate the meals without ever knowing who sent them." Dennis said, hoped he was right.

"If not, the killer would have to have stalked his victims first, something that seems unlikely given that they were from out of town. What information did you get from the ID in the women's purse?" he asked, knowing Chuck had made note of the information once the forensic team had arrived and processed the purse.

"As usual they're from out of town, New York. Pretty soon word is going to get out and no one will want to come to Chicago." Chuck answered, referring to his black note pad. "It seems someone wants to kill off our tourists and it isn't good for business when they turn up dead. This makes visiting Florida look like a walk in the park."

Chuck was referring to the carjacking's and murders that had plagued Florida years before. "Whatever else we find out will have to wait until the reports are finished. I'm sure Corrine will be only too happy to fill you in on the rest of the details over a drink." Chuck's tone was solicitous, and the strange look returned to his face.

"What the hell do you mean by that?" Dennis asked, irritated by Chuck's tone.

"I think Corrine is going above and beyond the call of duty, doing a rush on the reports and then inviting you for a drink. Why not just email you? Information and refreshments seems a little out of line don't you think?"

"What's out of line? I think this case has us all spooked. Corrine has been the lead CSI in this investigation from the beginning, and I for one am grateful that she has been willing to pull all the stops and get us the information back so quickly." Dennis said defensively.

"Why not invite me? I'm on this case as well. Let me assure you she wanted only you to meet her for a drink, and I'm not invited." Chuck's tone was sharp. "Hasn't she noticed you are married?"

Dennis knew Chuck was usually easygoing and enjoyed a good laugh at anything that would embarrass Dennis, but the usual humor was lacking in his tone at the moment. He would likely get a laugh out of seeing Dennis uncomfortable at the thought of having a drink with a female colleague if it meant more than a work-related event, especially a female with all of the abundant talent displayed by Corrine. But Dennis was sure it was just the heat of this case that had prompted Corrine to extend the unusual invitation.

"Look, I'm sure she assumed you would come too. After- all, we're a team. Why would she want to meet me alone? Corrine knows I'm married and she has never been anything but professional."

"Corrine has been divorced for more than a year, maybe she's lonely?"

"There are lots of single guys. I'm not the one to fill her lonely nights." Dennis gripped the steering wheel tightly as he maneuvered through the traffic.

"Are you sure of that?" Chuck asked, letting his question hang in the air.

Dennis tried to ignore his partner, saying nothing in response to Chuck's question. Things had been different lately. He had been wondering about life and hadn't come up with any answer that seemed to make sense of how he was feeling. There was a restlessness that seemed to gnaw away at the pit of his stomach. He loved his wife and he loved his job. But somehow each day seemed a little flat. Maybe it was that each day offered more questions than answers; questions about his personal life and these crazy murders. Dennis had chalked his restlessness up to his inability to solve this case, but the fact was, he had been feeling this way for a long time.

Veronica, his wife was going through her own change of life and the hot-flashes were fierce. It had forced her to move into the spare room, an arrangement that didn't make intimacy easy. And as usual, she was as busy as ever. It seemed as if they had been drifting apart for the past few years. Often weeks went by before they connected. Dennis knew he loved his wife, but he seemed to be asking the same question lately. "*Was this all there is?*" He hadn't been able to find the answer.

"Look. Right now all I need is a hot cup of coffee and not a hard time from an old fart like you. I'm not about to get into trouble with Corrine or anyone else on the force," Dennis said bluntly, hoping Chuck believed him.

With an obvious end to the conversation Dennis continued to wind through the late morning traffic, his thoughts turning back to the case where it seemed safe. Thoughts of murder were a lot more comfortable than thinking of having a drink with a woman like Corrine.

He pushed all thoughts of Corrine from his mind.

This case was getting to everyone and was now considered a "heater," a high-profile case. The press was all over it like gaudy makeup on a prepubescent teen, and the more murder victims that turned up the more the press piled it on. By now it would take a carving knife to peel away the muck and get to a likely suspect. Because the blood had been drained from the victims, every cult and weirdo in the city was on the carpet for the murders. But so far nothing had turned up. The teams of investigators that Dennis had assembled to help solve the case were frantically chasing down every lead they could find. Chicago was a city with a raw underside and if you wanted to find something that suited your fancy, from the weird to the wacky, you didn't have to go far to find it. And these killings qualified as just about the most bizarre case Dennis and Chuck had ever seen.

After the first three bodies had been found it hadn't taken them long to interrogate many of the satanic cults and devil worshipers in the hope of finding a clue, but so far nothing. Now even the sickest members of the night world of Chicago were trying to give the police a helping hand. The murders were bad for business and many of the after-hours clubs had seen a decline in attendance because of the series of shocking murders.

The detectives would have to dig a little deeper into the habits of the many night crawlers of Chicago to find out what the blood might be used for. And it was tough enough dealing with the usual thugs, let alone a killer that left his victims looking like they had made a trip to a slaughterhouse.

* * * *

It was now bright out; the clouds had disappeared as the sun shot gold beams of light on the frozen marshmallow world. Chuck could see Dennis's reflection in the window as they passed a large grove of trees. At fifty, Dennis was what one would consider good-looking. Not great, just good; square jaw, straight nose, gray eyes, and medium-brown hair. Once it all came together he had an "All American" look. His moustache covered a generous mouth and the dimples in his cheeks gave him a slightly Magnum look. His broad shoulders tapered into a narrow waist. Chuck envied him the fact that he never worried about his weight, a worry that was a fact of life for Chuck. One of the most outstanding characteristics about Dennis was how neat he always was.

As detectives, they wore their own style of clothing, but Dennis seemed to put it together better than anyone else. You couldn't really say he was a fashion plate but he usually wore his clothes in a way that made everyone else look slightly out of date. Maybe it was because Veronica bought his clothes for him, but he managed to make them look better than anyone else. He could have been the CEO of a Fortune 500 company. He looked as if he came from money, but Chuck knew that was far from the truth. He just had good taste and a way of standing out in a crowd. Maybe that was why Corrine had asked Dennis out for a drink. Chuck had a bad feeling about the invitation.

Lately Chuck had seen his partner fall into a slight case of the blues. It had started right after Dennis's fiftieth birthday. Veronica had thrown him a small birthday party with close friends and family. She was usually a great hostess but for some reason the party seemed half done, something out of line for the normally vivacious Veronica. And neither Dennis nor Veronica seemed to connect. This wasn't the usual loving couple that Chuck had learned to envy. It would be terrible if Dennis were to go through a mid-life crisis. Chuck decided he would have to keep an eye on his friend and make sure he didn't do anything stupid at this point in his life.

Chapter Two

Once back at the station, Dennis and Chuck headed for the conference room that had been converted into "Command Central" for the special task force assembled for the multiple murder cases. As he swung open the double oak doors he was still impressed with the expensive furnishings in the room, a result of a recent renovation. The Superintendent had been able to twist a few arms to get the quality furniture, not the usual cheap crap they were used to. The twenty-foot, solid, mahogany table was rounded at either end, giving the illusion that the table was oval. Thick padded leather chairs were drawn neatly up to the edge of the table on either side, sixteen in all. Currently there were only eleven detectives assigned to the case, but more could be added as needed and often the superintendent or the mayor would sit in on updates. Along the south wall, directly to the left, was a huge, whiteboard. Written on it in big letters were all the key words that tied this baffling case together. In bold capital letters it read.

TIME OF DEATH: Three to six hours

from last meal.

All of the victims ate the same meal; steak, potatoes, salad, along with dessert and wine.

METHOD OF DEATH; Hung by heels, throat slit, and blood drained from body, traces of Halcion in stomach.

PROFILE OF VICTIMS; All under the age of thirty. Victims were all from out of town, upper to middle income, victims single, white female. Other victims white couples.

OTHER COMMON DENOMINATORS FOR ALL VICTIMS; None apparent so far, may have been random. Killer probable didn't know his victims.

B.O.S.F.O.B.

This cryptic code of initials stood for "bag of soil found on bodies." It had been agreed upon that no one would speak about the soil beyond the confines of their team for fear of alerting the press to this valuable clue. Pictures of the victims lined the west wall. All had been taken post mortem. Pictures of pale human beings, all with a different story, except that they had all died the same way. But why? Dennis hoped that he and Chuck would find the answers to that question soon. If not, the body count would continue to climb. Together they sat saying nothing, both going over their notes, and typing their reports.

Chuck was ready to go home to bed with his report finished. He liked to keep the Paper-work simple, while Dennis was methodical and meticulous. They had been going around the clock and Chuck could sleep on a dime. Dennis on the other hand, couldn't.

"Go home, Chuck. There's nothing to do until today's report is in. I'll head home in a few hours as soon as I'm done here."

"You don't have to ask twice. Call me when you hear something. I'm bushed and can hardly think straight. Half of my nights are spent seeing our victims swinging from their heels with blood gushing from their throats. I sleep better in the day-time." Chuck stood facing Dennis with a great-full look on his face.

"Let the ghouls deal with these murders…for now I am just going to forget about what kind of sick mind comes up with these kinds of killings." Chuck grabbed his heavy winter coat as he went out the door.

Dennis was just about to call it a day and head home when two veteran police officers who had been assigned to the case, came into the boardroom. Both were in an animated discussion about another case they were currently working on. They followed calls generated by the press and Dennis's case was their primary investigation while the death of socialite Margaret Mendoza, the wife of lawyer Jackson Mendoza, was their secondary case. At the moment, most of the team that had been assigned to Dennis's and Chuck's unit had several unsolved homicides to deal with, in addition to the blood-les murders.

Margaret had been the daughter of Robert Grey, one of the richest men in Chicago and the great-grandson of one of the original Rubber-Barons. Grandfather Grey held the majority of control over the rubber industry, which sold raw material to the tire-manufacturing companies, making him a very rich man and one of influence. It was a shock to Robert Grey when his only daughter fell in love with the handsome Jackson Mendoza. Mendoza was a third generation Colombian, who was rumored to have ties with the illegal world of the South American drug lord, General Zaragoza.

"I don't care what you say, Mrs. Mendoza would never have gone to a Doctor like Clarence Fielding. She's probably never even been on the south side of Chicago, let alone gone to the office of that loser." Detective Ferine O' Donnell sounded miffed and irritated at his partner who seemed unwilling to let the discussion end.

"Who knows what these rich socialites will do? And maybe it's like the husband said, she didn't want her friends to know that she wasn't feeling well. I can understand that, especially in a town that "tells it all" like Chicago." Detective Patrick Getty shot back.

"Hey, don't you two have something better to do than argue about how the rich get medical treatment?"

Dennis welcomed the diversion. He liked the two officers, who were ten years his junior. Ferine was well over thirty-something, a man whose rugged good looks had most of the female staff drooling over the "Irish Stud" every time they came into contact with him. He was often the butt of many of the other officer's clumsy sex jokes. After all, Ferine was single and could get laid anytime he wanted. At this point he seemed less interested than he had in the past, the result of a crush on one of the new female rookies, who so far wouldn't give him the time of day.

On the other hand, Patrick was bald and a little paunchy, the result of a fifteen-year marriage to a wife who was rumored to be a gourmet cook. From the look of Patrick's protruding belly, Dennis felt the rumor must be true. Patrick was a man of great humor and joy, which made him one of the most popular lunch and after hours' drinking partners on the force.

"Hey Dennis, I didn't see you there. I was so busy trying to knock some sense into this lazy partner of mine." Ferine turned toward Patrick and gave his shoulder a friendly punch.

"What are you still doing here? It's OK to go home once in a while you know!" Patrick said as he approached Dennis.

"I was just heading out when you two loudmouths came busting in. By the way, what's the argument about?" Dennis always found it amusing to watch the volatile but loving chemistry of the two partners.

"It's the other case we're working on, the death of Margaret Mendoza. Her husband told us that she had two doctors." Ferine said. "One has been the family doctor for over thirty years, and apparently she had a second doctor for the past three months, a Doctor Fielding. But he's a scummy low life who has a major drinking and drug problem and I can't see why a classy dame like Mrs. Mendoza would even go to the south side, let alone to the grubby office of this slime-ball. It just doesn't make any sense, yet he was the last one to treat her before she died. My partner here is giving me a rough time and says no one can figure out the rich." Ferine gave Patrick an evil look. "Besides, I think there is something fishy going on and that there is a tie-in on our case to the new Doctor. It all just seems too convenient to have a new doctor and then die so suddenly."

"Hey I didn't say I didn't agree with you, I just said who can figure out the rich? They sometimes do some strange things. If this Mrs. Mendoza were anything like what her friends say she was, I agree. She wouldn't go to a man like Dr. Fielding," Patrick said, a wicked smile crossing his face.

"I think I'll let you two boys figure things out on the Mendoza case without me, I have enough on my own plate. By the way, how are things going on the phone leads?" Dennis hoped something would have turned up that could lead them to even one suspect.

"Every nutcase in Chicago has us running all over the place. Half of the weirdoes and mental patients have confessed to being the killer, especially the ones with a fascination for blood. They think that they have killed the victims by sucking them dry, but none of them know about the soil so we've had to rule them all out."

Ferine aimed his answer directly at Dennis and turned his back on his partner letting him know he didn't appreciate the rough time he had been given in regards to the Mendoza case.

The team of men and women that were assisting Dennis and Chuck with the case had been sworn to keep the information about the soil secret. It was only spoken of among the members. It would be the one thing that would help them to determine if they had the real killer. Often in high profile cases they would have some unbalanced "son of a bitch" confess to the crime. It was only the small details that could confirm or deny if the confessor were the real killer. The press was often their biggest problem. If too many details were published about the case then the fake killer could fool the cops into thinking they had the murderer, often letting the real killer go free until he struck again. The result was egg on the face of the investigating officers. The details about the bags of soil were guarded within the investigation circle, and Dennis hoped it would stay that way.

"All right, I have a bunch of other leads on my desk. If you two could follow up on as many as you can, we may turn something up."

"No problem. We have a lot of delay time on the Mendoza case. We have to get access to the medical records of Mrs. Mendoza and the husband is giving us a rough time. We talked to the original doctor and you could tell he wanted to co-operate with us but he can't unless we get a warrant to get access to his records. We're just waiting to get a request petition before a judge." Ferine said.

"Well good luck but I'm out of here. I'll see you both at tomorrow's briefing. Let's hope someone on the team turns something up."

Dennis grabbed his coat and left the two detectives still bantering different theories back and forth. They were a great team and debate seemed to be what held their ten-year partnership together.

Just as he was getting into his car, Dennis received a call from Corrine. The report was finished and she wanted to go over it with him. Veronica was still working in her salon. She had been a stylist for over thirty years and after selling her chain of salons, she went home based and had never been happier. After all, getting to work was just a step away. As Dennis looked at his watch he figured he had time to meet Corrine at O'Malley's for a drink and still be back for supper with Veronica and his daughters, Natasha and Katrina.

As he walked into the bar shortly afterwards, he noticed several other officers that he knew. It seemed strange to be meeting Corrine at a bar. It was the first time he had ever met with her outside of the crime lab. Still, it was work and this case was different from all of the others. Everyone needed more than a drink to get through this one. What harm could a few drinks be?

He knew even as he asked the question of himself that he was wading ankle deep in water that was rising fast, and he was without a lifeboat. Was something about to bite his ass? He hoped not. How far he was willing to go before he was pulled under, he still didn't know. Hell, he loved his wife. Corrine was a colleague and he had no idea what she was thinking. All she wanted to do was to give him some information on the case. He was making stuff up in his mind that he had no business thinking.

Dennis shook off his thoughts and tried to stay aloof. He had a job to do and it was up to him to stay focused. As he walked up to the table where Corrine was sitting he noticed that under her bulky coat she was wearing a low cut, V-necked top that exposed her abundant chest. The smile that greeted him showed even, white teeth. Dennis hoped he could stay focused. He cursed himself. What was happening? He'd never felt so disconnected.

"What's up Corrine?" he asked, as he sat down beside her.

"I wish I could tell you we'd found something different with these two but I can't. It's all pretty much the same, still no prints or fibers. I even got the toxicology reports back from the lab, Halcion, like all the others." Corrine said, looking sheepish. "I shouldn't have called you out again tonight. I could have e-mailed you the reports but this case has me so frustrated I needed a drink and I hate to drink alone." Her voice was soft and apologetic.

Dennis knew how Corrine felt. This case was taking its toll on him as well. Something was different about how he felt about life, his family, and his job. He didn't want to look deeper. It would mean making the right decision and right now Dennis didn't feel like doing the right thing.

Chapter Three

The Beef Chateau, one of Chicago's best-known steakhouses, was full of the sounds of success that Saturday night, back in early in November. Waiters and waitresses were dressed in the famous red and gold of the Beefeaters "sixteenth century" guard regalia, setting the tone for an authentic glimpse of the past. The eager young men and women hustled to pick up their plates loaded with hot potatoes, salad, mushrooms, and thick slabs of homemade bread smothered in sweet garlic butter before they went to the hot sizzling grill to pick up their individual cuts of beef, cooked to perfection.

Back in the kitchen, plates clattered and silver resonated with a low-pitched "clickity-clack" the way heavy cutlery sounds when it's dumped onto cooling trays fresh out of the dishwasher. The atmosphere was upbeat and it had a rhythm and pace that was unique.

The owners of The Beef Chateau, Lexy and Bara, had found a surefire recipe for success. Everything was brought in fresh daily except the beef. It was cut and hung in a huge meat locker at the back of the twelve-thousand-square foot restaurant for a full twenty-eight days of perfect aging. Lexy Cohen and his wife Bara had lived for well over six decades and for the past four decades they had been in the food business. It was only in the last ten years that they had come up with the idea behind the Beef Chateau. The problem with most eateries was that the menu had too many items and spoilage often ate away at profits. The Beef Chateau featured steak, steak, and more steak. Everything was streamlined. Their prep chefs had it down to a science.

Every night things came together like a symphony; the movement, flow and rhythm reaching the crescendo around nine when the crowd in the restaurant would hit its peak. The number of out of town guests often rivaled the locals and The Beef Chateau had developed an international reputation. Grade A Prime Cut Beef, the finest in the world. Grain fed, it had a taste like no other and the citizens of Chicago loved it. But it was the secret to the special steak marinades prepared by Brian Bentham, Lexy and Bara's head chef that soon became the most sought-after secret recipe in town, a combination few could beat.

The Beef Chateau was located off of Columbus Drive not far from the Goodman Memorial Theater. This had added greatly to their success with a large before and after theatre crowd.

Lexy looked around the dining room at the end of the evening, feeling a great deal of pride. November was a great month for business and Christmas parties were well underway. The red and gold décor seemed to be especially appropriate at this time of year. As a good Jew his reason for loving Christmas was mainly due to the increased dining traffic, but some of the sounds and spirit of the season flowed over into his joyful soul, making him especially happy during the holiday season, and Hanukah was also his favorite time of year.

Everything about Lexy made you think of circles. His round head, big blue eyes, round button nose, full round lips, round, wire rim spectacles, round shoulders, round tummy sitting atop short legs, all seemed to add to the impression of a big butterball. Even his temperament was well rounded; always smiling, he seemed to enjoy each minute with just the right level of excitement or dismay.

Most of the staff had been with Lexy from the beginning. And a few had even followed him from his very first venture forty years ago, a specialty deli. His maître d' André was now a little over sixty and Lexy remembered how young Andre' had been back then and still seemed to be now. As he looked back at the many years he had been with Andre, Lexy hoped his old friend would be with him for many more. One more look around. As usual everything seemed perfect. Chairs were tucked neatly under the tables, white tablecloths, stemware, and coffee cups were all in their correct places. Everything was clean, crisp, and perfect.... lights out.

Next Lexy waddled over to the kitchen where his wife Bara was overseeing the final cleanup. Once through the double swinging doors his eyes were assaulted by the bright lights of the kitchen. All was quiet. The dishes were piled neatly in stacks of forty covering a long row directly behind the huge cold and hot preparation area. Stainless steel gleamed from everywhere. When the late morning shift arrived they would fill the huge cooler trays with fresh crisp lettuce, shredded carrots, green onions, bacon bits, and all of the other items needed to compliment the steaks, a huge row of deep silver trays ran along the south wall near the prep station, full of over a dozen different dressings, all prepared fresh by the head chef, Brian Bentham. His secret recipes like the steak marinades were unique to the Beef Château.

"There you are my little dumpling." Lexy cooed to his wife Bara as she rounded the corner coming from the office at the rear of the restaurant.

"Where did you think I would be? Ten years and every night you find me here checking out the kitchen to make sure everything is clean and put away. Did you lock up the cash and transfer the debits to the bank?" Bara launched back at Lexy.

"What else? Every night I do the same thing and every night we have this same conversation."

With that final remark, Lexy kissed Bara on the forehead, slipped his arm through hers and headed for their coats at the back of the restaurant. Like clockwork it was always the same. As they donned coats and gloves, Brian Bentham, the head chef, emerged from the meat-cutting room.

Lexy knew Brian still had another two or three hours of work left. He had to finish cutting hundreds of steaks, some with the automated processor and dozens more by hand. Only the very best cuts were good enough for their clientele. Next Brian would prepare his special marinade. Most of the steaks would soak in his "world famous" secret recipe for up to forty-eight hours while they were kept in a special cooler to ensure their freshness. Brian was the best chef the couple had ever had and they loved him like a son. It had taken several years for him to open up to the couple and even after a decade of service he still seemed guarded. But Lexy and Bara knew Brian was giving them all that he had of himself and they were grateful for him being a part of their business.

"Another great night," Brian said as he came forward to give his customary hug to Bara. "Drive carefully and I'll see you both tomorrow."

Brian stepped back and gave Bara a loving look. "Are you losing weight? I swear you're at least ten pounds lighter than yesterday. If you don't watch it you'll melt away to nothing and then how much fun will it be to pull your chest into mine." Brian winked down at Bara.

Hugging Bara was great. At only five–foot-two inches, she was almost as wide as she was tall. With a full, forty-eight inch chest that felt like a soft cushion when you pulled her into your arms for a hug, she was a wonderful pillow of a woman. Bara still had a beautiful face surrounded by thick, naturally curly hair, cut above her shoulder and dyed dark. Her hair framed her clear, creamy-white skin and made her bright blue eyes seem almost bottomless when her intense gaze fell upon you. Dark brows and long lashes made it difficult to pull your eyes away. Forty years ago she had been a real beauty but now she was a bit of a dumpling, although still beautiful.

"Oh you bad boy, you tease me so!" Bara laughed, beaming like a schoolgirl as she looked up into Brian's handsome face.

"You know I love you and think you're the most beautiful woman in the world and I never want you to change. So just stay the same so I can get the best hugs in the world." Brian squeezed a little harder making Bara give out a happy, girlish squeal.

This completed a customary ritual that ended

every night just before midnight for the past ten years. Although the evening's custom remained the same, tonight would be an exception. Tonight Brian's life would change forever.

Once Lexy and Bara left through the back door, Brian pulled the deadbolt back, locking the door securely. He usually set all the alarms but tonight was different; he would have to open the front door for a special guest set to arrive very soon, so the alarm would be of no use. As Brian walked through the kitchen toward the double swinging doors, his thoughts turned to the past, to a day he would never forget, a week before his ninth birthday. It was the day his life had been altered forever, the day his mother left. At least that's what his dad had told him but Brian never believed it. Not then, not later, and not now. He knew with all the heart and might a little boy could possess that his mother would never have left without him. He knew his father's secret and he had learned to hate himself for keeping it. He'd never told anyone back then and now it was too late.

Brian still remembered that night so long ago when the police showed up to investigate. His dad had made his story sound pretty truthful. She had run off with her hairdresser, Max Fielding, who was also missing, along with all of the stuff in the hairdresser's apartment, but the lady who owned the salon where Max worked said he would never leave without his paycheck, so she had called the police. She told them he had been friends' with Brian's mother and that's when they came to investigate and talk to his dad.

The taller cop introduced his partner and himself when his father came to the door. "Mr. Bentham. I'm

Officer Crain and this is Officer Butler."

"We have had a complaint about a friend of your wife's who's gone missing and we were wondering if Mrs. Bentham was in and could answer some questions."

Brian stood behind his father when the door was answered. His heart beat faster, waiting for his father to give an explanation.

"Don't hold your breath, Officer, you won't find my wife here or that slimy hairdresser, seeing as my wife ran off with him last week. He can have her. She's nothing but a slut. The whore was dicking him for the past year and now she's gone off with the bastard." Joe Bentham's face was a twisted mask of contempt.

"Do you have any idea where she is or if you will hear from her?" This time it was the second cop, Butler, asking the questions.

"I haven't a fucking idea but if you'd like to come back next week who knows? Till then, I've got nothing to say about where she is. She can go to hell for all I care; no-good bitch left the kid and me. Now I gotta do everything myself."

"Well, if you hear from her, will you have her call us?" Butler said handing a card to Joe.

"If I hear from the bitch I'll pitch her ass onto the sidewalk."

"If we don't hear from you within the week we will have to come back and reinvestigate."

"Fine!" Joe slammed the door in the officer's face as he turned toward his young son slapping him across the head as he passed by heading for the kitchen to get a beer.

"Don't even think you know anything. Your mother left for a faggot hairdresser. She never loved you and she never loved me. They will never find her, she's gone for good, and no one but the devil knows where she is."

No one asked Brian where his mother was. No one cared what he had to say, he little boy that was left behind the little boy that knew where his mother's suitcase was and all of her things. The box filled with her jewelry and all of her bathroom stuff. The stuff she would never leave without. And he knew she would never leave without him. No one had asked about the secret place in the basement behind the wall. The place only his father was supposed to know about. The place where his father kept "those" magazines and the video's he would watch late at night. Brian had prayed the officers would ask him a question but they never even looked at him.

They came back a couple more times, but Brian's father managed to convince them that she was just another runaway wife. And each time they ignored the little boy who stood by his father, his eyes pleading to be asked about the secret place. He couldn't tell and they never asked. He was just too scared to cry out that his dad was a liar.

At night in his dreams he did cry out for his mother's arms. But it was his dad who jerked him from his sleep, shook him hard, and told him to stop crying like a baby. It was his dad's fist that slammed into his face and twisted his hair while telling him no one cared. Not about him or his "fucking" mother. Brian could smell the stale whisky on his father's breath from an evening of drinking. He never forgot the stale smell of his father or the sweet smell of his mother.

* * * *

Brian was startled out of his dark glance at the past by a loud rap at the large oak door at the front of the restaurant. As he swung it open, he knew he was about to cross a threshold that few ever had, and once having done so, he could never turn back.

Standing outside the door was a beautiful, tall redhead. He had spotted her earlier that night and had asked Sherry, her waitress, if she was from out of town. She was dining alone and often that meant a visitor to Chicago of which The Beef Chateau had many. Sherry confirmed his suspicion.

As was his custom, he went to the customers table to welcome her, making sure the food was to her liking. While he engaged her in a conversation, he felt as if a dark cloud had lifted from his brain and suddenly he knew he had a solution to a problem that had been keeping him up after his late-night shift. Long nights and little sleep were taking their toll. He had felt a strange surge of power as he approached the woman's table. He knew that women found him irresistible and he hoped his charm would hold for the invitation he was about to make. It was in the instant that he introduced himself that he knew that the dark side was about to take over. After all, hadn't his father told him often enough that he was no good?

"Hi, my name is Brian Bentham, and I'm the head chef. I hope the meal is to your liking." He leaned over to get a whiff of her perfume.

She seemed flustered that he had come to her table and he planned to take advantage of the moment. Brian took her hand after a formal shake, refusing to let go. Her hand was cold, his warm, and he could tell she felt a connection in the instant that they touched. Her face went red and she lowered her eyes, unable to keep contact with his piercing baby blues.

"If you're not doing anything later I would love it if you would come back and take a private tour of the restaurant. Please don't think I'm being forward; it's a custom to ask a special guest back each night and share the secrets of the marinades and dressings. And tonight I can't think of anyone more lovely to spend the rest of my evening with." Brian flashed a brilliant smile few could resist.

He hadn't known if anyone would fall for a line like that but she had and now she stood just inside the door. Brian locked the door behind her just before he took her coat and flashed one of his most glorious smiles.

* * * *

Gloria couldn't believe her luck. She was in Chicago for a week staying at one of the better hotels just a few blocks away. Gloria was from New York, working for a promotional company featuring a new computer disk business card. She knew the electronic card would be a great success. She had been pitching the disk to a high-level brokerage firm for the better part of a week. With the sale closed she was ready for a little rest and relaxation. Tonight would be special, an evening she was looking forward to. The Beef Chateau was one of the best restaurants in Chicago and she wouldn't have missed eating here for the world. As it turned out, the food wasn't the only great thing being offered.

When the head Chef came to her table she didn't know what to expect. His long legs, lean body, and broad shoulders were magnificent, but it was his face that made her heart stop. Blue-black hair, dark skin, and flashing blue eyes made her heart flop once. Then he smiled and her heart did a second flip-flop. His even white teeth covered by a full sensuous mouth, made her feel weak in the knees. He was glorious and he wanted her; she could tell by the way his eyes seemed to devour her. There was a moment when their eyes met that she thought she could see a flash of light. She got a feeling unlike anything she had ever felt before. It was like Brian was having a sudden realization, as if a solution to an unanswerable problem had suddenly been solved just by looking into her eyes. It was intoxicating and now here she stood in front of him. Hopefully there would be more than wine and a secret sauce. Hopefully there would be sex. Great sex if the looks this man gave her, were any indication.

* * * *

"Welcome Gloria. I wasn't sure you would take me up on my offer. It's the first time I've ever invited anyone back. It was just a line when I told you I did this every evening. This is really my first time."

Brian took her coat as he guided her into the dimly lit interior of the restaurant. He could tell by the red glow starting to run up from her chest to her pretty face that Gloria was excited and flattered by the attention he was showering on her. He knew he had her in the palm of his hand.

"No problem, I was hoping tonight would be something special too," Gloria said, her breath catching in her throat.

"More special than you will ever know." Brian guided

Gloria into the recess of the restaurant knowing tonight would be delicious, simply delicious."

* * * *

It was easier than he had ever dreamed. Cattle were more difficult to lead to the slaughter. The rest of the evening had gone exactly to plan. With the chit-chat over, he had gone in for the kill. The final drops of blood were now just dripping slowly over her chin. He spun Gloria around once, looking objectively at his delectable sacrifice. She hung limply from her ankles, the strong ropes cutting into her flesh. Swinging from the meat hook, her hands dragged along the cold concrete floor, still bound by the duct tape. Gloria's red hair dragged softly against its cold surface. Brian had drained all of the blood from her body. He had to hold her head to one side to ensure that the flow of blood would leave as little mess as possible. She had been alive and fully aware when he brought the small automatic blade to her throat. She had struggled for the first few minutes and it wasn't until near the end that she stopped jerking around. As the blood drained into the plastic bucket, Brian was excited by the amount he had collected.

He would be able to make a wonderful batch of his secret marinade with this warm, red elixir. When he was finished he poured some of the blood into a new marinade pan. He thought it was nice to have the bright, shiny, stainless steel pan used only for this sacrifice. Gloria would never know it, but her blood was needed like air. It had become as important as his very breath and Brian knew he could no longer live without it. They say once an animal has a taste for blood, it can no longer go without. Brian now knew it was true. The thirst for blood and the sense of well-being it gave him had driven him to do what he had never thought possible.

* * * *

Brian had spent the first hour of the evening sharing with Gloria, a wonderful white wine, Kaiserstol 98, and asking all sorts of questions. They sat in the front of the restaurant, music softly adding to the sense of romance Brain was trying to create. Did she have any family in Chicago? Friend? When was she due back? Where did she work? Did she have to check in back at the office? He tried to get as much information as he could…after all he knew how important it would be if he wanted to get away with the murder.

Murder, he had never imagined that one day he would do to someone what his dad had done to his mother. Kill. He had imagined the murder of his mother in his head a thousand times. How had she died? Strangled? Stabbed? Shot? Was it an accident? No! When his dad moved the other woman in, Brian knew his father had planned it. The bitch was still living in his house years later, sleeping in his mother's bed and he still hated her.

But he hated his father even more. "Like father, like son!" No! Never! He just had to do this. It wasn't personal. He just needed the blood. Everything in his body yearned for the feeling he got from devouring what was forbidden.

When Brian felt he had enough information to complete his plan, he invited Gloria to take a tour of the restaurant. Opening the cooler door he knew she would find the meat-processing room, fascinating.

“This is where we cut the steaks,” Brian said as he welcomed her into the room. “Come over here and I’ll show you how everything works.”

He walked into the middle of the room where a very large wooden block stood. Overhead a rack of knives hung, each one a special tool for the carving of the steaks.

“We cut our steaks here. But it would be much too difficult to cut them all by hand so I have the help of an automated processor.” Brian said as he turned around and opened a small door off to the side of the wall. “It’s tucked in here and runs on a special arm.”

He pulled the round, saw-like apparatus from its small chamber. It looked like a small buzz saw and ran on a pulley that would allow Brian to maneuver it with exact precision. He walked over to a large set of doors that was off the right of the room. He opened it and showed Gloria a room full of trays stacked on dozens of shelves. They were wrapped in layers of what appeared to be cellophane.

“This is a flash freezer. It hits sub-zero in seconds. We can freeze our extra steaks and they will still be as fresh as the day they were cut. This process makes it impossible to tell that the meat was ever frozen once it is thawed.” He said with pride.

Once out of the flash freezer, Brian moved Gloria closer to the middle of the cutting room. On the meat table he had a wooden mallet used to beat and tenderize some of the cheaper cuts of steak. In an effort to give Gloria a kiss, he turned Gloria so that her back was against the table. She moved in closer, her head turning up to receive his lips. Brian knew he had her. As he slipped his hands up her skirt to the warm recess of her body he knew he would be able to enjoy her in more ways than one…sex and murder, an intoxicating mix.

* * * *

It was finally over. Now he had to make sure that the cleanup and disposal of the body was meticulous. He knew what to do. After he had enjoyed the warmth of her body Brian's hand closed in around the mallet. Gloria lay face down on the wooden table. As Brian withdrew from her body he had the mallet in his hand. Before she knew what was happening he brought the mallet down upon her pretty, red head. She had no idea what had happened. By the time she came too, Gloria was bound by her ankles with rope, and had been hoisted off the ground by a hook that usually supported a hind of beef, her hands bound by tape. Her mouth was also taped shut. Brian had heard enough from her pretty lips. Why spoil the moment now by listening to her pleading for her life? He preferred to stay aloof. He simply swung Gloria around, bringing the automated blade to her throat. He knew how to slaughter his prize and take advantage of the blood her body would provide.

The terror Gloria would feel in the moment would provide a wonderful mix of hormones, a very powerful combination. Once Brian soaked his steaks in the special blend of wine, blood, and herbs he knew that the human blood would provide a special kick. He would once again get that unique feeling. But first he would have to make sure he cleaned up. There would be no evidence. Brian knew what to do.

As he laid Gloria out on the floor, which he had covered with bubble wrap, he stroked her face and kissed her lips once more. . He carefully washed her hands with warm soapy water. Finally he brushed her hair with the brush he found in her purse, afterwards placing it back in her handbag. He made sure that there would be no fibers or hair from his body found on her. After he had hit her with the mallet, he had dressed himself in a full, white, disposable body suite. He usually used them in order to keep the cutting room hygienic, making sure that the beef that was served would never have a human hair. Now it would protect him from leaving any clues for the police.

Next he carefully examined her lifeless body to make sure there was nothing on her clothing to tie her to the meat cooler or to him. He ran a large piece of tape over her dress, panties and private parts, making sure he removed any of his hair that might have attached itself to Gloria. He had made sure he wore protection when he came inside of Gloria. No DNA and the rope fibers around her ankles were a standard issue, the kind you found at any hardware store....nothing unusual there.

The floor of the cooler was unpainted and washed twice daily with a water-soluble detergent: the kind of soap common to ninety percent of all commercial buildings, again, a tough lead to follow. The cops could follow the smallest clue and Brian would try to give them as little as possible to go on. He knew that the contents of her stomach would be examined and he would have to be sure that no one would suspect that her last meal had been at The Beef Chateau. He would be sure to dump the body a few days later, but for now a little hocus-pocus.

He had a sure fire way of confusing the police. If they could pin down the time of death they could trace the murder back to the restaurant but he had a way to baffle the police and he knew he could get away with it. Next he dragged her body into the special freezer.

Brian wore his latex gloves, the kind you find anywhere. This would prevent him from contaminating the body and leaving any evidence. After he laid the body in the center of the freeze zone and closed the door, he turned the dial slowly. She would be frozen in less than thirty seconds.

The process was called "flash freeze" but in reality it took a little longer. He had removed the bubble wrap before placing Gloria in the freezer. He knew it couldn't stand up to the sub-zero temperature that was needed to freeze the body quickly. Once done, he re-entered the cooler and gently rolled the body onto the wrap. Frozen, she needed to be handled with care. Again he examined the floor to make sure it was spotless. He didn't want any evidence that the meat freezer might give the CSI team that he knew would eventually investigate.

Brian would have to load the frozen corpse into the back of his van. He would then take the body home with him and put it into his empty deep freeze before dumping it a few days later. He would have to lay out a clear plastic tarp over the van floor to ensure that fibers would not be found in the wrap, nothing that could lead the police back to him. Now all that was left was to load the body into the van, lock it up tightly and return to the restaurant to finish his evening's work. Later he would plant the rest of his evidence to lead the police on a wild goose chase.

Chapter Four

Dennis sat at the supper table with his wife Veronica and his two daughters, Natasha and Katrina. It was late, almost seven. Their conversation covered the mundane and the bizarre. It was difficult at times like this to hang onto reality, one moment you're at work staring into the faces of people you've only met post-mortem, lifeless, cold and silent. They want to tell you a story. Talk to you if they could. But they're silent and it's up to you to drag the details of their lives and deaths into a story that makes sense. A story that will tell you what happened, and why. A story that takes a team of investigators, each of them experts in their own ways to decipher the last moments of the victims lives.

The patrol officers, detectives, medical examiners, forensic team, witnesses, friends, and family, all of the things seen and unseen. Somehow the stories develops and no longer are they unknown corpses in a murder investigation, they take on a personalities. Some you like better than others and every once in a while, one even hooks you in. Even though they no longer walk among the living they become friends. The spirit or essence of what they were and in some ways still are, speak to you from beyond the grave. A piece of them stays with you every minute of the day and night, even in your dreams. They speak to you and they don't stop until it's over. You have to solve the case! They never rest until you do.

Right now Dennis felt as if eleven friends had joined him at the table with his family and they would continue to stay with him until the whole mess was over. He tried to bring his mind to the table and give his family the attention they deserved. But the conversation he had with Corrine kept drifting back into his mind. It was bad enough that this case was driving him crazy, but the added complication of Corrine was enough to take him to the edge.

* * * *

Corrine had finished her third glass of white wine when she suddenly got silent. Up until then it had been a none-stop line of chatter with Dennis doing more nodding and listening. The conversation had been work-related and listening to Corrine talk about her love of the job had been a welcomed diversion for Dennis, even if most of the information was about the case.

"Why are you so silent all of a sudden?" Dennis asked, almost afraid to hear the answer.

"I was just thinking about how selfish it was of me to take you from your family. I know with this case you and Chuck have been going around the clock. For me it's no problem. I have no one at home to miss me, only my cat," Corrine said. "But you have a wife and kids..." She said, letting the last statement hang.

"I've never even asked you how things have been since

the divorce. I'm not even sure I understand what happened. You have any kids?" Dennis asked, he didn't want to get into a conversation about his family.

"Bill never wanted any. As a lawyer he was married to the firm. I was knee-deep in my career for the first ten years and by then I was in my mid-thirties. I started to think about a family, but Bill put the lid on anything that might derail our upwardly mobile journey. By the time I knew what was happening, he'd used so many delay tactics that I was nearly forty…much too late." Corrine took another sip of her wine.

A waitress came to the table to see if they wanted another round. It was almost five-thirty. Dennis would have to leave soon.

"Why did the marriage go south?" He asked.

"We drifted apart. It's like that when your first love is your career. And for both of us our marriage was second on the list. It doesn't give you a common ground to keep the important things front and center. Sometimes the cases have so many twists and turns, keeping your family and that part of your life straight can be tough. I found out over a year ago that he was going to be a daddy, but I'm not the lucky mother. Just a little detail he forgot to mention. It threw me for a loop. It has been over a year and I am still not over it, I guess that's why I wanted to go for a drink. I know it was a lame excuse, the case and all. But I didn't want to drink alone. I hope you don't mind." Corrine gave Dennis an apologetic shrug.

"I can't imagine how you feel, but I'm glad you asked me. I have been feeling dragged down by this case and a rum and coke was just what I needed." Dennis said; suddenly feeling a little more relaxed. The Bacardi was starting to take effect.

Just then Dennis looked up and saw Chuck heading towards the table. Dennis felt the blood rush to his face. He knew he must be looking guilty and his partner would likely give him a rough time.

"I was wondering if I would find the two of you here. I thought you had to be at home for a family supper?" Chuck asked, giving Dennis another strange look.

This new look Chuck kept giving Dennis, was starting to become all too familiar. It made Dennis feel as if he had been caught with his hand in the cookie jar. It was time to go home.

"Corrine will fill you in on the latest details. Call me later and well see where we go from here." Dennis said, as he stood, and put down the money for the bill on the table.

Chuck could keep Corrine company. After all, Chuck was the single one. Dennis felt a small twinge of regret as he hastily left the bar.

* * * *

"Dad, I asked you a question. Could you look at my car? I think it's making a funny noise." Katrina, his youngest asked.

"Sure sweetheart, right after supper." Dennis said, trying to bring his full attention back to the dinner table.

His daughters were over for a rare visit; the youngest, Katrina, was happily married, while the oldest, Natasha, was footloose, happy to just enjoy her friends and puppies. Their lively chatter was a welcome intrusion. It kept him away from his thoughts. As he looked at his daughter's innocent faces, he felt a twinge of guilt. *For what?" he* thought. He shook off the strange feeling and tried to concentrate on his daughters.

Natasha was a tall, Slavic beauty. She had inherited his family's facial structure with his wife's big green eyes. Her hair, now cut short, made her look even more outstanding. High cheekbones, a long elegant neck, and a jaw line to die for, she was made for the movies. Natasha had a beauty that made you stop and look twice. Clear pale skin in contrast with the dark hair and pitch-black, finely arched brows complemented a face that could have graced the cover of any fashion magazine. With a university degree in Slavic languages, Russian and Ukrainian, Natasha had brains and beauty. After deciding that academic life was too boring, she made the leap into the beauty industry and became a hairdresser like her mother. Who could understand kids now a-days? A fifty-thousand dollar education, and now she was working with Veronica as a hairdresser. Oh well, whatever made her happy!

Katrina was always the center of attention. When she was cheerful she was delightful and full of stories about her day. She had decided to try her hand at Real-estate, a career her grandmother had mastered. As a junior partner she was learning the ropes and loving it. Katrina had always been pretty…at five foot six inches, her curvy figure would have given any Diva a run for her money, but it wasn't until she dyed her hair from light-brown to black that she became outstanding. She had a look that was reminiscent of the 1950s pinup girl, Betty Page. Her olive-green eyes were framed with the same black, finely arched brows, as her sister's, but Katrina took after her mother with a soft oval face and a perfect set of lips. Her tiny, straight teeth, gave her a sensual, exotic look. Her short bangs and shoulder-length bob said, "I know who I am, so don't mess with me!" And few did.

As the conversation shifted, none of it requiring his interjection, Dennis turned his attention from his daughters to his wife, Veronica, a woman he had come to rely on for over thirty years of marriage. Veronica Kortovich was in one word, majestic. At five feet nine inches, her large frame had put on a few extra pounds over the years. Dennis was glad they had been put on fairly evenly, so she wore them well. Her face was a combination of both daughters or vice versa. Big green eyes, straight nose, medium lips and even teeth made her a beauty. When one looked at her you got the feeling that she was much younger than she really was. Her incredible clear, white, flawless skin and her unbelievable eyes usually had strangers giving her a second look. But when she spoke she made you think of someone who had a hundred things going on inside her head. When you met her you felt her excitement and energy. Often people would feel overwhelmed by her presence, and quite frankly, there was a side to her personality that was wacky. Call it what you will, but her love of reading had led her down a few strange paths. Conspiracy theories, space aliens, and corporate socialism, every topic, not discussed in polite company became her obsession. Religion, politics and little-to-unknown facts about things no one cared about or thought about rattled around in her pretty little brain. No one could say she wasn't a hell of a lot of fun, but few understood her. With tongue in cheek she would expound on the latest tidbit that she had read, mostly at the frustration of the listener. Dennis thought the reason she shared many of her uncommon ideas with friends and family was to shake them up and get them thinking. It worked. The only problem was, most people just thought she was nuts. Not that she cared. She had always marched to her own, offbeat drum. As a hairdresser and former owner of five salons, she always kept herself busy.

Five years ago she had sold the chain of salons and put a small, professional salon in her beautiful home in the Ukrainian Village on Wood Street, an old section of Chicago with a rich past. Now her daughter, Natasha worked with her. Veronica had never been so happy. No pressure, just lots of fun, friends, and family.

"Girl's, I hope you aren't going out clubbing tonight. We still don't know who's behind these crazy killings. Even if all of the victims are from out of town you still can't be too safe," Veronica said as she stood to clear the table.

"Your mother is right. I don't want you going to any after-hours clubs or eating out where you don't know everyone. Don't talk to anyone you are not familiar with. Until these cases are solved, I don't have a clue what's happening so you can't trust anyone," Dennis said, looking at both daughters to let them know this was the cop, not the dad talking and they had better listen.

It was hard being a dad as well as a cop in Chicago. You became all too aware of what was happening to the young people in the city and what kind of trouble they could get into. Even good kids from good families sometimes found themselves in enough trouble to affect them for the rest of their lives.

"Don't worry, we won't get into any trouble and being killed isn't on our agenda." Katrina said as she bent to kiss her dad on the side of his cheek.

“Well Dad, Mom, we’ve gotta go.” Natasha stood up with her parting words. “Katrina and I are footloose tonight and we’re off to a movie. Supper was great thanks and don’t worry, we won’t go anywhere or do anything that will get us into trouble.”

“Yeah thanks, I hate cooking and I love coming home and being fed even if it means getting the third degree. I know you love us but we are big girls and can take care of ourselves,” Katrina interjected. “I’ll leave my car and go with Natasha. Thanks Dad” was Katrina’s parting words and off they went: both of them knowing that their father’s words were based on his fear of the past few months’ events.

Dennis pushed his chair away from the table and automatically started to clear his dishes and put them in the dishwasher. He had the weirdest feeling that somehow he should just ground the girls and forbid that they even go out until the killer was found. It would be difficult to control grown women, but he somehow felt he should try.

“What’s the matter Dennis? You’ve been quiet and distant all night. I don’t think I’ve seen you this way before. What’s up?” Veronica asked as she joined him in the cleanup.

For just a second Corrine’s face flashed before his eyes.

“We found another two victims this morning. So far there doesn’t seem to be any new clues or evidence. I’m as stumped today as I was with the first killing. He’s getting bolder and the murders are happing more frequently, and when you have a killer that’s slicing up two victims at a time, its hell.”

Veronica moved in to give Dennis a hug. She put her

arms around her husband and laying her head on his shoulder. He moved in to give her a hug back. He started to feel excited. He tried to keep the image of Corrine from his mind. Suddenly Veronica moved away, her face a bright red.

"What's the matter?"

"It's just a flash. I hate this. I think I'm going to have a melt-down. When you touch me it sets off a heat wave that could melt the ice caps." Veronica said, reaching for a cold glass of water.

For a second Dennis felt almost thankful that Veronica had pulled away, though it would usually irritate him. It was hard watching his wife go through the change of life. She was more distracted and irritated by everything. And sex seemed out of the question. It would set off a heat wave that almost caused an atomic melt down. Was he just getting older or was this case starting to get to him at a deeper level than he had experienced before? Or was it something or someone else? He shrugged off the feeling and thought about his daughters. The victims were all from out of town and serial killers seldom changed their method of operation. He was sure the girls would be safe, but something kept pulling at his gut.

"You'll solve this case. Whoever the bastard is that is doing these terrible things, he will make a mistake. They all want to be caught. You said so yourself." Veronica offered.

"Hopefully before the body count climbs any higher, it's all bullshit and I feel helpless." Dennis sat back in his chair.

Veronica put her arms around her husband once again and gave him a comforting hug, moving away quickly before the physical contact caused another hot eruption.

"Just let go and stop thinking so hard, when you relax and focus on something else, you'll find the piece that's missing. That's how it always seems to work." She kissed the top of his head.

"Yes, you're right," Dennis agreed reluctantly. "I'm going to put my feet up and watch a little TV. I'm giving myself a night off. I won't let this case get to me." With that statement Dennis disappeared into the family-room, leaving Veronica to finish cleaning the kitchen.

Once Veronica turned back to the sink, Dennis reflected on the events in their lives that had brought them to this point. Their families had lived in Chicago for nearly one hundred year. .Dennis's grandfather had escaped Russia during the revolution and his grandmother had come from the Ukraine. As immigrants from Eastern Europe, they settled in the area of Chicago now known as the Ukrainian Village. Originally it had been settled by Eastern European immigrants, but as the years passed many of the original families had moved to the suburbs. Now the area was more bohemian and eclectic, than European. Young yuppies and artistic types had moved into the area giving the neighborhood a unique feel. Dennis knew Veronica loved the neighborhood. It suited her diverse taste and need for excitement and color. As far as Dennis was concerned it was Veronica who added color to the neighborhood. Dennis had been well into his late twenties when he finally decided to become a police officer, a choice that would prove to be perfect for his analytical, perfectionist nature and bright mind.

Athletic, strong, and fit he had kept himself in great shape and often beat many of the younger officers on written test and physical skills during their rookie years.. Even now, twenty years after joining the force, he had stayed in great shape.

Most of the men he worked with were Irish, a tradition in the Chicago Police Force, and Dennis had learned to love their daredevil ways as well as the stories they could tell about their fathers, uncles, brothers, and friends in the force. Some of these went back to a time before the late 1800's, in a city that had a reputation for being a little unconventional. It was easy to fall in love with the old stories about heroes like Elliot Ness and villains like Al Capone, although it was sometimes hard for the public to decide whom they liked more…. the criminals or the cops.

Veronica on the other hand was an adventurer and "entrepreneur extraordinaire." With her flair for the dramatic, the beauty industry fulfilled her need for constant change and excitement. Now, at nearly fifty, she had calmed down enough to be happy with just one project at a time. Cutting hair out of her home allowed her to read, work in the garden, and listen to some of her weird radio programs like The *Art Bell Show,* a program that delved into all of the conspiracy theories that Veronica loved. She continued to drive her friends and family crazy, with a variety of wacky, outer-edge ideas. Dennis and Veronica were the sensible and insane. They were perfect for each other and he knew it, thinking once again about the late afternoon drink with Corrine.

Dennis flicked the button on the channel changer hoping to find something that would engage his attention and keep him from thinking about the so-far unsolvable case. As usual, his mind drifted to what seemed to be hundreds of pieces of information. Few that fit together. The first victim, Gloria Crow, had been from New York. She had been discovered at the back of an old warehouse. The coroner had concluded that she had been knocked unconscious before she had been hung upside down, had her throat slit and the blood drained from her body. There was some evidence that suggested she may have had sex, but no evidence of rape, it seemed consensual, no bruising or marks between her thighs. Time of death had been determined to be two to three hours from her last meal, a steak. She'd had some wine, a coffee and a dessert only a few minutes before she died.

This meant one of two things. Either she'd had supper at one place and dessert and beverage somewhere else before she was killed, or she had simply delayed the final part of her meal until later. At first Dennis thought there might just have been a delay between the meal and dessert; he often ate a big meal and waited for dessert. The only problem was that after the other ten victims were found, all with the same contents in their stomachs, he knew that they had eaten at one place and the follow-up murder likely took place somewhere else. There was always a two-hour lag after supper, with only a few minutes from the time of dessert to death. They say coffee, booze, and sweets aren't good for you, but this time they were real killers. Dennis didn't find it funny. Someone was going to a great deal of trouble to set up his victims.

There was no trauma to the body other than the emotional terror she would have felt before her death. All of the other victims but Gloria had been drugged by an overdose of Halcion, a medication used by many dentists to knock out their patients before a difficult surgery, and a great medication for the sleep deprived. After the second and third victims had been found with the medication in their stomachs, Dennis's team had done an exhaustive search to see if any Halcion was missing from its registered source.

It wasn't until the fourth and fifth victims had been found that they discovered that Gloria Crow had just recently been prescribed one hundred and twenty tablets to help her sleep on her many trips from home. Only two tablets were required to knock out a full-grown man. How convenient for the killer. He now had enough to render at least sixty victims incapable of fighting back. He had killed eleven innocent people, and at the rate he was going, another couple of dozen would mean a long, hard spring and summer unless they could catch this bastard; and so far there were no leads. More murders were likely to follow.

"What was the blood for?" Dennis wondered, as he turned off the television, he lay back and reviewed the last few days of the investigation. Dennis felt the blood was the motive. The killer needed it for something. Once that became clear, the solution would follow.

Dennis and Chuck had followed up every clue they could on the known cults. They even discovered in their exhaustive research that a "Buffy the Vampire Slayer" cult was thriving in the underground world of Chicago, mostly twenty-something, middle class kids belonged to the cult, which had developed as a spin off from the TV show, but they took their roles very seriously. Dennis wondered if they took it seriously enough to kill.

He and Chuck had been shocked at how serious the

many young participants were in their make-believe game. The night in late November when the detectives had gone to check out the weird lead about the group was cold and crisp, and thankfully the wind was making mischief in upstate New York not Chicago. Dennis's personal hatred of the wind bordered on obsessive.

An old warehouse in the south side of Chicago had been converted into a Vampire world and many of the participants took on the roles of the characters in the TV Show, "*Buffy the Vampire Slayer!*" When Dennis and Chuck had showed up at the club they were greeted by a Buffy Summers look-alike.

"Hi, my name is Detective Dennis Kortovich and this is my partner Detective Chuck O'Brien. We would like to ask whoever is in charge some questions, if we may."

Dennis flashed his badge at the blonde woman who looked no older than fifteen. Her long, blonde hair and short skirt, along with her school sweater made her look much younger than Dennis suspected she really was.

"That would be Angel but I don't think he would like it if I let you in. This is a private club and we only allow members." The young girl looked defiant and ready to challenge his authority.

"I'll tell you what. I'll just wait here while you go in and get this Angel guy. Then you won't give me a look that says you'd like to kick my ass."

Dennis tried to give his most charming smile, something he hated doing. Charm seemed like a waste of time but it was a tactic he would use if he had to. The young girl disappeared into the big gothic doors of the dark building, giving both Dennis and Chuck the impression that she had been swallowed by something that was a living thing, rather than a building of brick and mortar.

"Holy shit Dennis, have you looked this building over? Someone has gone to a lot of trouble to make it appear as if it's come from some nightmare out of Stephen King's mind." Chuck said, looking up at the building, mouth wide open.

Dennis joined Chuck in looking up at the five-story building that should have been torn down decades before. You could tell that a great deal of money and effort had been put into its restoration. The outside was a pale-gray and the upper edge of the roof had been refaced with gables running all along the building. At each interval where the gable attached itself to the front of the warehouse, a different, winged, underworld demonic figurine, stared down at whoever entered, making it appear as if they would take flight at any second and attack those who dared to darken the doorway uninvited. That in itself was a spectacle to behold. Two winged demons flanked either side of the double doors while a two-headed serpent wound its way around the curved overhang of the doorway. It would be enough to give most people the creeps, but these kids flourished under the imaginative theme. They obviously took this Vampire stuff seriously.

The big doors opened giving both Dennis and Chuck goose bumps as the creak of the door announced the arrival of Buffy and her companion, Angel. What a piece of work. The guy was obviously very handsome, but far older than the field of other players, who were mostly kids. This guy was at least forty or maybe even older. From what Dennis could gather on his research about the TV character Angel, he was supposed to be a 242-year-old Vampire who had recognized his evil past and was now hell-bent on helping Buffy rid the world of Vampires and their blood-sucking ways. Dennis got a very different impression from the guy in front of him. In fact he was sure that the whole set up was a way to lure young girls in for the kind of adult fun that was not just sucking on the necks of other kids willing to play the game. Dennis and Chuck walked up several steps leading to the door.

"Hello."

A deep baritone voice of velvet and honey greeted both men before they could say anything to the owner of the club, a man whose real name was Christopher Keller.

"I understand you would like to speak to me."

He held out his hand to the men, allowing Dennis to take the lead and shake his cold clammy hand. His fingernails were long beyond belief.

Dennis stared into eyes that were of the deepest blue. They seemed to hold his gaze in an almost hypnotic trance and when Christopher smiled Dennis was flashed a smile that had the long eyeteeth of a Vampire. Dennis gave a *"You've got to be kidding"* look over at Chuck and saw that he too was having a hard time not laughing at the charade of a full-grown man giving in to the make-believe world of a TV show as a way to lay young chicks. If ever there was a sexual con, this club was it, but it was the detective's job to make sure that nothing unusual was going on.

"Yes. If we could look around and ask you a few questions in regard to the murders that have been taking place lately."

Chuck had decided it was his turn to get a closer look at the guy and by his asking the question; Angel had to turn his full attention toward Chuck.

"You mean the 'Vampire Slayings' don't you? And I suppose just because we run a theme club we're going around killing people and drinking their blood. I assure you that although blood is the elixir of life, we prefer our Bloody-Mary's with tomato juice, and of course if anyone is under age we don't even allow them access." Angel turned toward the double doors indicating by his action that Dennis and Chuck should follow.

As the men entered the foyer of the building they were astounded by the number of young people wandering around. From the looks of it, the whole building was divided up into different theme rooms and the kids were able to roam from room to room listening to different music and role-playing different characters and themes from the show. It seemed casual and a bit spooky, but Dennis quickly became aware of just how young the girls seemed in contrast to the males. This was just a front for a bunch of dirty old men to seduce younger women in a fun but dangerous game. If all of the girls were of legal age there wasn't much he could do, but if the girls weren't, he would have the club shut down as fast a stake shoved into the heart of a vampire by Van Helsing, the real Vampire slayer from the book *Dracula...*

Angel led the men into an old creaky elevator. He hit number five, and when they got out of the elevator they weren't surprised by the obvious sexual theme of the room.

Tall candles lit the room from every direction, their soft glow illuminating a large, hand-carved desk of dark, rich mahogany. Directly to the side of the desk was a bed of gothic design and proportions. Dennis guessed it was hand-made; it was enormous, the dark-red, velvet canopy semi-enclosed the bed giving it an exotic look, while red tulle allowed the candlelight to give the bed a soft, inviting glow. It was the kind of bed that screamed of group sex and Dennis guessed many of the club's female members had seen the inside of its covers alone or with several others. The only thing being sucked on in that bed wasn't from the neck up but rather… Dennis decided to turn his attention away from the bed and get to the business at hand...murder.

"So, what can you tell me about the play acting going on around here? Do you think anyone would take their role seriously enough to want to drink blood from a live human victim?"

"I can tell you that I can't personally think of even one person who would take their play acting that far and I must say it bugs the hell out of me, because even though it may seem busy to you, business is down. This club is the first place where someone would think a member could be involved in something like this; after all, blood is the Vampire's food. And yes, there is always some nutcase that may take this stuff seriously but I can't think of one person who would."

Angel put his feet on the desk and leaned back, showing a tanned, fit body beneath his open, white, flowing shirt. His face looked dangerously handsome in the candlelight, and Dennis knew what would draw young women to Angel; his rugged good looks and the sense of danger that oozed from every pore.

Chuck decided to try another angle to see if Angel might have some insight into what would make anyone want to drink human blood, seeing as this Vampire stuff was Christopher's specialty.

"Why would anyone want to drink human blood, even in cult worship like Vampires?"

"What do you know about Vampires and the myths around them?"

Dennis and Chuck could tell by the tone of Angel's voice that this was a subject of great interest to the man, not the character Angel. He moved from behind the desk and leaned toward the men, with nothing separating them, he was about to share his passion.

"There have always been mythical creatures like Vampires from the beginning of time, even the ancient Greeks recorded them, but today's Vampires have a more recent history beginning around the Middle-Ages. Between 1600 and 1800 it was almost an epidemic and spread across Eastern Europe .But it was back in 1476 when Prince Steven Bathory helped a Romanian Prince named Dracula regain his throne that things really began to grow in mythical proportions.

It seems that Bram Stoker did base his Count Dracula character on the real life historical figure of Vlad III Dracula, also known as Vlad Tepes or Vlad the Impaler. It seems the only way this guy could find to amuse himself and deal with his enemies was to impale them on pikes and place them around his castle so that he could watch as the buzzards ate them alive. Some even say he drained the blood from his victims and drank it in a death toast. Myth had it that he lived for a long time and looked forever young in a time when forty was considered old. They said it was in the blood."

Christopher stood up and went over to a bookshelf behind him. It held hundreds of leather-bound books, many of which looked very old. As he ran his hands over the books he turned his attention back to Chuck and Dennis.

"If you study other cultures, like the some of the tribes of Africa, you will see that the drinking of blood; albeit from cattle, is imperative to the survival of their people. Blood is like a whole food; it passes into the system without having to be digested because in fact it already is. It can then pass its nutrients directly into the blood of the one drinking it. It is rumored that all of the properties in the blood, including its hormonal advantage can pass the blood brain barrier and give the drinker an immediate feeling of well-being. The blood even makes them feel as if they have more energy and are stronger and better than they have ever been before." Veronica looked at the faces of her friends as she delivered her speech, noting their interest.

"It is said that Genghis Khan and his Mongolian horde would drink the blood of their horses, stabbing them in the rump and drinking directly from the warm animal. This sustained them during their long rides across barren land. From all of these stories, the myths that Vampires have super-human strength is probably based on the fact that drinking blood would make a person feel good."

Christopher looked at both men, sensing their skepticism. If they only knew what a rush all of this could be they wouldn't be so anxious to knock it.

"So, do you think that any of the members of this club might want to get a little extra bolt of energy by drinking human blood, and if so, could any of them be capable of these killings?"

Dennis knew that a direct question like this would likely not bring forth any answer that would lead them directly to suspect but it was worth a try.

"I can't say I know of anyone off-hand but there is one guy who likes to play the role of Rupert Giles and he takes his role much too seriously."

Chuck asked the questions this time. "What exactly is his role and why do you think that he would be a character to look at?"

"Rupert Giles is a Watcher, as was his father's father. It is a very serious role and he mentors Buffy and tries to keep her safe. It is a great role around here and we have at least a hundred of our members currently playing this role, but only Harold Gainer takes it as seriously and the result is that a lot of our 'Buffy's" won't play with him. I'm afraid he's down to being allowed to follow only a couple of the girls and his pretense at being Rupert does not fool anyone that he is really just a creep." Christopher smiled. "But then again this club is really all about following the girls and rescuing them."

"Can we find this guy and talk to him?" Dennis asked, tired of the history lesson and wanting to get things moving on the investigation.

"Sure. He's here every night and I think you'll find him on the second floor, the school-room. Just take the elevator and if you need any other answers just come back up and ask me."

"How will we know which one he is?" Dennis headed toward the elevator as he asked the question.

"He'll be the oldest-looking one and he will be hanging out at one of the school lockers talking to a Buffy lookalike or another young girl called Cordelia Chase, a dark-haired girl who acts like a self-absorbed snot. You know the kind."

* * * *

The ride down the elevator to the second floor only took a few minutes, but the sounds of screams and loud rock and roll music was enough to make you think all hell had broken loose. If both men hadn't known differently, they would have believed that the screams were real. Once off the elevator it was apparent that a great deal of work had gone into making the second floor look like a genuine high school. Neither of the men had ever watched the show, but the walk down the hall to the gym and then the girl's locker room and shower was a bit of a shock for them. Several girls dressed in short skirts were lined up at the lockers and a couple of men who were obviously Rupert wannabes were' chatting' them up.

True to form there was one man who stood out. He was incredibly thin and well into his late fifties, but you could tell immediately that the girl he was talking to seemed bothered by his attention and didn't want to role play with him. This must be their man, Harold Gainer. As the detectives walked toward the locker they passed by a series of open showers and couldn't help but notice that two young women were buck naked and standing under the warm steam of water. In the corner were two other young men who were obviously playing the role of Vampires about to spring on the innocent young women. The girls were about to be attacked and Dennis wondered if one of them was a Buffy who would drive a stake into the heart of the Vampire. He was sure the only thing that would be driven into anyone's flesh tonight wasn't going to be anyone's heart. And the only wound anyone would receive was a fleshy woody attached to one or both of the young men. Dennis looked over at Chuck who returned his indifferent gaze with a shrug. No big deal, this was Chicago and both men had seen a lot more disturbing behavior than this.

They continued on their way toward the tired-looking, thin man who was the objective of their investigation. As they approached the locker the man looked up and although they were in street clothes they could tell by the look on his face that he was aware that they were police officers. For one brief moment he looked like he was going to run but the only exit was behind Dennis and Chuck and he stood little to no chance of getting away.

"Harold Gainer, we are police officers and we would like you to answer a few questions."

Dennis closed the gap between Harold and himself. The young woman Harold was talking to took the opportunity to get away from the bothersome man who was using his character to get close to her. They obviously took the roles they were playing seriously and, it was difficult for them to be rude to the character of Rupert Giles, but they found it revolting to be with Harold. An exasperated Harold dropped his character and responded with a curt. "Yes," to Dennis.

"We have a list of dates that we would like to show you and find out where you were on these dates and until what time." Dennis pulled out a list containing the dates; the approximate times of when the murders had taken place. They had already given the list to Christopher and had him write out whom he was with at the times. They would check them out later, but first things first….Harold.

"I don't know what you mean and why do you want to

know? I haven't done anything."

A defensive Harold jutted out a thin jaw-line that reminded Dennis of a ferret's

"Maybe not but we just want to check things out and find out what you may have been up to. We are investigating the murders of several young couples."

"You mean the Vampire Murders?" Harold seemed very excited by his discovery of their investigation.

"I can't imagine who would do such a thing and if I knew of anyone doing these horrendous crimes it would be my duty to eradicate such evil beings." His response was intense.

Both Dennis and Chuck could tell that Harold was serious about getting rid of such evildoers. They would have to make sure that he wasn't unbalanced and simply role-playing.

"So what would you do if you found out someone was killing these young people?"

"If it wasn't a Vampire I would call the police. If it was a Vampire I would call Buffy and make sure she drove a stake through his heart."

Harold was dead serious in his response and both Dennis and Chuck knew instinctively this wasn't their man, although he was certainly very strange.

"Can you think of anyone who might do such horrific crimes?"

Dennis thought it wouldn't hurt to see what kind of a spin this strange little man would put on the murders.

"I know I shouldn't say this because we feel that the Great One would never bother himself with us here in Chicago. But who else could pull off this many murders and drink such a vast amount of blood? Only Dracula could do such a thing and never leave any prints or clues.... not even The Master could do such a thing." Harold's voice lowered in a conspiratorial effort. "I think you had better look into some of the darkest places in the city to see where Dracula may be sleeping during the daytime and end this reign of terror in the city. If you need any help I will coach Buffy to aid you in your quest." Harold's voice held the most sincere tone.

The Great One was a reference to another character played in Buffy the Vampire Slayer and both men knew that Harold was a nut case and they were likely at a dead-end. As they left the building all Dennis could think of was that he was glad that both of his daughters were rooted in reality and would never resort to role-playing for kicks.

Chapter Five

Brian Bentham's life now had a new meaning. With Gloria Crow's impulsive murder he felt as if everything in his life had led up to these last few months. Brian was sitting in his reclining chair in the living room of his modest, two-bedroom bungalow, in the old part Chicago. His home was tastefully decorated in a soft array of color and unusual design. Japanese' Feng-Shui' made the flow and set up of the rooms seems sparse, although each piece of furniture had a special meaning and design. It was very masculine without seeming harsh and left many of his guests feeling as though they were only being shown a small glimpse of the man, while they guessed that there was so much more.

"Still waters run deep,"-was a perfect description of a man who showed you everything in its simple design and arrangement, but the story it meant to tell always fell short on the personal details. Brian had spent years perfecting a style that made people feel comfortable. As the evening wore on, often guests would find that they had shared intimate details of their personal lives as a result of his easy manner. Once the relationship grew they would eventually figure out that they actually knew very little about this charming, handsome, likable man. That was the way Brian liked it. Eventually this became a way for Brian to gain power over the people he knew. They gave all, while he gave nothing.

As Brian sank his body into the plush, burgundy leather chair he reflected back to a night in late October, a night that had started out like many others. Lexy and Bara had just finished their usual tour of the restaurant, making sure everything was ready for the morning shift. Brian had given Bara his usual nightly hug with a warm farewell.

Once they had gone he'd returned to the beef locker. It was completely encased in stainless steel and state of the art equipment for hanging, aging, and cutting the finest beef found anywhere in the world. Brian would now spend three to four hours cutting, freezing, and hand-preparing hundreds of steaks, which would find their way onto the plates of their clientele over the next two days. All of the steaks would require at least a forty-eight hour marinade and this was the secret of The Beef Chateau's success. The marinade's base was from the freshly drained blood of the beef.

This beef blood was shipped over in pails from the slaughterhouse where they prepared their beef. The blood was always marked, as were the great big slabs of beef. The special cuts were marinated in the blood of same animal. As the young steers were swung off their feet at the slaughterhouse they would have their throats cut quickly and with great precision. A loud gurgle would be heard as the blade cut the animal's throat, accompanied by a last thrashing as the animals finally succumbed to the sudden, violent loss of blood. The slaughter master would then gather the warm dark blood into the collection trays below. The sweet smell of warm blood over-shadowed the violent death of the helpless beast.

Once Brian identified the slab of beef, he matched it to the appropriate pail of blood. Then the first stage of his evening would begin. All of the blood would be poured into shallow pans that would hold two steaks deep and ten across. Brian could then stack ten trays at a time for one hundred steaks and ten across for a total of one thousand cuts, each marked clearly for their type, T-bone, Sirloin, Rib eye....

Later he would cut the large chunks of beef needed to make the prime rib roasts, which were also available to their clientele.

Every marinade consisted of beef blood, wine, spices, and light oil. Each cut would have a different marinade using a combination of several wines and many different exotic spices. The delightful smells of wine and spices overpowered the sweet aroma of animal blood. No one but Bara, Lexy, and Brian knew that the main ingredient for the marinade was blood, the best meat tenderizer of all.

It was on that fateful October day that Brian's life would change forever. He was cutting the last of the steaks for the evening, when the processor blade stuck. After tinkering with it for a few minutes, he reached over to turn on the switch and in an instant caught the corner of his thumb on the blade. The sharp edge of the blade cut through his thumb, making a deep gash. Brian's adrenaline pumped through his system, clearing his brain and heightening his senses. He only had to take two steps to the left of the meat cutter to get to the sink. As he leaned over to turn on the tap and wash the wound, now dripping heavily, a marinade pan full of wine and spices caught his eye. Instead of letting his lifeblood run into the sink, he deliberately held his hand over the pan.

It was as if time had slowed down. Brian could hear his heart beat in his head as it pumped the blood through his body, finding its way out through the gash on his thumb, bright-red, perfect blood. Not the black, purplish blood of the steers, but a crimson and thick gush of his blood. He let it drip into the pan for what seemed like forever. As the hypnotic dripping of the blood continued, the marinade pan seemed to fill before his eyes. Brian felt weak and he remembered a time when he and his friends had shared a gruesome conversation.

It was about a fateful Arctic crash where the survivors had to eat each other to stay alive. They then turned their sick thoughts to Jeffrey Dahmer and his cannibalistic tendencies, and finally to the subject of Dracula, myth or fact, and his need for human blood; a thick, sweet substance that gave eternal life to the dead. The conversation was sick and funny at the time and Brian remembered being told that human meat was the sweetest, tenderness, and tastiest of all.

Thoughts filled his head, formed and formless. He let the wound on his hand drip a few more drops of colorful blood before he finally put pressure on his thumb to slow the bleeding. Next he took a sterile strip and wrapped it around his hand and thumb. The pounding of his heart slowed and although Brian still felt as though he was in a trance, he picked up the best cut of the evening and placed it in the marinade pan full of blood, wine, and spices. His blood was red, thick, healthy, and sweet. It would be his prize, his moment of darkness. Something he could tell no one. It would sound too sick. Brian put his nose close to the steak as it soaked in the elixir. Yes, sweet, with a pungent aroma of musk, unlike any other. Beef blood was totally different from human. He could tell he would like it. It would need forty-eight hours to sit in the unholy blood, a taste few would ever know, only those who crossed the line.

* * * *

He would never be able to eat another steak prepared the old way. After cutting into the rare, pink, perfect cut of beef, Brian's trained pallet knew within seconds that the taste was like no other.

He ate slowly, his heart pounding as he enjoyed the private moment that his delectable prize gave him to savor the unique taste. As his mind wrapped its self around the idea that this was a forbidden food he knew this one moment would change his life forever. It gave him a feeling of power and in some way, a sense of sexual excitement. He ate his unholy steak with Bara and Lexy. They too ate a rare cut of perfect beef, but not like his. He remembered another time when he dined out with friends and had felt this same sexual excitement, a time when his date had let him know that she had only worn her expensive, red silk dress and little else.... bare legs, breasts, and butt. As they dined and drank expensive wine all seemed normal above the table, while below a steamy sexual encounter took place.

Shoes off, bare feet roamed over bare legs, his feet, her legs, till they found that spot. Her pupils dilated and he knew that she was excited by their secret exchange. It was the forbidden, their secret unspoken. It made him hot as the blood rushed to the intimate parts of his body. He had to lean back to let his body stretch out to make more room. His foot plunged deeper into the warm recess between her legs. He nearly exploded. That was how he felt now as he dined on his special steak. Hot, and ready to explode. He ran his tongue over his lips making sure he tasted the last drop of the marinade. A slight shiver ran through his body before he felt an explosion of awareness unlike anything he had felt before. Mind, body, soul, all slamming together at once, he could feel every cell in his body suddenly become alive and invigorated as if by some unseen force. It was the way sunlight brings a feeling of well-being and health after it bursts forward on a cloudy day. Suddenly he could feel his senses lift to an altered state. The world was perfect. He was perfect. He knew in a second what was happening. The human growth hormones as well as the adrenaline and endorphins had found their way into his system via the steak. The way medication does, but this was even better. As he digested the steak, the nutrients moved through his veins and he became truly alive for the first time. He needed more.

Twice over the next few days after he had devoured the first steak, he deliberately reopened the cut on his thumb. It hurt like hell, he had a good body; it wanted to heal. Reopening the wound was more painful than the first cut but he needed the blood.

Somehow the knowledge of his secret indulgence as well as the hormones found in human blood became a powerful mix. He couldn't remember another experience that seemed so intimately his. How would he continue to get this feeling? A week later he found the solution. A new game was about to begin.

Chapter Six

The overhead lights were bright, dancing off the gray walls, everything seemed dull, the walls, the flat, cold tables, the floors, all gray, flat surfaces that seemed to blend into nothingness. This was the place where all the bodies came to rest for a while before they spent time telling their story to Dr. Shelley MacPherson, Chicago's finest Medical Examiner and Pathologist. By the time they got to the morgue, she was the only one who could listen. Few had the expertise to know the terrifying last moments before their deaths. She could understand the reactions that might have taken place in their bodies as they faced the cold, sharp slash of stainless steel slicing across their throats with medical precision, or the feel of the ropes as they cut into their ankles. Ropes that bore the full weight of each body as it hung helplessly upside down, arms held at their sides. They had been wrapped from ankles to shoulders by something like a large tensor bandage. Shelley could tell by a few unique markings. She leaned over the body of the latest victim; a female, twenty-nine years old, five feet six inches tall, one hundred forty-seven pounds, Caucasian, brunette. Shelley always felt as if she was betraying the side of her that was female, the soft side of her. As a Medical Examiner she found life a little too reality-based and lately she was getting enough of that on TV. Here at the Coroner's Office, she had to stay detached and professional.

But every once in a while she could see the cold, stiff, lifeless body as it once was; vibrant, smiling, full of life and promise. This young woman was once an example of what everyone wants to be; exceptionally beautiful, healthy, and intelligent… absolute perfection. Her naked body lay stretched out on the cold stainless steel gurney. She was a lovely example of womanly perfection. Round full breasts, small waist, full hips, long legs and slender, perfect feet. Her hands and feet were well cared for with fingernails that matched the color on her toes. Both had been professionally manicured. Shelley could tell that the victim's skin had been well attended to, as well. The woman had likely been a regular at a fancy spa. She looked like money and success.

Shelley had removed and bagged all of the victim's clothes and sent them to forensics. The body now lay naked, fully exposed, and Shelley needed to tell a story that would allow a team of experts to find out who was committing these terrifying murders. It was always the same. The perfect cut across the throat, and every ounce of blood gone. The content's in their stomachs was barely in the first stages of digestion. No bruising, cuts, or trauma to the body except for the rope burns around their ankles. Two things stood out. There were no unusual fibers or out of place evidence on any of the bodies and each and every one of the victims had their hands washed and fingernails scrubbed underneath before the killer dumped his or her body, the contents of their stomachs was always the same, the full meal deal with steak, potato, and dessert with wine.

Shelley concluded time of death was less than a half hour after consuming their dessert and wine, approximately two to three hours after eating a steak dinner. A few had soup or salad… either-way it was always the same, a steak supper, then dessert and wine, followed by death. Other than the first victim, each had been given a dose of Halcion just enough to put them out for only several minutes, but long enough to be bound and hung, leaving them helpless.

They had all been only too aware of their impending deaths and while they were alive they had been emotionally traumatized by the knowledge of what was to come. They were bound too tight to struggle physically, but their minds and emotions must have been assaulted by terror as the adrenaline and other hormones rushed through their blood to aid them in hopes of helping them survive. Each victim was painfully conscious of the last few moments of his or her life. They would have felt the initial rush of warm sticky blood as it gushed forward and downward from their throat as they hung upside down. Whoever had killed them would have had to hold their heads in his arms to avoid having the blood run down the victim's faces into their hair. Each of the victim's faces were cleaned, and their hair was brushed and tidied afterwards in order to leave little in the way of trace evidence. The killer was a perfectionist and obviously had killed them to collect the blood, but for what? No one seemed to have an answer.

The autopsies were finally done. Shelley pushed the

body tray with job #11027A, back into the cooler locker. The brunette's partner, job #11026A, lay one locker over. It was nearly lunch and Shelley had a few personal errands she could run before returning for the afternoon. She would send her report over to Dennis Kortovich later that afternoon, but for now she needed to attend to some personal business, apron off, gloves in the disposal bin, grabbing her coat, and heading down the hall to the rear doors. Outside, her old, blue, 2001 Topaz was parked in the staff parking area. She hoped someone would steal it, but each time she walked across the rear of the parking lot of the M.E.'s office, like a loyal sentinel, it was still there. *Why were the loyal and good ones always old or ugly?* Shelley laughed to herself; just like men; the good ones were always too old, too ugly or were already taken.

Shelley was a real Ingénue, a pixyish beauty. At only five foot three, her cute figure was always a source of pride. At nearly forty, she could honestly say gravity had done very little harm to her toned, muscular body. Her calves were full and strong reaching up to well rounded, smooth thighs. But the greatest envy expressed by other females when they discussed their bodies was her flat stomach that inched up to her tiny waist. A full chest, well-toned arms, and long, graceful neck completed a body that if taller would have been near perfect. Her face was a soft, heart shape with a wide forehead and small dimpled chin. She almost had a slightly romantic, innocent look, but her small freckled nose, expressive lips, and wide, golden-brown eyes gave her an impish, mischievous look that belied any thought of innocence.

Together everything matched her impulsive spontaneous personality. If Shelley got an idea, look out! She would soon be absorbed in it up to her delectable neck. Over the years she had managed to run several very successful businesses, return to school to complete a medical degree, specialize in forensic medicine and raise a wonderful, over-imaginative daughter, Tiffany, now nearly twenty. Friends often ran out of breathe just thinking of her accomplishments. She also had a passion for trying to do everything on her own. Why buy when you could make it or do it yourself! Her friends always wondered if it was because she was cheap or brilliant. It was probably a little bit of both. As a single mother, dollars were hard to come by, especially after she returned to school in her late twenties.

Presently her home was turned upside down with renovations. Actually, her home was always partway through one project or another, anything from a giant fishpond in her back yard to ceramic tiles throughout most of the home. Even the removal of half the walls was accomplished with the help of "How To" library books or Videos. Every tool imaginable, electric or manual, was stored in her garage.

Shelley was almost out the double back doors when a familiar voice halted her steps. She turned, a wide grin reaching across her face and lighting her brown eyes with a resigned but cheerful expression of welcome.

"Dennis! I knew I couldn't slip away without you on my tail. A few more minutes and you would have missed me," she blurted out. "You have an unusually accurate sense of timing. I'm sure you lurk in the halls just waiting to corner me so you can pretend you were just in the building anyway and no, my reports are not finished. I've got to drop some other papers off then I'll be back and email them to you when they're complete."

"Wow! Now that you've stopped long enough to breathe, let's take some time together." Dennis put a guiding hand on Shelley's shoulder. "I really need your insight and I've got to go over to The Beef Chateau and finish a few questions with the owner and some of the staff and I was hoping we could do lunch."

Dennis finished with a solemn half-grin, making him look vulnerable and helpless, a sure heart sinker that usually worked with the women. It was all an act, but it still worked.

"Dennis you're an ass if you think I'm falling for that wounded, I need help look. Forget it. But I could use a nice lunch. You're buying."

With that exchange Dennis escorted Shelley over to his car and they were off to The Beef Chateau a good twenty minutes from the Coroner's office, enough time to fill in the latest developments. Once seated behind the wheel, Dennis jumped straight in.

"As you know these two newest victims are number ten and eleven and we're so far away from even having one good suspect that I'm afraid the number of victims is going to go even higher. Was there anything different about these two? Something he may have missed?" Dennis inquired hopefully.

"Not really." Shelley turned to Dennis with a resigned look. "Whoever is doing these murders is good. Maybe the best I've seen. He leaves us nothing and I've truly never seen this before. Every victim is killed the exact same way."

Shelley pulled on the seat belt that had become twisted under her coat collar. "When the lab goes over their clothes and belongings there is nothing there. I am sure he has some forensic experience, and uses scotch tape to remove all evidence from the victims. There is never a struggle because of the Halcion, which puts them out for a few minutes. By then it's too late, I imagine when they come too they must be terrified. In the autopsy, the hormone systems were on overdrive. This psycho has them bound so tight they can't struggle while he terrifies them. This helps to get the hormone levels on overdrive and then once he drains their blood, he cleans everything up, washes their hands and dumps them." Shelley paused for a moment to sort through the facts.

"The most unusual part is that there are usually fibers from the car that the victims would be transported in but there is nothing, so he must lay a clean plastic tarp down and wrap them from head to foot in something to avoid contaminating the bodies with any evidence. Everything is clean. If you ever catch this guy you better get him cold because we won't be able to back you up with additional evidence, so far we have none." Shelley's tirade was over and again she fumbled with her seat belt, irritation showing on her face.

Both Dennis and Shelley sat in silence for a few minutes, each sorting out all the details of the case in their minds trying to make some sense of it.

"What about the soil we found on each of the victims, anything new there?" Dennis's question was hopeful as he navigated the pre-noon traffic with ease.

"Again, nothing new, all of the soil is in a standard baggie. The kind anyone can get at a grocery store. There are no prints on the bags. Everything is clean as a whistle." She looked into the rear-view mirror making sure her face and hair weren't a mess from the morning's work.

"The soil itself isn't unusual, you could find it anywhere in Chicago. I can offer you one little hope, or prayer. If you find the right location I could give you a 99.9 percent confirmation. Soil may look alike and in many areas it is but when you have the spot I'll know." Shelley said with confidence.

"Soil samples are easy to match to their exactness once you have the right location. My gut is he's trying to tell you something and it's usually close to home."

"Why didn't we find a bag of soil on our first victim?" Dennis inquired, staring ahead at the road.

Shelley turned her head to look at Dennis, his profile straight and strong. His teeth clenched, making the muscles in his jaw flex back and forth. Even his gloved hands on the steering wheel were clenched firmly. He was wound tight, like a rubber band. The difference was that Dennis would never snap. He was too good for that, one of the best. Shelley knew he already had an answer. He just wanted a fresh perspective.

"My guess is that the first murder was done on impulse. Something snapped in this guy's brain to start this string of killings. The next two may have moved him deeper into his psychosis and now it's an all-out game and he doesn't want to get caught. I would just like to know what he wants the blood for." Shelley's face was thoughtful.

"Maybe he thinks he's a vampire and is drinking it. Have you checked into any of the cults to see if it's a ritualistic killing or anything like it?" She undid the seat belt, throwing it off in irritation.

"We've already gone down that road, as far as we know

the few weirdoes that see him or herself as Dracula or any other ghoulish thing are all accounted for."

Dennis's voice lost its even tone, raising a little as he continued. "They even disclaim any involvement in this kind of behavior, not that anyone would confess. But still, it seems to be a dead end, meanwhile we're still keeping an eye on it."

"Now to a more cheery topic," Shelley interjected. "Where is that partner of yours, Chuck? I haven't seen his chubby face around lately and I miss him. He always makes me feel good, kind of special, you know." Shelley turned back to face the front window, the seatbelt having been dismissed.

"I'm sure he does make you feel special." Dennis gave her a sly smile.

"He has a crush on you ya know. When are you going to give the guy a break and go out with him?" Dennis's attitude turned more serious.

"What have you got to lose? Some of the guys you've dated have been pretty bad, big-time losers."

"Thanks a lot." Her eyes widened in mock indignation.

"You know nothing about being single. It's damn hard to find a good guy. Especially when you work the hours I do. Shift work, long hours, and kids. You try finding someone." She crossed her arms, her lips pouting.

"Yeah, you're right. I've been married forever and I like it that way. Veronica and the kids are used to things now and my home life is finally smooth sailing." Dennis shifted gears. "It hasn't always been this easy, but it is now and I try not to take it for granted."

* * * *

Once again they each drifted off into their own thoughts, sifting through their memories of the past years. Shelley had to admit it to herself, in the area of romance she was a dud. She couldn't tell a 'Pig from a Poke' and her self-confidence in the romance department was at an all-time low. Besides, some of the lazy ones, boring ones, driven and obsessive ones, and even a few good but dull ones had managed to find their way in and out of her life. One guy she'd thought was perfect. It ended up being a classic textbook case, but she couldn't see it until it was too late, even if her friends could, a stalker! In the end he had become so obsessive and controlling that she finally had to admit that he had crossed an invisible line that once stepped over, became abuse. She had tried to end it several times. Nicely at first, but finally she had to tell him in plain blunt terms that it was over. She never wanted to see or hear from him again.

* * * *

"Look Roger, It's over. I don't want you calling me or coming over to the house or showing up at work. I never want to see you again. I don't need someone in my life who thinks he can run me. I have been on my own for too long." Shelley faced the man who at one time she had thought was Mr. Right.

Roger Grant was a tall, thin man whose looks had gotten him his share of women, but his relationships had never gone anywhere and Shelley now understood why. He had told her of all of the heartbreak he had gone through when they first met and at the time she had been a sympathetic listener. Now she felt disgust at his neediness.

"Look little miss, I need nobody. I'm tired of being dumped by girls like you that think you can bat those big, brown eyes and we come crawling with our tails between our legs, and then when it's not good for you anymore, it's over. This time I decide, and I say it's not over." He put his face in hers. She could tell he had been drinking.

There was no use in arguing further. He wasn't going to hear a thing she had to say and he was hurting at the rejection. He would just need a little time to cool off and get over the end of what had started out as a great romance.

"You contact me and I'll call the cops. So get off my doorstep." Shelley slammed the door in Roger's surprised face.

"Fine, who wants to be with a cunt of a bitch like you, anyway? I can get a dozen women just like you. So go fuck yourself and stay an old maid." Roger stomped away, leaving a trail of cuss words in his wake.

At first she thought she had finally gotten through to him and then funny things started to happen. Mail went missing. Doors that were supposed to be locked were left open. Her drawers in her bedroom and office had been gone through. The list was classic. Finally there were calls, at first pleading and finally threatening. It went on for over a year. Restraining orders and visits from the police had little effect. But finally Lady Luck smiled on her after a year of hell. The bastard took sick and developed double pneumonia. Who would guess he had developed a resistance to all antibiotics? Once he got a good case of staph infection it was soon over. He died from complications. She had only felt relief at the news of his death. The dating game was over. And a nice guy like Chuck wouldn't shake her resolve, even if he had been there for her during her ordeal. Yes, she was sure. No more dating!

* * * *

As they pulled up in front of The Beef Chateau, they noticed a police cruiser out front. When they walked to the double oak doors, Chuck was soon at their side, the cold crisp air of February making his round cheeks seem even rosier because of their natural high color.

"Hey, what took you so long? I've been here for over half an hour?" He asked Shelley. "You look great." It was all Chuck could add to his initial out-burst his eyes softened as he took in the perfection of Shelley's face.

"I picked up a little extra help on my way. I thought Shelley could add some insight to our investigation." Dennis replied, seeing Chuck's obvious pleasure.

"Once again, all roads seem to lead us back here to Lexy and Bara's restaurant. They agreed to meet us and see if they can add anything new." Dennis drew his hood up over his head.

"We now know that most or even all of the victims ate here at least a few days or weeks before their deaths, not unusual for out of town guests. It is the number one restaurant in Chicago for beef, but none of the victims were here, near or around the time of death. So far it's the only thing all of the victims have in common. Credit card receipts prove that at some time during their stay they all ate here. Let's take one more shot at it, maybe we will come up with something." Dennis reached for the door.

Before he could grab the large, finely carved antique ring and knock, the door opened and they were greeted by a big smile and warm hello and hug from Lexy.

"Come in, come in, you will freeze out there. Come and get out of the wind and cold!" Lexy admonished as he took their coats and motioned for them to follow him. "Bara's in the back preparing a special lunch. We want to help all we can."

Lexy motioned for the threesome to follow him to the back of the restaurant. Once they were seated comfortably, Bara brought in a basket of the hot buns fresh from the oven, smelling like hot yeast and warm butter. They were being treated to a new steak, recently added to the menu.

"How much did you say this steak would cost?" Dennis asked with disbelief in his voice.

They all went into shock when they heard the price, nearly four hundred dollars for all of them to eat the perfectly cooked filet Mignon that was done to a rare perfection. For each of them lunch was a culinary experience they would never forget. The meat was sweeter than usual. The spices and wine were a soft contrast to the undertones to the taste of the meat; tender, moist, and grilled with a charred spicy taste on the outer edges. The steak was sheer perfection.

As the steak hit the recesses of their stomach and the first stages of digestion began, the juices and blood of the marinade were assimilated through the walls of their stomachs into their bloodstream. POW! Something began to happen. By the time they finished the last piece of the steak there was a definite sense of well-being and awareness that was different from after any other meal.

"What's in this meat?" questioned Dennis who had the look of a Cheshire Cat on his face. "I've never eaten anything like it."

"Yeah! Unbelievable, I feel great." Chuck added as he put his hands behind his head and leaned back making a little more room for his protruding belly. He was definitely stuffed and feeling great.

"I almost feel like dancing or maybe doing a twenty-six mile marathon. I even bet I could win." Shelley stood and did a couple of fancy turns as she too responded to the new feelings of delight that spread through her body.

"It's a secret," Bara chuckled, "one of Brian's new recipes. He didn't want to put it on the menu, but after we tried it we felt people would pay the price for such perfection. It was hard to convince Brian, but it's become a great hit on the menu. Few can afford it, but once they do they usually come back for more. Now, how can we help you? The rest of the staff will arrive soon and we will have to get back to work as well." Bara's earnest request brought them back to the present.

Dennis stood up and began to pace. His brain seemed clear and his senses were aware of all the subtleties of the room. Not unusual for his analytical mind, but there seemed to be more color and clearer sounds. He swore he could even see a slight source of light coming from all of those who had gathered for lunch. He blinked twice, but the light and feeling of awareness remained.

"I need to ask a few more questions." Dennis launched in quickly trying to dismiss the unusual scene before him.

"We know most of the victims ate a meal here a few days before their deaths and we also know that most of your staff have been questioned and checked out. So far no one can be tied into any of the victims. Only Brian Bentham has no real alibi, but that too isn't in and of itself suspicious." Dennis paused for a few minutes stroking his mustache before continuing. "Brian works late and alone every evening, leaving for home between three and four a.m..." Dennis looked at Bara for confirmation.

"He lives alone so no one can confirm his presence there. Nevertheless, no-one seems to know any of the victims beyond the service given to them the night they dined here." Dennis kept his monologue direct and precise.

"There seems to be no other contact with the victims by anyone who works here. My only reason for going over everything again, it is the only thing all the victims had in common is that they all ate here a few days or weeks before they died. What do you make of it?" Dennis turned his attention to Lexy, hoping his astute people skills might come up with an overlooked thread of information that would tie things together.

"Nothing, nothing that makes any sense and none of my people would do such a thing." An excited Lexy replied as he too paced in step with Dennis hoping to add his energy to Dennis's much faster stride.

"I have over a hundred full and part-time people," Lexy continued. "They are usually finished by eleven. Bara and I leave at midnight and later Brian leaves at four. This has been going on for over ten years and I've noticed nothing unusual."

"The only thing different is the addition of the deluxe steak to our menu, and for us, what's so new about steak?" Lexy stopped his pacing long enough to turn around and face Dennis with a blank look on his face.

By now Chuck felt as if he too had to get up and get moving, an entirely new sensation for him. He could definitely be described as the original couch potato. He drove everywhere and never walked if he could help it. Why walk if you could drive, stand if you could sit, or sit if you could lounge? This need to move and think was a new experience and he liked it. He felt alive and his brain was racing. Some idea was trying to form in the recess of his mind. The steak was a new item on the menu. Brian, the only one left late at night. Chuck couldn't put his finger on it but something about all of the victims eating at The Beef Château was staring him in the face, he just couldn't get a fully formed idea. It still hung back somewhere in his brain but he was unable to bring the idea forward and give it a tangible form or thought.

Chuck took three long strides over to the double stainless steel doors leading to the kitchen where he was almost knocked over by Brian Bentham, the head chef and the object of their discussion. Brian pushed open the left door leading out of the kitchen.

"Oh! Sorry, sorry. I didn't know anyone was standing here." Brian's deep voice boomed with concern.

"Left door for out, right for in, so no one will get knocked out like this." He bent over and offered his hand as well as his apology.

Brian's heart started to pound. The police were back. They had only recently showed up after several of the victim's' credit cards tied them all to an evening at The Beef Chateau. It was the only thing that Brian could not control. He never had access to any of the money, so removing the credit card receipts was impossible. As he stood up, he pulled Chuck with him. Brian turned around and stood face to face with Dennis, his new adversary and a long-time friend.

"Hi Dennis, Chuck. A little early for supper wouldn't

you say?" His voice was smooth and welcoming.

Brian looked over at the table near the kitchen doors, the one at which the staff usually sat at. He could see they had finished a special lunch prepared by Bara; a lunch only he could really appreciate. Bara sat at the table next to a dark-haired woman about his age, she was very attractive and he was sure he had never met her before. He would have remembered anyone as delectable as she was.

"Well yes and no, we came by to cover a few more details and Bara as usual had to feed us the new specialty of the house. A secret recipe of yours, I understand." Dennis's questioning glance was directed back at Brian.

For a few seconds Brian wasn't sure he knew how to respond. Did they know? He doubted it. No one would even try the steak if they knew the secret to the marinade. Hell, once again the cops were too stupid to know what was right under their noses. Brian cleared his face of any emotion, something he was very good at, and looked Dennis straight in the eye. "Yes it is new and I can tell you it's a huge success but the main ingredient is very expensive, almost priceless you might say. How may I help?" was his earnest reply.

"If you could walk me through the back again and go over your evening after everyone leaves, it might help to give us a time frame for your whereabouts." Dennis gave him back an equally even look.

"This time I'd like Chuck and Shelley to come along." Dennis stated, leaving no room for discussion.

Dennis had taken a brief walk through the back shortly after they had found the common denominator for all of the victims, at the time he had seen nothing unusual. The rule in good police work was to look for the obvious. "If it looks like an apple, it isn't an orange." If the restaurant was the only thing tying the murders together, then there was a high percentage of chance that someone here was involved, but whom? Bara and Lexy didn't seem to be the type and so far there had been few serial killers who were married and had waited till their mid-sixties to start a life of crime. Most of the other staff had worked a variety of shifts and no one had been working each and every one of the nights that the victims had dined there, only Brian.

Brian could fit the profile; white male, middle age, single, and a loner. Dennis had known him for nearly a decade. He and Veronica had eaten at The Beef Chateau many times and Bara and Lexy had become good friends. Often they would dine late on a weeknight and the couple would join them as the evening wound down. Brian would also sit with them if all were well in hand. Dennis had liked the chef's easy manner and wit. He felt a little guilty at having to question Brian like this, but it was his job. However thin the thread was that linked the victims to Brian, Dennis had to follow it to the end and somehow he was reluctant to let go.

"Not until you introduce me to this lovely woman," Brian countered, his brain racing.

What were they up to? He had to keep things short and to the point. "*Keep it simple.*" He thought to him-self. They were simply following up the only lead they had. All of the victims had eaten at the restaurant. He knew they would show up and they had, but he also knew that they wouldn't be able to find any concrete evidence leading to him. He had been very careful and he was sure he hadn't slipped up.

He already had a plan forming in his mind for a future airtight alibi. Brian turned his deep-blue eyes toward Shelley, looking at her directly as he flashed his beautiful smile.

"Hi. I'm sure we've never met, my name is Brian."

He lowered his head so his eyes would be directly even with hers as he took her warm strong hand and engulfed it into his finely formed hand. He could feel her tremble as their bodies exchanged energy, leaving them both a little shocked.

"Nice to meet you." was the only thing she could come up with? It sounded a little simple even to Shelley's ears, but at this moment her brain was on hold while her hormones shifted into overdrive. She even felt a little faint. Could this be love? No, just lust. It felt good. Maybe if someone like Brian asked her out she could break her no more dating rule.

"Enough with the starry eyes you two, we have things to do and these detectives have to get back to work and solve these terrible crimes." Bara broke into Brian and Shelley's private moment. With a stiff push up, she rose from the table and launched into her usual scolding and bossing around. When Bara wanted to get you going, you got moving.

"Now let's get to it. Brian you take everyone back into the kitchen, and tell them what they need to know. Then let's get going, we have a busy night." She said as she pushed everyone toward the kitchen.

Brian opened the right swinging door and led the way. He held the door open until they were all assembled in the kitchen and then turned his attention toward Shelley, turning on the charm.

"I still don't know your friend's full name or what she does and I won't answer any questions until I do." Brian continued with a flirting tone to his voice.

Chuck gave Brian a dirty look and kept on walking. Like hell he was going to help out this Romeo. Why did all the girls go for good-looking, smooth talkers, who always broke their hearts? What was wrong with a guy like him? He looked over at Shelley and he could tell she was a goner. Smitten and down for the count.

"Brian, I'd like to formally introduce you to Dr. Shelley McPherson, our Medical Examiner and one of Chicago's top forensic experts on trauma. If anyone can find out what's going on when these bodies go under the knife, it's Shelley." Dennis finished with an obvious pride.

Brian could tell that Dennis and Chuck thought a lot of this woman, enough to bring her here. It would be dangerous to show too much interest, he would have to be careful. This was someone he would have to get to know and get close to. Shelley would be able to provide a perfect cover for him without ever suspecting that she was being used. What she knew, he must also know. He would have to get her card and call her later.

Chapter Seven

The day was finally over. Brian played the events of the early afternoon once again in his head. He had gone over every detail a hundred times and could find little that would alert or set up any red flags concerning him, other than the fact that he worked at The Beef Chateau. His work hours left him with little or no alibi, but nothing unusual made him a strong suspect. His only reason for being a suspect is that he didn't have an alibi and he was about to fix that.

Brian made sure during the questioning and the inspection of the back area that his energy stayed even. When he was asked a question he gave only enough information to satisfy the cops; never too much or too little. Brian had spent a lifetime studying crime and he knew that guilty people would often give too much detail or information trying to prove their innocence. Often they would say something that would set up red flags for the cops and eventually it would "undo" them, causing them to get caught.

After his dad had killed his mother he had devoured "True Crime" stories like a junkie needing a fix. He never got enough. He watched *American Justice* on TV as well as any other program that covered murder investigations. *"Investigative Reports"*, books, anything! He even bought books on forensics and in his late twenties attended a few night classes with Continuing education; "Scene of the Crime 101." The topics included evidence collection and analysis, fingerprint identification and development, footwear comparison, physical matching, bloodstain pattern analysis. It was through these classes that he learned how things were done at the Medical Examiner's office. Downstairs in his basement was a library of books, videos and taped TV shows that would put any professional to shame. When it came to crime, he was the best. But he wasn't interested in solving murder. He was only interested in getting away with it.

Brian looked around one more time before sitting down with a second glass of wine. He laid his head back against the plush, semi-circular booth and closed his eyes, going over all of the details of the afternoon visit from the police. Now, one more time, had he given anything away? He had taken the lead, holding Shelley's arm like a gracious host escorting a very special guest. Dennis seemed amused while Chuck looked irritated. He was stepping on some toes but that was Chuck's problem. Obviously Shelley wasn't interested, she had eyes for Brian only.

Brian had given Dennis a brief, step-by-step account of a usual evening for him at The Beef Chateau. He arrived at work around two p.m. Saw to the preparation of dressings and garnish, and then made sure all of the different cuts of steak were ready and available for the evening dinners. Over one thousand steaks went out to the half-a-dozen open charcoal grills, all with a special marinade for each cut.

The rest of the evening was spent overseeing all of the cooks, making sure each plate had the right garnish. Over the years he had developed an eye that could spot a sloppy plate before it was even one step out of the grill area. The junior cooks took a great deal of pride in their plates, so his job was easy until after close. Brian would then cut steaks, and prepare marinades and special dressings. After his cleanup, he would go home. He tried to make it sound simple but Dennis wanted to access the meat-cutting room, and he seemed determined. Brian knew that there was only one thing that could give him away. He would have to be careful.

"What's in here?" Dennis asked as he pointed to the heavy locker door that led to the cooler and meat room.

"This is my pride and joy, where all the magic happens." Brian kept his voice steady and remained open and helpful.

He had nothing to hide. He knew it would look all right. Once they were inside, the white walls and bright lights assaulted their already overloaded senses. Hinds of beef were hung on several hooks to the left. Next to them was a large freezer. Inside, were trays upon trays of already-cut beef. Brian figured they would have to know what to look for to really see anything that could draw any suspicion.

In the center, a very large wooden cutting block stood alone, above it, knives of every description. To the right halfway up was another sealed locker about the size of a small fridge. Brian held Shelley's arm and deliberately stood in front of the sealed locker, giving everyone a full view of the room and hoping they would not see the small door behind him.

"A lot of sharp knives, I'm sure they would cut with exact precision." Dennis slowly stroked his mustache, a frequent habit as he looked up at the distinctive blade of each knife.

Shelley stepped forward and joined Dennis as he slowly took each knife down and examined it. Now it was her turn to do what she did best. She had seen enough to be able to give an accurate guess if any of the blades matched. She put on her gloves and picked up each knife slowly. She knew the gloves wouldn't help much; each knife was clean and well disinfected, it was just a habit. Nothing! Not one blade was thin enough to cut as finely as the wounds on the victim's necks, which had been made with such clean precision. Each blade was either too big and would have left a few jagged edges, or too small, which caused several starts and stops on the victims' necks.

She looked up at Brian, his face clear and open, like a man who had nothing to hide. She could feel herself blush, knowing that she had hoped all along that they would find nothing. After all, she was just doing her job. She turned her eyes to Dennis.

"None of these blades are a match. We're at a dead end here." Shelley stepped back over to Brian's side, removing her gloves and stuffing them into her pocket.

Dennis took one last look around. It was all clean, very, very clean.

"I see you freeze a lot of your meat. I always thought it was fresh." His tone was even, with no hint of suspicion.

"It's the only way to stay ahead of the demand. The steaks stay "same day" fresh, but it also helps to kill any bacteria. This freezing prevents any chance of food poisoning." Brian hoped his response would be enough and they would leave. Well, Shelley could stay, but he could get to her later.

With one last look around, Dennis went towards the exit door. Chuck, Shelley, and Brian were close behind.

Dennis halted just before exiting.

"What's the electronic key pad for?" He asked as if surprised by the security.

"There's one outside as well." Brian offered.

"Only Bara, Lexy, and my-self can get in. Once we're in, it locks and only by knowing the numbers can we get out. The secrets to all of our recipes are kept in here. We guard them with our lives."

Brian finished his response with an innocent wink toward Shelley keeping the mood light. With that statement he moved forward, pressed four keys on the pad, heard a click and opened the door. The only reason that they hadn't noticed the key pad before was that Brian, surprised to find the cops here that early in the afternoon, had not locked the cutting room when he came into the dining room.

Shelley looked down at her watch surprised at how late it was; nearly three.

"Oh my, I've got to get going. I still have some papers to drop off at the court house and I have a report to type for you if I remember correctly." She turned a reproachful eye toward Dennis.

"Wait, you can't go without leaving me a card or number where I can reach you. I'm sure I have a few questions of my own." Brian's flirtatious response brought a blush to Shelley's cheeks.

As she pulled a card from her pocket she could feel her cheeks grow warm at his comments.

"Here, call me any-time. I'm there most days and I check in for messages." She tried not to sound too hopeful.

Chuck could stand the flirting no longer and turned to make an obvious exit out the kitchen doors to the dining room where Lexy and Bara were waiting to give their farewells. *Why watch and listen to such dribble?* He thought as he pushed open the doors to the dining room.

Dennis and Shelley exchanged a, "We're in deep shit" look and followed Chuck. Brian waved a final good-bye.

They were finally gone.

It was now several hours later and Brian finished his wine and steak, a deep sigh of relief exploding from his lungs. It was as if he had been holding his breath all night and only now could he let it go and relax, now that he was sure they had seen nothing to cast any suspicion on him. They never saw it, the small locker behind him. If they had asked what was in the locker they would have had their answer to the precision cut on the victims' throats. But, they hadn't and Brian felt safe. He knew life was all about the small details. If he had stood even a few inches to one side Dennis would have seen the small door and asked to see what lay behind. It was soon time to go.... Brian had two new bundles to take home and put in his deep freeze. Once again he had some extra work to do to keep the cops from finding out when or where these two new victims were killed. He loved it. Everyone was so stupid. He could hear an ancient echo in his ear as the voice of his father once again came to mind.

"I'll show you boy! You'll never be smarter than your old man. Don't think you can get away. Hiding won't help! Gotcha!" Whack, Whack, Whack! He could almost feel the sting of the belt as his mind raced to the past.

The smell of his father's breath and the sweat from his skin could still come to mind and seemed real whenever the old thoughts broke into his everyday world.

"You are nothing but a little bastard, your head always in a book. I bet you think you're better than your old man, with all your fancy marks in school, but you are nothing. You'll never go anywhere and if you think you can outsmart your dad then think again, cause it don't matter, I can still lay a licking on your skinny, no--good hide. You're just like your mother and if you know what's good for you you'll keep your' nose clean and keep your smart mouth to yourself. Just remember boy, I can send you anywhere I want and no one's even going to give a damn. After all the cops never found out where your mother ran off too and they wouldn't even waste their time on a little fucker like you."

The sound of the belt was the last sound Brian heard as he quickly put all thoughts of the past from his mind. He slowly finished the last of his special steak before going home. She was good, very, very good. He'd always liked brunettes.

Chapter Eight

Dennis had gathered the team of other detectives in the boardroom for most of the morning. It was beginning to become one of the most depressing parts of his day. Each time the team gathered around the table to go over the hundreds of leads that poured in daily, there was a sense of doom as each member reported the lack of progress in each area of the investigation. This morning most of the team left the boardroom in order to follow up the new leads, in the hope that just one call could lead them to the killer. As Dennis turned to leave he heard a loud conversation brewing at the end of the boardroom table. It was officer Ferine O'Donnell and his partner Patrick. Once again a heated argument was well underway.

"I can tell you for certain it's a clear-cut case of murder." Ferine seemed determined to get Patrick to see things his way.

"Look Ferine, I agree with you, but we still only have hunches and innuendo. It's not enough to get a warrant for the arrest of a guy like Mendoza. He'll have a team of the most high-powered lawyers on us like syrup on hot cakes. We can't rush an investigation like this." Patrick at this point wasn't trying to get Ferine mad. He was just trying to make a point.

Dennis tried to get the two officers to lighten up "Hey you two, don't tell me the honeymoon is over and you still haven't settled this case?"

He could tell Ferine was genuinely frustrated with his partner's hesitation in pushing forward and going for an arrest. Not that Dennis blamed him. Patrick Mendoza was a mean son of a bitch and few ever crossed him; especially the police. He would have little compunction in arranging for an accident for anyone who got in his way.

"Dennis, you know what we're up against. Give us your opinion on this case. I just can't seem to get my stubborn partner here to see that if we rush this case we'll get fucked in the left ear by Mendoza. He'll pull every string he's got to bury us. And if it means he can't do it by calling on City Hall and have us walking a beat then I don't doubt he could arrange an accident. We have to go careful and get the bastard cold." Patrick turned to Dennis for confirmation and backup.

"Go slow and tell me what you've got."

Dennis was all ears and his analytical mind was prepared to listen to the details and give what advice he could.

It was Patrick who took over the task of unfolding the story for Dennis. "It's the Doctor, Clarence Fielding. From what we can gather over the past two days, this guy has a real drug problem. It seems his finances are also in a shambles and he decided that he would be a "mule", making a few drug runs to Colombia, and get a cut of the action. He could pay off a few bills plus snort some of the stuff on the side. That's how he came into contact with Mendoza."

"It seems that Mendoza was tired of his wife and had a serious affair going with one of the daughters of his partners in the law firm where he is the senior partner. Mendoza may have built up a seemingly legitimate front by being a lawyer, but the word on the street is that he's a major player in the import business of illegal drugs. One of two things may have happened. Margaret Mendoza got wind of the affair and took it hard. She either asked Mendoza to give up his girlfriend and stay with her, or she demanded a divorce. If she knew of Mendoza's real business then she may have seemed like a threat to him, or else she wanted more of the fortune than he felt she was entitled to. Either way he wanted to get rid of her."

Patrick stood up. He seemed to think better by walking back and forth as he outlined what information they thought they had.

"If Mrs. Mendoza went missing or died from something other than natural causes, then her father would pull every string he could to launch an investigation and all the money in the world wouldn't solve the problem if Shane Grey called in all of his favors. He could bury Mendoza in enough financial investigations to make sure he would have to spend a fortune defending himself. From what everyone says of the man, money is everything, so death by a natural cause was the only option open to Mendoza, thus the need for a man like Dr. Fielding. He would have to kill the wife and make it look like natural causes. We think Mrs. Mendoza never even met Dr. Fielding until the morning of her death and that the file he has on her is a fake. It appears that she had a blood clot to the lungs only hours after Dr. Fielding came to the Mendoza home to treat her for what the family says was hypertension. The secretary says she walked into the room and Mrs. Mendoza was getting a blood transfusion.

"The doctor had several bags of blood and told Mrs. Mendoza that her hemoglobin was low and that a transfusion would help her to feel like a nineteen-year-old again. At least that's what she told her secretary. Mrs. Mendoza was fine when he left but within a few hours she collapsed with a blood clot to the lungs. The secretary thought that at the time it was funny because Mrs. Mendoza's blood type was O and she was sure the bags were A-. At the time it didn't register with the secretary that the blood type was wrong, it was only later when Mrs. Mendoza collapsed that she remembered. If Mrs. Mendoza was given the wrong blood type, then it was murder. The problem is that we can't seem to prove that the blood given to Mrs. Mendoza wasn't type O or that anything was done on purpose. If she did get the wrong type though, she would have gotten a blood clot to the lungs.

"The secretary now says she doesn't remember seeing what type of blood was in the bags and we are afraid that Mendoza got to her. The coroner says she didn't find anything unusual in the blood because she wasn't looking and now it's too late. The poor woman was cremated and we can't do a follow up based on the blood with-out a corpse. All we have is a weak theory that Mendoza wanted to get rid of his wife and made a deal with the Doctor to "do her in" in return for money. The Doctor was desperate and we think he would do it."

"What about his bank account? Has he come into a large sum of money that he can't explain?"

"He has over one million dollars that was just

transferred into his account yesterday. But when we traced it, the money seems to have come from an inheritance from some uncle who just died. And guess where his uncle lived and where the money came from?" Ferine spoke up for the first time, hoping his question would lead Dennis to an obvious conclusion.

"Colombia. His uncle was a lover of a warm climate and just happened to live in a country where Mendoza has rumored ties." Dennis stated the obvious.

"That's the problem! It's all rumors. We can't prove anything, at least not with the budget this department has. If we could get approval to go to Colombia we're sure that we could prove the uncle is bogus and the money is tied to Mendoza. But until then we're at a dead end.

"Then you'll have to do what we all have had to do at one time or another. Grease a few palms around the bar where the doctor hangs out and wait until the good doctor gets too drunk or high and tells the wrong person. I have never seen a man like him not break at one time or another. Check his background and find out exactly what his story is. Then you'll find his weak spot and break the case. Mendoza will never make a mistake. You'll have to get to Mendoza by way of the doctor. A man like that is weak and he will make a mistake sooner or later. Now let's hope our killer makes a mistake and tells someone with a conscience before several more bodies turn up." Dennis excused himself, wished the detectives well, and left the boardroom to go back to his office.

Both of the detectives knew that Dennis was right. They would have to bide their time and wait. At this time they only had hunches and no judge would come up against the powerful Mendoza without a confession from the doctor on his part of the murder. It was the doctor who was the weakest link. The detectives would do exactly what Dennis suggested and dig up every detail of the good doctor's life and put it under a microscope. Nothing that had ever happened to Doctor Clarence Fielding or his family would go undiscovered by Detective Ferine O'Donnell or Patrick Getty.

Chapter Nine

It was another Monday night and Veronica was off to her usual Weight Watchers meeting with Judy, a long-time friend, as well as Terry and her sister Jodi, who were clients of her salon and good friends as well. Together they had all joined Weight Watchers to get off an extra forty to fifty pounds that had slowly found its way onto their already well- rounded bodies, except for Jodi, who was still slim. Jodi liked to join them for supper after the meetings. It was a great opportunity to be with new friends. Veronica heard the front door slam and knew that Dennis was home.

"Hey honey, I didn't think you'd get home before I left, supper's in the oven." Veronica turned around as she spoke to see a dejected-looking husband standing in the kitchen door, looking like he had nowhere to go.

"What's the matter?" Veronica was surprised to see her husband of so many years, look so worn and emotionally beaten.

Dennis could barely keep the tears from forming in his eyes and he was sure his throat was going to close up tight. He could barely speak. "We found another two victims – sisters. They were only twenty-one and twenty-four, the same ages as Natasha and Katrina. I just finished calling their parents in Seattle. I can't stand it anymore. What if it was our girls?" Dennis choked on the last words in a horse whisper.

"God have mercy." Veronica responded as she stepped away from the stove and engulfed her husband into her large, ample body. Her hands instinctively stroked the back of his neck and tears flowed down her shocked face as she pictured the parents receiving the news.

"They were here for a dance audition with the Chicago Ballet. They were staying at the Hilton Hotel, a gift from their parents. They were only here for a week, one week, and now their lives are over. I just can't take it anymore!" Dennis whispered, gripping his wife tightly, his face pale and drawn.

"I'll stay home, we can talk, and you need me," Veronica offered, reluctant to let go of Dennis as he moved away from her arms to sit down on one of the chairs at the kitchen table.

"No, I need to just be alone and sort things out, you know me. Give me a couple of hours and I'll be able to work this through with you." Dennis bent over, putting his head in his hands.

"For now, all I need is a good long soak in the hot tub and an hour of TV. I need time to separate from this string of brutal murders or it will kill me." Dennis looked up at Veronica with pleading eyes. "You understand don't you?" he asked as he gripped her hands, knowing that her touch would help to ground him.

"I do sweetheart. I'll be home by ten-thirty, if you want, we can talk then." Veronica bent over and kissed her husband tenderly on the lips, her heart sinking to her stomach as she drew away from him. "I love you and you will catch this bastard." She finished with a big hug.

* * * *

The display of emotion was unusual for Dennis…. he was always able to stand back from the crimes. Veronica knew these cases were different. They had become too overwhelming. He really did need the time. A horn honked noisily outside, and Veronica had to go. Once in the car she turned to Terry and Jodi and blurted out the terrible news.

"There have been two more murders." Her voice caught in her throat. "They were only twenty-one and twenty-four years old…. sisters. I feel physically sick and Dennis is a mess." The horror of it all shone in her eyes as she shared the details.

Terry drove away from the house…. she usually drove. Veronica's kids always seemed to have her car and it was common knowledge that she was a terrible driver anyway. With over sixty speeding tickets in twenty years and a few weird accidents, all with Chicago City Transit, she wasn't one to make her friends feel safe with her behind the wheel.

"When's it going to stop? Someone has to do something!" Terry said with disbelief turning into anger. She maneuvered her car through the light traffic, trying not to let her anger get in the way of her driving.

"We have no leads and Dennis says this guy is the best he's ever seen. He won't go into specifics, but he says they have nothing." Veronica's reply did little to settle Terry's ruffled feathers.

After hashing over the horror of it all for several minutes, they decided to let things go; it was only causing them a great deal of fear and anger. Who knew where the killer would strike next? They knew that they personally had nothing to fear, all of the victims were from out of town. But still, murder had a way of involving a whole community. Veronica looked over at the two sisters, and a smile crossed her face. She really did enjoy their company.

Terry and Jodi were both very attractive young women, but few would guess they were sisters. Terry was four years older than Jodi who at thirty, still maintained a muscular, but trim figure.

Terry's build was also very muscular. A dedicated horsewoman for many years; the muscles in her legs and upper arms could rival those of most young wrestlers. Motherhood had added a few extra pounds to what would always be a full, curvy figure. Both girls were short, only five-feet-three inches, but the way they carried themselves made up for any lack of height. The contrast between them was always amazing.

As curly as Terry's light-golden hair was, Jodi's was straight. As turned up as Terry's nose was, Jodi's was equally as straight. Both had golden, hazel-brown eyes, but Terry's were turned up at the edges just like her nose, while Jodi's round, wide eyes added a look of innocence to her open, trusting face. Their personalities also differed. Terry was always direct and to the point, sure of her ideas and opinions while Jodi, like all younger sisters, could hold her own when opinions differed. But she usually held back, offering little to the conversation until all opinions were in and she felt sure of her ground.

"Where are we going after Weight Watchers?" asked

Veronica as she dialed a number on her cell phone.

"Judy can't make it in time for the meeting but she'll join us later," she offered as her call was completed.

"Let's go back to The Beef Chateau. Where else have we gone for the past year?" Terry interjected.

"Andrew is working tonight and I thought we could share that new expensive steak on the menu, as well as a few extra side dishes." Terry's voice took on a dream quality.

"That new steak is something else and I for one would like another taste of it." She finished, licking her lips as she did.

"Count me in." echoed Veronica. "Good service, great food. What else motivates a bunch of food-obsessed women?" She laughed as she thought of the irony of Weight Watchers and eating out.

They had been going for over a year and supper was the perk for going to Weight Watchers. Jodi was outnumbered, but it would have been her choice as well, so her consent was given by her silence. Veronica gave the details to Judy over the phone as they drove into the parking lot of the mall, where the meeting was held every Monday. She hoped they would all be down a few more pounds....supper was always a lot more fun on the nights they were successful. With their meeting over it was off to the Beef Chateau.

The dim lights of The Beef Chateau added to the effect of a sixteenth century chateau. The chandeliers were replicas and reminders of a time long past when candlelight was all that kept the shadows from the night. Now, small electric bulbs tried to give the illusion of softly lit candles as they danced upon the dark wooden walls. The sounds of the hustle and bustle of the many waiters and hundreds of patrons were softened by the many small rooms that surrounded the central grill. It dominated the back wall, just in front of the kitchen while several other small grills were spaced throughout. The semi-circular theme and three-quarter partial walls divided the restaurant up in a way that made each table feel private, giving the diners a feeling of intimacy. This was rather unusual when you considered the size of the restaurant.

Soft, plush seats of deep crimson and antique gold made the customers sink into unaccustomed comfort, while the room was enhanced by the low, wooden-beamed ceilings that were lit by dozens of ancient-looking chandeliers. Clients found it amazing that a restaurant ten times the size of its competitors could be so busy and yet retain the feel of quiet intimacy. Many said that the spirit of Lexy and Bara pervaded every seat and table, giving a special energy to "The Beef Chateau".

"Hello ladies. It's nice to see you again." Came the authentic French accent of Andre, the maître d' who for the past ten years had greeted the large clientele. Andre could remember the names of most of the clients, often after only one visit, making everyone feel special. Once seated, Andre asked a few questions of each of the girls, inquiring about their children and husbands well-being. It always amazed everyone that he could remember so many details about his regular clients. It was a gift and one that made him irreplaceable to Bara and Lexy.

"I shall get Andrew to see to you in one moment," Andre offered. "Let me know if anything is not to your satisfaction."

He finished with a bow, his language very formal with

a slight French accent. The look of his costume added to the ambiance, giving the diners the added feeling of stepping back in time.

The girls settled in, with Veronica, as usual, taking the lead in the conversation.

"I sure do like a man in tights. It must be a requirement that the guys have great legs and buns. Look around, every one of the guys has legs and asses to die for," she gushed as she gazed around the room.

"Yeah, but remember we're old married ladies and all we can do is look." Terry interjected as she turned to look for Andrew, their waiter.

"Speak for yourself." Jodie pulled herself up to her full five foot three and gave the group a 'don't insult me' look.

"After all, you guys may be old, but I'm the baby of the group, and looking is good for us, it helps to keep the blood pumping." she finished, placing her red linen napkin in her lap.

No sooner had she stopped talking, than a warm masculine voice interrupted all of their discussions of young male flesh.

"Well, here are my favorite girls. No Monday would be complete without you beautiful ladies gracing my section. How did Weight Watchers go tonight? Or is that a subject I should just leave alone?" Andrew stood beside Terry as he handed out menus.

"Andrew, you know we come here only to see you. It's all we have to look forward to now that we're fat and married." Veronica reached for Andrew's hand and gave it a motherly squeeze.

It was partially true. Besides the great food, Andrew had become a friend and their weekly visits were now a ritual. Often they would invite him to sit with them at the end of his shift. Andrew was the kind of boy that made mothers wants to go home and round up their daughters. Everything about him was perfect. His combination of boy-next-door, I'm an average kind of guy, and quick, electric personality shone like a beacon on a foggy night. He was the kind of guy who by the very nature of his perfection, would stand out in any crowd. Then, there was one last quality that was sure to make most women melt. It was Andrew's smile. Even, white teeth, the kind you thank God, or your orthodontist for, were a part of a grin that lit up Andrew's face all the way to his eyes. Eyes that were framed by perfect, dark brows, giving you the impression that he hung on your every word….and he did. When you spoke you could tell he was listening, really listening. He wasn't thinking about the dishes he needed to clear or what he needed to get for the other tables or when he would get off work. He had a way of slowing down time and making you feel as if yours was the only table that mattered. He was here, just for you.

"Where's Judy? Surely she won't deny me the pleasure of serving her as well." Andrews' pretense at the pain of Judy's missing presence caused all of the girls to smile.

"You're a rascal." Terry laughed as she took a menu from Andrew.

"Yes, Judy's coming, so just leave an extra menu. She'll be here any minute." Veronica answered.

Just as they opened their menus, Judy's laugh could be heard as Andre led her to their table. It was a laugh that was so beautiful, if it could have been boxed, it would have sold for millions.

"Thanks Andre, I'll tell Bill you were asking about

him, but don't worry, he's doing fine." Judy sat in the chair as Andre pulled it back for her.

"The doctor said medication, diet and exercise will allow him to stick around for another couple of decades and keep me from spending his money." Judy's laugh filled the room once again.

It was a laugh that was like no other on earth; it was perhaps her best quality, among dozens of great attributes. Judy was an old childhood friend of Veronica's, one who would and had endured through all the many events of their crazy lives. Her laugh was full, rich, and perfect in every way. It reflected the whole of who Judy was; Mother Earth Her dark hair was dyed a rich copper-red, cut in a trendy, short style that framed a round, full face. Creamy, dark skin and full, rosy cheeks complimented her even features and big, romantic brown eyes; a mother's eyes that saw everything with love. You always felt she knew the real you. A you that isn't perfect but she loved you anyway. Judy could scold you while making you feel safe and secure. Huge, ample breasts dominated her full figure. The best way to describe Judy's body was to think of a woman who was painted by Rubens and then amplify the proportions one more time. Then you'd have Judy; full figured, beautiful, warm, funny, and perfect. The kind of person you wanted to spend time with when things were good or bad.

"I hope you didn't order without me because I was hoping we could share that new steak on the menu. I can't afford it alone, but four forks are better than none." Judy laughed again at her own pun while everyone joined in. You couldn't help it; that was the effect her laughter always had on everyone.

Later they had just finished the last bite of steak when that familiar look crossed their faces. Andrew was clearing up the last of the side dishes when he saw it happen. It was beginning to be a joke with the staff. Within a few minutes of completing their special steaks, the patrons would get a dreamy; all-is-well-with-the-world look. Then soon after, they would become energized and flamboyant. The quiet would become loud, the loud almost obnoxious in a happy "ain't life grand" kind of way. It was almost irritating to the staff except that tips would soar, sometimes topping thirty percent of the tab. This new steak was the best thing that had ever happened to The Beef Chateau and tonight the girls, his girls, were no exception.

"Can I get you ladies some dessert? We have a new special on the menu, cranberry and apple cheesecake baked in a thin, flaked pastry." Andrew offered, knowing that even though they were all dieting, they would likely share a couple of desserts.

Andrew had no sooner finished tempting them with his offer of cheesecake, when Evelyn Brooks, another friend, arrived looking like she had just lost her best friend. Her brown, fashionably cut hair framed her pretty face making her expressive eyes even more intense.

"Did you hear? Veronica, you must have, with Dennis on the case." Evelyn paused for only a second to catch her breath before continuing. "Two more girls were killed, both the same age as our kids." Evelyn looked at Veronica and Judy only, knowing that Terry and Jodi's children were still small.

"It makes me feel sick. I was driving by when I heard and had to come and see you." she finished, sitting with a thud as she dejectedly accepted a chair from Andrew, joining the girls at the table.

Evelyn was also a childhood friend of Judy and Veronica's. Since grade ten they could trace the best times of their life with each other. Their teenage years had been spent growing into womanhood during the 'sixties and seventies'. Looking back, the three of them had decided they would keep a vow of silence about their misspent youth. There were things they would one day tell their daughters when they were fifty or sixty, or maybe never! When it came to their daughters, they were glad that their girls' attitudes toward sex, schoolwork, and love were far better than in the wild times of the 'seventies' times now kept silent and only discussed away from the kids.

As they paid the bill and finished their conversation about the murdered girls, Evelyn voiced her concern about what the killer did with the blood.

"Well, I for one think that there is some blood-sucking vampire running around town killing people," she stated as matter-of-factly as she could on a subject like murder.

"Why would anyone want to drink human blood?" Jodi spoke with a twinge of disbelief.

"Blood is a very special elixir. The Maasa of Africa and other tribes have lived off of the blood of cattle and warm milk for thousands of years. It's almost a perfect food. Iron and nutrients are all a part of its makeup and human growth hormones as well as all of the other hormones are in the blood. When you drink the blood, it passes through the brain barrier straight to the brain. Pop! You feel good, real fast." Veronica continued; "Did you ever watch the episode of *"Survivor in Africa"* when they drank the cow's blood and afterward everyone appeared to feel better? Well that's what blood will do for you. That's why Dracula has super-human strength…. human blood. Someone must be feeling real good if they are drinking the blood. I'm just glad it's not me, it would gross me out." She made an ugly face to indicate how distasteful it would be.

Everyone just seemed to accept Veronica's statement as truthful. They all knew that she read some pretty strange stuff and it would not be unusual for her to know just exactly why Dracula would want human blood. It was just one idea and as the theories went around the table they became even wilder, with each speculation.

It was still a mystery to everyone and after a half an hour of a very lively, imaginative, discussion they couldn't come up with anything that made any sense. What did the killer do with the blood? Who could really guess? It would remain a mystery and for now they were just happy to share a great meal. They all still felt dreamy and energized after eating their special steak, their senses were still sharp from its effect. Veronica double-checked the cash on the table, making sure there was enough change. Andrew always got a great tip from them.

"Boy, that steak was great." They would have to share another next week, Veronica thought to herself as she grabbed her coat. She decided she would splurge next week and eat a steak of her own. After all, what harm would it be? She could afford it. The only one it could hurt was her and it sure felt and tasted good, after all, money wasn't everything. So what if it cost an arm and a leg?

The girls gathered their coats. They would have to wait for another week.

Chapter Ten

Brian was feeling great as he walked through the kitchen doors to the dimly-lit dining room. He always loved the contrast between the two, the kitchen ceiling bouncing beams of light off the stainless steel, giving everything in the kitchen a cold functional feeling, and then melting into the warm, soft glow of the dining room with its rich, red and gold, plush furniture with gilt-framed pictures. It always made him feel as if he were stepping back in time.

As he walked past the grills, the smell of charcoal and steak assaulted his nostrils. He loved the aroma and sounds of the steaks as they sizzled on the grill, leaving a light trail of smoke rising upward to the overhead fans that were hidden by the overhanging encasements covered in shingles of cedar. The shingles added a look and smell all of their own, making an even stronger impression of a time long past. Brian surveyed the room before he moved past the grill, making sure he was aware of the movements of the staff, as well as those of Lexy and Bara. Tonight he would make his usual rounds, greeting old and new clients alike. No one would ever suspect that he was a predator checking for the weakest prey, the way a wolf-pack surrounds a herd, looking for the most likely target before going for the kill.

Brian spotted two young people in Section D, directly in front of the grill. Their table was separated from the cooking area by a small partial wall, done in artificial gray bricks, giving an authentic medieval look to the divider.

West Coast… he could tell by their choice of wine; a Californian, their taste in fashion; casual, as well as their mannerisms, self-centered. This combination of drink, clothes, and personal traits gave Brian a strong indication that they were from San Francisco. The woman, a blonde, reminded him of a Barbie Doll. Her hair was too blonde, the kind of color that came from the drug store. Her deep-gold roots and over-processed ends only added to the look of someone who cared too much about her looks, but didn't want to part with her money for a more professional color. Her hair fell well past her shoulders, framing her small face, and making her fine features seem overly painted with makeup, which was more reminiscent of the seventies, than today's softer, more neutral colors.

Her companion seemed somewhat younger, maybe mid-twenties. His dark hair and skin were in strong contrast to his pale partner, making him seem to be the dominant personality; a false impression Brian was sure. From the intense exchange of looks and touch, Brian guessed the blonde was a master at the game of manipulation. The boy had no chance at winning this one. She had him eating out of her hand, while making him feel like he was in control.

Brian could always tell who was from out of town; there was a way about them. He had often made bets with the staff, waging even higher odds if he could tell if they were from the West or East Coast; New York or Los Angeles. He always won… it was his gift. He had learned to observe people, developing an instinct that was now becoming even more important than ever. He couldn't afford to be wrong. Brian had to make sure that who-ever he invited back for wine and dessert would fit the profile he had developed, ensuring the success of his new game.

They needed to be young; under thirty, at the height of their hormonal development and he had to know that they would not be missed by family, friends, or co-workers for a least a few days-time enough to remove any connection to their time spent at The Beef Chateau, although now, there seemed to be a connection; their credit-card receipts.

Brian had developed a few key questions that he needed to ask his prospective guests as he made his rounds before closing up for the night. After the staff left, his victims could come back for their private tour of wine, dessert, and a terrifying farewell. As Brian approached the table he noticed the blonde's quick appraisal of him while the male continued to hold her hand, unaware of her shift of energy. She was good, very, very good. These two could prove to be a little more exciting than the others.

She too was a predator, a hustler of young flesh. She and Brian both got what they wanted from their helpless victims and then moved on to new prey; discarding the old. The only difference was that Brian's game was played for bigger stakes. He laughed at his pun. A slight smile lit his eyes with an unusual light. She would prove to be a worthy adversary and so would he.

Brian interrupted their conversation with a smile.

"Hi. My name is Brian Bentham, the head chef here. I do hope you are enjoying your evening and your meal is to your liking." He offered his hand to the female, noting the male's discomfort at being interrupted.

He quickly shifted his attention to the male not wanting to ruffle the young man's feathers. As he reached across the table he noticed that they had ordered the special steak, and were both enjoying a fine cut of their own; a special couple, for a special couple of steaks. He knew they would enjoy the meals immensely.

For a split second Brian could see the couple from upstate New York. The steaks on the plates of this couple had been soaked in the easterner's blood. She had been a stunning brunette and he was an athletic, handsome young man. Both of them were fashionable young entrepreneurs; their mohair coats and watches, status symbols. The look of terror embedded across their faces flashed one more time before Brian's mind's eye, as he was drawn back into the conversation with the blonde.

"Hi. My name is Candy," the blonde offered as she took Brian's hand.

He knew it. Candy was a fitting name.

"And my friend here is Brock and my yes, its great here. We just had to come while we were in town. Everyone does." She eyed him up and down one more time.

"Where are you from?" Brian paused. "No, don't tell me; let me guess, California….even better, San Francisco." Brian smiled as a look of surprise crossed both Candy's and Brock's faces.

"How did you know?" Candy took the lead once again. "Are you psychic or just sexy?" She gave him a look that was unmistakably obvious about her intent.

Brian noted once again that her companion was uncomfortable.

"No just an old pro when it comes to noting details about people and being able to draw some obvious conclusions."

He looked directly at Brock as he spoke, assuring him with his smile that he was no threat, something he had had to do often with the males over the years. It was always important that his own gender be as comfortable with him or their testosterone levels jumped and they became too competitive.

Brock spoke up slowly. "Well, you'll have to share your secret with us. Will you join us?" The reluctance in his voice was obvious.

"No thanks," Brian responded. "But I'll tell you what…." He set his eyes evenly on Brock.

"Every once in a while I invite out-of-town patrons back after hours for wine and dessert. I'll take you on a tour of the back area, I'm sure you'll be impressed. Then if you're real good," Brian paused, shifting his gaze to Candy. "I'll share the secret of our marinades with you." Brian never broke his gaze knowing it would be Candy who made all of the decisions.

"Of course you'll sign an agreement swearing to keep our secret and I assure you it will be worth your while. It will be an unusual way to finish your evening. Only you and a few, select others will ever know the secret to the steak you are enjoying right now." He flashed a warm, friendly smile at both Candy and Brock, noting their pleasure at being invited back.

"As a matter of fact," he continued, "I have gift passes for 'Zanies' Comedy Club on North Wells Street. The show starts around nine, ending after midnight. If you could return after that, I'll help you cap off the evening with wine and dessert." Brian flashed a warm smile at the couple, winning them over to the idea.

Candy loved the idea, after all, it would be a great deal of fun and they would be among the few who knew Brian's secret.

* * * *

The evening was slower than usual, giving Bara and Lexy a much-needed chance to leave the restaurant early. After the usual farewells, Brian had a chance to sit back and enjoy a rare glass of Southern Comfort on ice. He closed his eyes, letting the warm liquid surge through his body. He had treated himself to one of his special steaks and noted that the supply was getting low. Tonight would be timely. As the steak became more and more popular, he needed to use all of his skill to keep the details of each killing smooth. He had started to overlap his murders, doing them three to four days apart. This meant that he needed to fine-tune the evidence he needed to prove that even though the victims had eaten at The Beef Chateau, they continued to enjoy Chicago's hospitality for days after.

The ticket's to 'Zanies' were just one of the brilliant touches he had come up with. When the couple returned with the ticket stubs tonight, he would plant the stubs in their hotel room, proving that they had left The Beef Chateau alive and well.

Brian finished his drink, his mind turning backward as he fingered the stem of his glass.

* * * *

"Shut up, you little fucker." A voice screamed in his head, interrupting his thoughts. "You're just like that slut of a mother, always reading books. Good for nothing."

Brian could almost feel his hair being pulled, the big hand of his father yanking him off the bed. The feel of the floor as his father slammed his head against the course, shag carpet caused his face to burn from the impact of the rough fibers. The smell of dust and mildew assaulted his nostrils, and boots jabbed his ribs as his father kicked him one more time before stumbling to his bedroom for the night, dead drunk.

"Turn off that goddamned light and get to sleep, you little bastard or I'll really show you what for.'

The grating sound of his father's voice caused Brian's heart to beat faster, sweat appeared on his upper lip; his body responding to the memory as if it were real, not a fearful reminiscence from the past. His father had hated the fact that Brian was an introspective young man, who always had his nose in a book. If the man had ever bothered to see what his son was reading, like "How to Get Away with Murder" along with others on poison and different weapons. It would have caused him to pause and wonder just what it was that his son was reading. It wasn't good. Brian played the last moments of his mother's life over and over again. The only problem was he had never really known exactly how his mother had died. He could only guess. If his father had been true to form he would never have used a gun or other weapons; he was a bare-hands kind of guy, and Brian knew his mother's last moments would have been painful. Pain was his dad's' pleasure.

Hoping the moment would clear his thoughts and bring him back to the present. Brian stood, shaking off the feeling of dread as if it were a creepy-crawly thing.

He looked up at the clock; 12:15. It was time to go to the front of the restaurant and wait for his guests. As he swung open the front oak doors, Brian could hear the laughter of Candy and Brock as they discussed their favorite moments of the evening. The comic had been good and they were looking forward to the completion of their evening with the head chef, Brian Bentham. It would make a great story when they returned home and relived the trip with friends and fellow workers. They still had three days left in Chicago and they intended to make the most of them. Candy devoured Brian with her eyes as he greeted them; too bad she had to bring a sandwich to a banquet. Brian looked good enough to eat and Brock, although a good diversion for the trip, would never compare with the tall, dark man in front of her. They were cut from the same cloth; she could tell....it was one animal stalking another, the scent of the kill in the air. She could feel the sexual tension.

Brian too could feel the hormonal vibrations.... he was sure he could read Candy's mind. She was wishing she was alone and Brock was back at the hotel. Brian laughed. With what he had in mind, he needed all three of them, a ménage a trios of a different kind. Once they were seated, Brian poured a sweet wine and then a little later, after a long conversation, a special coffee and dessert. He needed at least an hour for the answers to a lot of important questions. Where are they staying? When were they due back, business or pleasure? Did they have friends in Chicago....

business appointments....parents that would miss them if they didn't call...children? Brian had decided he would never kill if there were kids, after all, a child would always need its mother and absolutely no one should interfere with that!

As the evening ended, Brian took out his measured dose of Halcion. It was just enough to put them out for under twenty minutes, giving him time to bind them in bubble wrap and tie their ankles before hoisting them up on the hooks used for beef. They could struggle but it would do no good. There wouldn't be a sound; just the thumping in his head as he felt their hearts beat. Hearts that raced with terror once they became totally aware of what was about to transpire.

* * * *

Brian walked up to Candy and knelt down, making his face even with hers. She became aware of her surroundings and the fact that she and her partner were hanging upside down with their feet and arms Bound and mouths gagged. She started to struggle.

"Don't bother," Brian cooed softly. "It won't help. The plastic wrap is unbreakable. You won't get out." He stroked her over-bleached hair, dry like cotton and unpleasant. He let go and took her face in his hands, kissing her forehead, nose, and chin. As he gazed into her eyes he was shocked. He didn't see the usual terror he had become used to, but rather a blazing anger of pure hatred combined with disbelief.

"That's right, feel the anger.... let it rip through you. It will only help me in the end. You see, I promised I would share the secret of the marinade." Brian shifted his hand from his knee, to her breast.

It wasn't sexual; he wanted to feel her heart shift into overdrive. He knew it would. "You see; you and your friend are a part of that secret. After all, it will be your blood I'll use for the next batch of steaks. Just like the others. The sweet, sweet blood of young, beautiful couples just like you. After all, you enjoyed some of it tonight. They were from Seattle....a new way for east to meet west. You would have liked them. Oh...." He laughed. "I guess in a way, you did."

He could feel her heart doing double time. A rumbling sound tried to make its way out from under the duct tape covering her mouth. He had wiped her lipstick off before placing it on her mouth. He hated making a mess of her pretty face. He had even replaced lipstick on all of the victims; the women should look their best when he laid them out for the cops to find. He could feel and hear the thrashing of her partner, as the sounds of deep masculine mumbles came from his direction, Brian chose to ignore him, it was always more effective to terrorize the female. The male's natural need to protect was being stifled by his inability to do more than wiggle like a big fish caught on a hook. Brock's testosterone levels jumped like crazy, as well as his adrenaline and cortisol levels. The more their endocrine system went on overdrive, the bigger the rush that was felt by anyone who dined on the sweet, blood-soaked steaks Brian would prepare tonight.

Brian stood, turning to the small, steel door halfway up the wall; the one Detective Kortovich had missed. He opened it and slid out a multi-functional, automatic meat cutter. The head of the thin, precision blade could be moved 360 degrees in any direction, allowing one to cut up, down, or across, in any direction. The sound of the blade as it cut smoothly into their flesh was the last thing they heard. The last thing they felt was Brian's arms and hands around their heads as he held them firmly, guiding the blade easily across their throats. The last thing they smelled was his sweet cologne, Drakkar, mingled with the sweat that beaded on his forehead and upper lip. There was the smell of an excited female; sexual, sensual, the hormones in full throttle, which were needed for the slaughter as Brian concluded his conquest, making the final kill.

Both bodies were then wrapped up tight, frozen, and were ready to be dropped into his deep freeze, which was stored in his double-car garage. But first he would need to do a little stage setting. He had Brock's wallet and Candy's purse, as well as a key to their hotel room secure in his breast pocket. Now he needed to make sure that for the next few days there would be little evidence to lead the police back to The Beef Chateau. He would go to their room and place the props needed to put the police onto a new trail. First he would make sure any surveillance camera would not be able to identify him. He dressed like a gang-banger, loose jeans, oversized hoodie, sun-glasses sneakers and a back-pack full of props he would need.

Their room was exactly as he had pictured it, although the maid had cleaned as well as she could. Candy's makeup and clothes were strewn all over. It was clear that she wasn't trying to impress her young man with her domestic skills.

First the bed.... he needed to rumple the sheets and pillows to make sure that the maid would testify that their bed had been slept in. He wore rubber gloves, as well as plastic coverings over his shoes. No prints, no fibers! Next, he planted the stubs from "Zanies"` on the dressing table. He had wiped all the prints off the stubs at the restaurant to make sure his prints would not be present if the police tested them. He then pressed Candy's forefinger and thumbprint on both tickets stubs making sure only her prints would be found. He would go home for a few hours and get some sleep. Over the next few days he would have to leave a trail for the police to follow… one that would lead them as far away from him as possible. Just before leaving the hotel room he would hang the "do not disturb" sign on the door and then return in the morning to continue the game.

Chapter Eleven

Shelley was excited. She had received a call from Brian, the head chef at The Beef Chateau. She had thought about him constantly, ever since they met three days ago and she`d hoped he would call. She was overjoyed when he did, all resolve to stay away from men having gone out the window only minutes after meeting Brian. His voice was smooth and confident over the phone; she liked that. After checking their schedules, they decided to get together two nights later. Now she was only a few short hours from picking him up after work. They had made plans to attend an after-hours club and go dancing. Maybe she would offer to make him breakfast at her place. If she were lucky, they would wind up with more than scrambled eggs.

* * * *

Brian was just finishing up; the clock over the cooler said quarter past one, Shelley should be here any minute. The bodies of Brock and Candy were already dumped. He had waited for Bara and Lexy to leave. Once he was sure all was clear he had gotten into his van and drove to the lower east side, to a deserted lot. It was unlikely he would meet anyone late at night. He made sure he dumped the bodies at the edge of the parking lot near the entrance. All of the other victims had been dumped at a series of different locations. Brian always made sure that the bodies would not be obvious to anyone unless they were walking along the edge of the road. It was important that other cars and trucks would drive over the same area that Brian's van had traveled, making it impossible for the police to identify his tire tracks.

He had carried the bodies to the trees along the road. They were difficult to move, so he pulled them along the snow, each wrapped in his or her plastic bubble wrap. He unrolled them quickly, bundled up the wrap to put in the van and burn later, and then took a multi-pronged rake over his prints and the tracks, which had been left by the wrap. All of their personal belongings were left with them; her purse, and his wallet. The only prints the police would find would be those of the victims, or whoever discovered the bodies. No tire tracks, no footprints, and bodies so clean that the forensic team wouldn't have a single hair or fiber that could be traced to anyone but the victims. The only item out of place on every victim but the first was a small bag of soil found in an ordinary baggie, with no prints.

There was nothing that could be traced to him, unless they solved a puzzle he had set for them. But to solve it they would have to know he was the killer. If he was caught, it would have to be a "tit for a tat." Brian knew that once the police found the victims, they would try to piece together the last few days of the couple's life. Like all of the others, it would seem that they had died within a few hours of the last meal, a meal eaten somewhere between eight and midnight. A meal they had enjoyed in their hotel room. Brian had found a way to ensure that the victims would seemingly have eaten the exact same meal from another restaurant the night before, only in their hotel. Once he knew where Bara and Lexy were, he called the hotel where Candy and Brock were staying, asking for room service. He then ordered the exact meal they had eaten with him and asked that it be sent to their room at precisely eight-thirty. It would be peak time for The Beef Chateau; a time so busy, few would miss him.

* * * *

Brian slipped out the back door and quickly made his way to the nearby hotel. Once in the room he unlocked the door and turned on the radio, making sure there would be enough noise that he would have to shout out to the room service waiter through the bathroom door. He then placed the cash on the dresser, leaving a generous tip. When the waiter arrived, Brian opened the bathroom door and shouted out to just leave the meal and take the money on the dresser, thanking him profusely through the open door.

Brian laughed loudly and talked to someone in the bathroom so the waiter could hear; leaving the impression that he was sharing the bathroom with a female friend. Once the waiter left, he put all of the food into a plastic bag that he had brought with him. He then put the trays back out of the door for room service to pick up later that night, making sure there was a record of the meal, as well as a witness. This would take about half an hour from the time he left the restaurant to the time he returned. So far he had been lucky. All of the hotels had been less than ten minutes from The Beef Chateau. He had pushed the food around on the plates using all of the utensils, poured the same wine they had ordered at the Beef Chateau, swirling the wine around before emptying the glasses in the bathroom sink, then rinsing the sink with very hot water and soap, to remove any evidence of wine stains being found. He had to make sure it looked like two people had eaten all of the food and enjoyed it so much they would have made their mothers proud; eating everything on their plates. Once back, he was seldom missed. Only once did one of the waiters ask him where he had been and the waiter seemed to accept the answer, "In the can`, allowing Brian to carry on with the rest of the evening.

Brian dumped the food that he had carried back in the plastic bag, into the garbage bin with all of the other scrapings that had been left on the plates of the guests of The Beef Chateau. The covers for his shoes as well as the baggie that carried the food were then left in the van to be taken home and burned in his fireplace. Brian continued on as usual until later, when Shelley would arrive. He felt confident that his dumping Candy and Brock`s bodies had been handled with all of the skill he could muster. He knew he was at his best. He had planned for a lifetime to know all he could about murder and he knew he would be difficult to catch. His father had gotten away with two murders; Brian`s mother and the hairdresser, Brian was sure of it, although he had no evidence about the hairdresser. Brian's death toll was now at nineteen, *Try to top that*, he thought, thinking of his father. So fuck the world and fuck his dad.

Brian heard the bang on the back door. He had told

Shelley she need only knock and he would be waiting. He looked up at the clock, one-thirty, right on time. After swinging the door open, he just stood in the doorway saying nothing. He let a slow boyish smile cross his face and gave Shelley a look that would have melted an old maid's lonely heart. But Shelley's heart was guarded. He could tell she had made too many mistakes and no longer trusted her own judgment about men. He would change all that.

"Well, are you going to let me in or have me stay out here and freeze my ass off" Shelley smiled, as Brian offered her his hand and pulled her gently into the brightly-lit kitchen.

"And a pretty little ass it is," he responded with a light laugh.

"It's cold out there, but I'm sure we can handle it, after all it's the middle of April and spring is just round the corner."

Brian continued to hold Shelley's hand.

"I'll have to change and get out of these clothes and put my dancing duds on. I've worked double time to get everything done. This way I can enjoy the night and sleep a few extra hours before I have to be back here tomorrow. How about you? Are you on a late afternoon shift tomorrow?"

Shelley removed her hand from his. She was starting to feel as if he was getting too close and she still hadn't made up her mind if she wanted to open up her heart to this, or any relationship. She could smell his after-shave and cologne, Drakkar, her favorite. She was in big trouble. He was much too handsome and smelled good enough to eat. Shelley moved further into the kitchen.

"As a matter of fact, I have all the time we need." She looked straight into his baby blues, holding his gaze. Her eyes twinkled and she hoped she didn't sound too hopeful, or too forward. The dimple in her chin deepened as she spoke.

"Please hurry, I'm starved. So go change and let's get out of here." She pushed him toward the men's bathroom, a teasing smile on her face.

Brian had picked up his clothes after she had dropped his hand. "OK. I'll only be a minute."

As he closed the bathroom door, leaving Shelley to linger outside to look around, he was thankful for the fact, that he was able have a date with someone who could provide an alibi. That he was attracted to her was an added bonus.

While Shelley waited for Brian to dress for their evening, she looked around the kitchen. The buzz around town was that Bara and Lexy were now opening a second location on Michigan Ave. Their recent super success was a direct result of the secret marinades, especially the new steak, a highlight for most Epicurean's. For those diners who ordered the new steak, it was a special taste of heaven, but few could tell why.

Shelley thought of the last steak she had enjoyed the day she met Brian. The steak had been like no other and she`d felt like she was on cloud nine. The feeling had lasted for hours. It was more than just meeting Brian. Her senses were sharper than they had ever been. She could see better; hear better, smell better, and think better than she could ever remember. As a matter of fact, even her memory was better. Well, at least for a little while anyway. She had started to wonder why the steak had given her such a sense of well-being, when Brian reappeared dressed to the nine's. All thoughts of the steak left her mind as she shifted her attention to the gorgeous man who stood in front of her.

"You clean up real good." Shelley stood a few feet away from Brian, giving him an appreciative look.

They decided to take her car, a decision Brian helped her make. He emphasized that his van had been there since three that afternoon and would take a lot of warming up, while her car was as warm as toast. So off they went to dine and dance at the hottest after hours nightclub in Chicago, The Dragon Room on West Evergreen.

The three-level dining and dancing club was notably not cheap but the sushi bar would still be open and Brian could stand a little variety in his menu, and Shelley would hopefully make a great dance partner. The night would prove to be wonderful, especially for Brian. After all, he would now have an airtight alibi and by tomorrow morning he would need one.

The music, food, and conversation had been wonderful. Brian noted it was well past six in the morning, but neither Shelley nor he felt tired and both hoped they could share more than early morning toast and coffee. He couldn't help but admire Shelley's wit and intelligence. Her big, liquid brown eyes, shone as she shared a variety of stories about her past years with the ME`s department. Brian was careful to ask few questions and let Shelley share whatever she felt comfortable with in regards to herself.

Her straight brown hair would fall over her left eye and he had to hold back the urge to brush it over her small, perfect ear and continue to stroke her hair, a movement that would be too intimate considering they were still strangers to each other.

* * * *

Shelley had never been so taken with a man as she was with Brian. He listened in a way that made her feel as if there was little she couldn't share. The stories about Tiffany, her daughter, had Brian erupting with laughter. At one point she was sure he would fall off his chair, he was laughing so hard.

"Tiffany sounds like an unusual child and it must have been difficult being a single mom. I'm amazed that you were able to accomplish so much, especially with all of the crazy things you had to endure raising a child like her. Why is it you never married?"

Shelley's face darkened and Brian knew he was on dangerous ground.

"It's OK, I won't push. We can share our love life stories once we get to know each other better." He shifted his questions away from the personal, back to a more professional direction.

When Shelley talked about her work, Brian's face took on a serious look. She felt as if he was fascinated with all the details of her job. She shared the excitement she felt as she cut into the bodies brought to her; bodies that needed to tell her the, who, what, where and whys of how they died. She shared her frustrations with the latest string of murders. The bodies were holding back, giving up little information. Information needed by the police to help end these horrendous murders. Shelley somehow felt as if she were failing these young, beautiful visitors, who were being returned to their families in body bags. They were humans beings shipped like so much cargo, rather than the young vibrant men and women their families would now mourn; families that so far had little closure. As long as their killer was out there she was certain that more parents would be shedding tears of grief as they met the airplane returning their loved ones' cold, lifeless corpses.

Brian seemed to hang on every word. It was if he wanted to see right into her brain and know everything she knew. No one had ever listened to her that way before. Brian never interrupted. Shelley was sure he would let her go on forever and she was sure she could. She needed to vent her fears, hurt, and anger at the frustrating lack of leads. Whoever was killing these tourists was doing all he could to cover his tracks, figuratively and literally.

Shelley accepted Brian's invitation to breakfast, after all, sushi just didn't stay with you long enough and she did feel a little hungry. She knew her hunger was for the contact of someone who could love and protect her; something she felt she needed lately. The drive over gave her a chance to look at his profile and admire the way he held himself, soft and relaxed. As she reviewed the evening in her mind she discovered that she had done all of the talking and that he had been a very good listener. She would have to draw him out and find out what made him tick. He looked like a man who would be easy to read, but so far she was coming up with little more than an itch in her crotch. No! Sex always made her goofy. This time she would take it slow.

"How do you like your cheese omelet, with or without onions?" Brian asked as he reached for the frying pan. Brian had insisted that he serve breakfast and Shelley had been curious to see his home….it would tell her a lot.

"Cheese and onions?"

Shelley answered, noting how organized Brian's kitchen was and how trendily his home was decorated.

Black and white, with a splash of cherry-red, the small, two-bedroom bungalow seemed sleek and stylish, much like Brian. The only problem was that the kitchen was also a little too sterile. It was as if Brian's home appeared one way; stylish, sharp and simple, but underneath something was missing. She would have to find out the secret hidden in the depths of this man. She hoped it would be fun and take a long, long time. While cleaning the kitchen with him after break-feast; Shelley couldn't help but stifle a yawn.

"I guess you're beat." Brian came up from behind Shelley and started to rub her shoulders. "We both need some sleep." His voice was smooth and warm. "How about staying a while and both of us just cuddling and really getting some sleep?" Brian's voice sounded sincere.

"It's been a long time since anyone just held me, making me feel safe." Shelley answered as she turned to face Brian.

His eyes were like dark-blue pools of water with hidden depths that Shelley found difficult to read. He would be a complicated man to get to know and she was sure he deliberately kept parts of himself hidden.

His bed felt wonderful. Deep foam accompanied the mattress making her feel as if she was floating on air. Full, light feather comforters were pulled up around her shoulders, wrapping her up like a butterfly in a cocoon. The king-size pillows were full of expensive down feathers, the kind of pillows you could wrap around your head and sink into deeply, feeling like you were surrounded by a little bit of heaven. The soft, flannel sheets provided cozy warmth, different from the cold sheets Shelley had to face nightly. Embellished with the light scent of Brian, it all added to the feeling of safety that she needed as she drifted slowly to sleep; Brian's arm's wrapped around her in an easy manner. She remembered thinking how wonderful it all felt. For the first time in months she felt safe, a feeling that had eluded her more and more as the body count climbed. Here finally was a man who could create a safe place to fall. She slowly drifted off into a dreamless sleep.

As Brian tried to relax, his heart beat faster. It had been a long time since he had felt the comfort of a woman for something more than just sex. He had spent a lifetime keeping his heart hidden from anything that could be a real relationship. Loving wasn't an option. It would make him weak. He would have to be careful but for now he would snuggle in and enjoy the moment. It was a rare event for Brian to drop his guard. Tomorrow would be soon enough to let things go back to normal. Tomorrow he would have to replenish his stock, but for now, the only warm-blooded body would have to be Shelley's, and it felt good.

Chapter Twelve

The night had turned bitter and as the evening broke into dawn, the cold, northern wind whipped itself into frenzy, like a spoiled child unable to get its own way. Dennis had pulled his hood up over his head hoping it would offer some shelter from the cold. It wasn't until after lunch that anyone had spotted the bodies and now he stood around with the other members of his team, wishing he were anywhere else.

The continual lack of evidence in the investigation was beginning to wear everyone's nerves thin, and the howling wind only added to their frustration. It was already April, but anyone who lived in Chicago knew that April could blow the most bitter of winds. The unrelenting gale also blew away any hope the team of investigators may have had that the killer would have left any clues. It was unlikely that even if the weather had been great they would have found much. Each time the killer dumped his victims it was at the edge of a busy parking lot or at the side of a road that would have some traffic. Cars would then grind down the tire tracks of the killer, leaving the police with little hope of identifying the treads or at least getting a handle on what type of vehicle he might have been driving. He had also raked all of the tracks he left after dumping the bodies, so it would be difficult to match his boot print to any of the prints left in the snow. Because of the wind there would be few prints, and as usual, there would be few clues today as well.

"Fuck this wind, and fuck this guy!" Dennis muttered under his breath as he squatted down in front of the couple. They had been discovered at the edge of the parking lot of the Schwab Rehabilitation Hospital.

"What have you got so far Chuck? And just once tell me this fucking freak has left his driver's license or his business card. I'm tired of it all and wish I could just quit." The exasperation in Dennis`s voice was also accompanied by a look of resignation.

It was as if he doubted himself and everything he knew about police work. Barring a miracle, he wondered if he would ever catch this psychopathic bastard. Chuck joined Dennis near the bodies. Their shoulders touched, causing a feeling of comradeship. They were in this together and for better or worse they were partners.

"You could just duplicate any of the files, change the name and location, and you'd end up with an exact copy of the other murders." Chuck's tone matched Dennis's.

"I've a feeling we're going to be at this a long time if this guy doesn't mess up somewhere." Chuck stood, feeling a slight cramp pull at this thigh muscle. Once again Chuck envied Dennis his slim, athletic build.

Soon the forensic team was on the scene, Corrine once again in the lead. When she approached Dennis and Chuck she slowed her pace. Because of the drinks a few months back, she had been reluctant to engage Dennis as anything more than another professional. She knew he was a straight shooter and that he loved his wife. With all of the single men on the force why was she attracted to the married ones?

Dennis stood after several minutes of silent contemplation. They both moved off to the side of the crime scene, while members of the team did their respective jobs. Photos were taken, measurements made, and bags were placed over the victims' hands, on the off-chance there would be some forensic evidence under the nails of the couple.

Dennis walked over to Corrine giving her a warm smile.

"I've got the girl's purse and the guy's wallet. They' are from California; the San Francisco area. Chuck and I will go over to their hotel while your team processes the bodies. Then you can come over to the hotel and collect whatever evidence we're lucky enough to find." he stated, suddenly feeling a little stupid, knowing that as a professional she would know what to do next.

Chuck gave Dennis a knowing look, fully understanding that the pressure they were under often made normal conversations redundant.

"No problem." was Corrine's easy reply.

"Let's just get over to the hotel and see if there's anything new. I sure hope there's at least one thread of evidence we can follow that will get us closer to this guy."

By the time Chuck and Dennis arrived at the hotel they were half frozen, they had been at the dump site for over an hour and the windy, early spring day had already taken its toll. They had gone through the contents of the purse and wallet at the crime scene hoping to find anything that would give them clue to where the victims had been, prior to their deaths

Tickets to ``Zanies` from the night before were found in the girl's purse and a signed Visa slip for flowers dated the day before was in Brock's wallet. It must have been a special occasion because the roses were over a hundred bucks. As usual, there was still cash in his wallet, over a thousand dollars, so the murders had not been committed for gain.

Candy Johnson's purse was exactly as Dennis expected. Several shades of lipstick, as well as an expensive Estée Lauder burgundy compact with gold trim were tossed carelessly to the bottom. Her driver's license confirmed his guess. The female was in her early-thirties while the male was only twenty-two but very mature looking, his bold features and large, husky frame belying his youth.

Candy seemed like the kind of woman who would need a man. Dennis could tell that her fashion and hair were all a part of a style that she had deliberately developed to attract the opposite sex. She was now on her way to a slab in the morgue, but the detectives didn't miss her over-processed hair and heavy makeup. As they processed the crime scene, several receipts for purchases from the many stores along the "Million Dollar Mile" could be found. The team would have to follow every lead they could, trying to fit together the last days of the victim's lives. Things were getting hot and many of the newspapers from around the country were picking up on the story, especially since some of the victims came from their towns. Trying to sort out all of the newest details, hoping something new would turn up and help them crack open this dead-end case, was their only hope of keeping the press at bay.

The Trump International Hotel on Wabash Avenue was still one of the best hotels in Chicago. So far, several of the victims had stayed there, and Dennis knew that the manager would once again be very unhappy when he saw Chuck and him at his office. The hotel was noted for its great food and above-average service, and the manager was beginning to take it personally after several of the victims were found to have stayed at his hotel.

The team of investigators would follow Dennis and Chuck within the half hour. They both knew that they would like some time alone in the room before the photos, prints, fibers, and personal belongings would be taken and then added to the pile of evidence collected and stored at the police department's evidence room. Chuck closed the door to the hotel room behind them, letting the manager, Charles Ranger, a crisp little man, know that they would handle things alone. Dennis moved to the middle of the room touching nothing. it was at times like this that he was at his best. His senses became more alert; his eyes slowly taking in every detail of the room, his ears straining to hear sounds from the outside hallway. There were none. He walked over to the chair where there were clothes piled high or flung carelessly on the floor. Picking up a heavy black sweater, hers, he put it to his nose. It smelled like cigarettes, but not in the way a smoker's should….it was secondhand smoke. They had been in a bar or club where smoking was allowed. He then walked over to the closet where two men's suits were hanging.

Again he put his nose to the jacket, and found it fresh with a light, lingering scent of male cologne, CKI, Calvin

Klein's fragrance for men and women. The male was definitely a non-smoker. The female however may have been, but was probably cutting back to impress her athletic young lover. She definitely did not smoke in the room. As Dennis walked over to a French-Provincial writing desk that Candy had turned into a makeup table, he picked up her large vanity bag. It dominated the table. As he riffled through it, he learned he was right. A half-pack of Players-Lite was in the bottom of the bag.

The bed was unmade so he had no way of knowing if they had returned to the room after leaving last night. They had to have gone sometime after eating their supper. Dennis had picked up a computer printout from the front desk before going to the room. It would have all of the charges made by the couple during their stay and it would give enough information to help the police figure out what had happened the last few days and hours of Candy's and Brock's lives.

They had ordered a last meal and it had arrived at eight p.m. Again, Dennis wasn't surprised; two steaks, one with fries, one with baked potato and a side salad, as well as bottle of California wine, and lastly an orange cheesecake. Although they had ordered room service, they had paid cash. Once again, everything was following the usual pattern. He would have to question the room server but he was sure he already knew all the answers. The bouquet of roses that dominated the room had a card written in a light feminine hand, it read, "Last night was great! Love Brock. He had sent flowers to the room but the florist had signed the card… again no lead.

Chuck just stood off to the side watching Dennis do what he did best; investigate. With his notepad in hand,

Dennis jotted down a bunch of scribbles, saying nothing. Several times he stopped and stroked his mustache, his gray eyes staring off into the distance reviewing other details in his mind's eye. He was comparing this room to the other rooms he had already investigated.

"OK. Tell me what you've got." Demanded Chuck, he knew the others would be here soon and he wanted the review to be uninterrupted.

"They were here on vacation." Dennis started "Not working, it was a shopping holiday from the look of the clothes on the chair. Several of the items still have their tags on."

Dennis walked over to the dresser where the top drawer was half open. He pulled out a flimsy pair of panties with a matching bra. There were other new items hanging in the closet.

"And of course a little physical activity."

He held the items high and pointed to the side table where an empty condom package lay. "At least they practiced safe sex."

He placed the package back on the table. The follow-up team would process and bag all of the stuff in the room.

Chuck piped up with an off-hand conclusion. "If she was robbing the cradle, maybe she brought him here to get him away from his mother. After all, there is almost a ten-year age difference."

The thought of the boys' mother reminded Dennis that they would have to make the calls to the families. It was a job they hated.

"She smokes, he doesn't." he continued. "Although she was trying to cut back to impress him, after supper he was so thankful for the great sex that he sent flowers to the room. The printout says the call was made from this room and paid for with his Visa."

Dennis stood up and referred to his notepad.

"They also called in yesterday and reserved two tickets for The Goodman Theater." He looked up at Chuck, finding him engrossed in a newspaper article that had been left by the side of the bed.

"What date does the *Chicago Tribune* have at the top?" Dennis wanted to confirm that yesterday was the last day the couple had been there.

Chuck pulled his eyes to the top of the page, "April ninetieth, yesterday. I'd say that all was well and fine until sometime after nine or ten last night and then once again the killer struck."

"We may be missing one thing. What caused every couple to order the same meal the night before they all die?" Dennis sat at the edge of the bed as he spoke.

"Steak, salad, a side dish, wine, and cheesecake....the chances against this happening a couple of times, would be small but for this many times, the odds are huge. Once again I feel as if the killer is connected to the food." Dennis looked back down at his notes again and stroked his mustache.

"Maybe he sends them up the meal and the Halcion is already in the wine. We have no receipts for any of the meals on the VISA slips and most of them have been paid for with cash." Chuck answered.

"Anyone could have ordered them and sent the meals to the couples." Dennis sat up. He heard the rest of the team approaching before they would knock on the door.

"I wouldn't rule out the possibility that all the couples

were sent the same meal by the killer. Whenever we talk to room service they always say the same thing; the door is open and the guests simply leave the cash on the table and are in the bathroom. No one ever pays in person. I'm beginning to wonder for the first time if the killer is in the room before the victims return."

"Maybe he tampers with the wine bottles and puts the drug in it. Shit, I'm at a stale-mate. Nothing makes any sense." Chuck added.

Dennis heard a commotion in the hall. It was the other members of the team and they would soon be at the door. He looked over at Chuck, who was fingering the clothes in the closet. Dennis just wanted to go over the details in his mind, he still wasn't sure of his conclusions. Once enough bodies begin to pile up, you start to get a picture of what must have happened to the victims before they died. But so far all Chuck and Dennis had were more questions than answers. Dennis started to pace, wanting to get his thoughts out before the rest of the team came into the room.

"What if the killer orders the food and when the couples come to the room they think the hotel sent them a complimentary meal?"

"Meanwhile, the killer simply waits till the meal is eaten and enters the room later. The only problem with my story is how does he get them out without being seen?"

Dennis tried to picture in his head what it must have been like for a killer to sling not one, but two bodies over his shoulder and try to get them down a hotel hallway into an elevator, or harder yet, down a flight of stairs and then out one of the doors to a car. It seemed unlikely that anyone could get away with one, let alone nearly twenty murders and not have anyone see something that looked this suspicious.

"Well it wouldn't be the first time someone was killed and no one saw the body being removed, but so many? I think there still must be another explanation. Maybe they eat the meal in the hotel and then go somewhere else? The Halcion might be in the wine and they have a drink with the killer."

Dennis moved over to the door, opening it before a knock could be made. "There is always a delay before dessert. So who knows? Maybe they have dessert somewhere else?"

"Hi guys. You look warm." It was Mac Thompson, one of the best print men on the force.

"You hero's leave the rest of us slobs to do the grunt work, freezing our asses off while you lay around a hotel room in style and comfort trying to solve this mess."

He put his black case on the desk, opened it, put on his gloves, and started to dust as he spoke. Mack was straight and to the point, a no-nonsense kind of guy; boring, but bright. He could lift the print off the head of a pin. Dennis was sure he used fairy dust – he was able to create pure magic with his print kit.

Walden King, their photographer, looked like Rudolf the Red-Nose Reindeer. His red nose probably glowed in the dark, especially after a couple of hours in the cold and a few rum and cokes. At sixty-four he hated all of the outside work and looked forward to his impending retirement. Between Chuck's prominent tummy and Brian's red nose, all the team needed was a few elves and they could sign up for a stint at the North Pole.

“These guys were sure messy you’d think they would have picked up a few things.” Walden sounded disgusted as he started to snap pictures of the room from every angle.

“Be sure to empty the contents of their suitcases and get photos of everything, it’s easier to look at a photo than refer to a list.” Dennis slapped Walden on the back as he moved past his team and motioned for Chuck to follow him into the hallway.

“What names did you get from the manager?” He asked Chuck referring to all the hotel staff that may have come in contact with the couple or their room.

“The guy from room service and the maid were the only ones in the room. I’ll still have to find out who booked them in for the theater.” Chuck looked up at Dennis briefly and then back at his list. “And talk to the staff at the front desk, and I still have to find out who was working all day yesterday in the dining room, just in case they had breakfast or lunch here at the hotel. If they met with anyone, maybe someone will remember.”

Chuck got a nod from Dennis. He shut his notepad and followed him down the hall. They were finished with the room and might as well get going on the interviews while the rest of the team would do their thing. A complete report would fill in all of the forensic evidence, and once that was done, the whole team would meet at headquarters in the large conference room. Then they would compare notes, looking for any new information; anything that might give them a new insight or a sudden flash of intuition that could lead them to at least one decent suspect.

* * * *

Once back at headquarters, Dennis looked at the team of eleven men and women gathered around the table in the large, elegant conference room. Computers had been brought in along with extra telephone lines. Additional filing cabinets that could hold the original medical examiner's reports and photos of the crime scenes were also strewn about the room, making it look like an office instead of a boardroom. Everything was also loaded into the computers but Dennis still liked accessing information the old-fashioned way, from an original file, along with copies of the hand written notes. Often it would be a single phrase that never made it into the database that would give fresh insight into a case; especially one that seemed to be going nowhere.

Dennis looked around the room for a few minutes before starting the meeting. This was the best team of investigators he had ever worked wit and having Chuck as a partner had made these past few months a little more bearable. Each and every team member was a professional of their own area of expertise and there was no doubt in Dennis's mind that this team would work twenty-four/seven to solve this case if they had to. Once more they were at a dead end, without one lead on any suspect who was even remotely capable of committing the now nineteen murders, represented in the files. Dennis felt as if this nightmare would never end.

"We need to go back over the profile of the killer that we got from Professor White out of Atlanta." He motioned to the file placed in front of each officer.

They had sent duplicate pictures of every crime scene,

as well as profiles on all of the victims to Professor White. Dennis had made sure that they had written meticulous reports on all areas of the investigation. Dr. White, a Professor of Forensic Medicine and a leading expert in profiling had followed up with several phone calls before he had sent his written report to Dennis. It was time to review the composite of a possible killer again and hope that it would match a suspect that might come up in the future, if they were lucky enough. He still had no face or name, but Dr. White's report had a lot to say about the profile of the killers mind.

Dennis looked over at the veteran of the team, Perry Larson, who was now in his middle sixties. Perry sat behind a computer, in-putting all of the small pieces of evidence, and looking for anything they could pursue further or that might seem out of place. A big, burly man with shaggy brown hair that only had a hint of gray, his ruddy complexion gave Perry a look more befitting an outdoor logger than a man in an urban office. His eyebrows always needed a trim and seemed helter-skelter, as if each brow had a mind of its own and wanted to go in several directions at once. Dennis was always a little embarrassed that his eyes found it difficult to focus on Perry's expressive face and in- stead always traveled up to his bushy brows.

Perry took his cue from Dennis and stood up, moving his big leather chair away from the table, allowing him to walk around the now-crowded room. His thoughts were clearer when he walked.

"First and foremost," he stated in a flat professional voice that did nothing to match his animated face, "this guy doesn't want to get caught. Dr. White says one of the unusual characteristics about this guy is that he hates the police and for him it's a game of wits….him against us. All of the murders have something to do with some kind of score he's keeping. Those of us in the profession that wear the "Blue" are on the opposing team and we're losing." Perry stopped long enough to twist his brows unconsciously, his face scowling as he unfolded the rest of his report.

"He's bright, quite possibly brilliant, and he probably went higher than grade twelve, but not university…. maybe a tech or a trade school. He's probably a blue-collar worker, but he has an artistic flair. He could be a hairdresser, graphic designer, carpenter, or sculptor, anything that may have him working with his hands. He may be borderline obsessive-compulsive. He'll be neat, very, very neat. When we find him there will be very little that is out of place in his own environment. He'll have a clean home, a spotless car, and a meticulous workplace."

One again Perry stopped to gather his thoughts and as he did so he reached back up to his brows and twisted some of the longer ones.

"The blood he gathers will not be used for a ritual; he's practical and pragmatic, the blood will have a particular function of some kind." The room felt warmer so Perry unbuttoned his collar.

"Because the bodies experience very little physical trauma, he's probably very calm when he kills. It's almost like a job, and the soil is like a personal message to us. It's like he's saying. "You won't catch me, but if you do, you'll have to solve a puzzle." I don't like it. Who the hell wants to play games?" Perry's vocal out-burst was more for himself than the team that was gathered.

"Each murder is well thought out, he even takes the time to wash their hands and brush their hair, so he's obviously not in a hurry. He feels safe and takes lots of time. Killing two people at once, which is often the case, is difficult but he obviously finds it just as easy to kill two as he does one, so he's in his own environment."

Perry paused, looking up at Chuck and Dennis.

"That means he's very much in control; he has no fear of anything getting out of hand. He's aware of all the ways a killer could get caught, and he's covered his tracks brilliantly in every area." With that statement Perry sat back down, signaling he was about to sum things up.

"So we're looking for a white male, in his late thirties or early forties, smart, articulate, artistic, and fairly educated." Perry became quiet for a few second. "Oh yeah, he probably drives a van or a recreational vehicle, something big boys drive but still practical. It will be a newer model." Perry put the file down and turned his attention to Dennis indicating he was finished.

Dennis slowly gazed around the room. "OK. Let's sum it up one more time so everyone's really clear on things. He's white, about forty, bright, artistic, hates us, drives a big car, is a neat freak but likes dirt well enough to plant a bag of it on the bodies." Dennis stopped long enough to smile at Perry.

"You forgot one thing," Perry started up again. "He's not doing one thing that serial killers usually do. He's hasn't taken any trophies from the victims that we can tell, something that is personal to each one, at least none that we are aware of. Instead he leaves something and that makes him more dangerous than anyone here has dealt with before."

Perry almost looked apologetic for having missed this important part before turning things over to Dennis and having concluded his report without this final important information.

"Most serial killers take something from the victims so that they can touch them and then relive the feeling of the event, but this guy may be different. If he isn't taking anything from the victims, and so far we don't think he is, then his reasons for the killings will be with a much greater purpose in mind. That means he is not completely crazy, only more detached from his feelings than most of us. This will make him less likely to trip up and make any mistakes."

Perry was unaware that as he spoke, he once again twisted his bushy brows.

"Our killer has deliberately forgone the pleasure of any trophies and it takes a lot of control and a deep understanding of himself and his psychosis to forego this part of the killings. He will not stop until we catch him and he's bright enough to try very hard not to get caught." Perry was finally finished.

Dennis had stood up and was running his fingers over his mustache; a sure sign that he was focusing on something, when a loud clamor could be heard coming from the hallway, diverting all of their attention. It was a team of TV reporters. They had somehow managed to get past the duty sergeant and make their way to the conference room. From the sounds being made by a loud female voice they were determined not to leave until they got their interview.

A look of determination crossed Dennis's face. "Chuck you take this one, I can't stand to give another interview. What more can we say that we haven't said over a hundred times during the past three months? He picked up his final report, dismissed the team, to go over the reports and finish the work at hand, and slipped out of a side door leaving Chuck to handle the questions the press was bound to ask. Questions that Dennis and the rest of the team could not answer any better today, than they could at the beginning of the killings.

Chuck rolled his eyes, giving Dennis the "*you owe me one"* look and headed for the doors, taking a deep breath and pulling his shoulders back, bracing himself for the barrage of questions that would follow once he was out of the door and into the arms of the circle of reporters that was about to tear him apart. "*Why was it that the sidekick always gets the dangerous job?"* Chuck thought to himself as the full force of the press assaulted his ears, now that he was within shouting range.

Once Chuck had gone out to face the press, the rest of the team scattered from the conference room to follow up on the leads and to do what they did best; solve crimes. Each detective hoped he or she could come up with an idea, they had none and time was running out.

The back of Dennis's neck started to tighten and he felt a heavy pressure starting to build in the back of his head, God how he needed some new inspiration.

He noticed Corrine had waited until everyone was out of the boardroom and was holding back to speak to him.

"I need to apologize about something. A while back I asked you to meet me at the bar when I could have scanned and sent you the report directly to your phone, I know this case is driving us all crazy, but it was a mistake."

"Meeting a co-worker at a bar to talk over a case is

not a crime. And with this case I was more than happy to enjoy a rum and coke. With no new evidence from any of these crazy murders, it warranted a drink. It was really no problem." Dennis said, hoping he sounded cool.

"My reason for inviting you had more to do with me, than the case. It had been a year since the divorce and I was feeling lonely. The problem is, you are a great guy and a good listener. You also treat me like a lady. You have no idea how many men on this force still can't look me in the eye." Corrine said, referencing her ample chest.

For a second Dennis had to check where his eyes were focusing. He was not immune to Corrine's ample charms, but he had always been able to stay in the moment and concentrate, and when Corrine was in the room he had to work at keeping his manner and conversation professional.

"You're married and I had no right to invite you in the state I was in." Corrine's confession sounded more like she was fishing than apologizing.

Dennis knew where she wanted to take this and although a part of him wanted, maybe even needed, to go in the same direction, his natural instinct to do the right thing, came to his rescue.

"I do understand, and if I was the cheating kind, you would be my choice. I like and admire you, and I find you attractive. But, I love my wife and although it's tempting, I am a one-woman man."

Corrine leaned forward and kissed Dennis gently on the cheek. Turning on her heels, she left the boardroom with one final whisper.

"I know."

Chapter Thirteen

Brian looked in the mirror at the face that was now starting to show the first signs of aging. He was aware of how his looks affected others, both male and female. When he was younger it had bothered him, but as time went on he had learned to use his looks to manipulate others into doing whatever it was that he wanted.

He was always surprised at how easily others responded in a positive way to someone good-looking, even if it meant giving up whatever it was that they wanted. If anyone ever said looks weren't everything then they must have been ugly, because his looks were usually enough to get his share, plus the shares of several others. Brian was glad that the face that stared back at him from the mirror was just like his mother's – it gave him a sense of who he was, beyond being the son of a bastard like his father.

His father! Dear old dad. Today would be only the second time in over ten years that Brian would return to his father's house. The first was months ago when the first murder had taken place. It wasn't until Brian had killed for the first time that an idea had formed in his head about how he could vanquish his enemies; his father and the cops. After he had killed the first time had known instantly, that he would kill again. These murders were about his mother....now buried under a few feet of garden dirt.

She had deserved better and if the cops had done their job she would be sleeping an eternal sleep in a satin-lined coffin with a headstone fit for an angel, rather than in the degrading, secret cradle of death. He would have gone to her gravesite over the years and mourned her death properly, knowing that her killer, his father, had gotten what he deserved. But he couldn't tell anyone. The police had to do their job! They never did!

Brian was willing to endure the presence of his father and his stepmother to get what he wanted, dirt. The dirt that covered his mother's now decayed body that would one day be shoved into his father's mouth, so that he would choke on it and all of the lies that he had said about Brian's mother and her virtue. It would be a short, ten-minute drive to his father's home, the one that Brian had grown up in, and that his father had dared never sell just in case it gave up his terrible secret. Brian would never tell. It was an unwritten rule.

If the cops weren't smart enough to catch his father, then they could all burn in hell and Brian was sure the cops' lives were a living hell lately, with all of the unsolved murders that were taking place.

The drive over to the house gave him enough time to breathe deeply and detach himself emotionally from the visit that was about to take place. If he hadn't needed access to the back yard, he never would have agreed to come over. He had managed to avoid seeing either of them for the past ten years and only the thought of his dad rotting in hell had prompted him to return. As he turned up the driveway in view of the old house, he regained a calm that would see him through the visit. There was nothing his father or stepmother could do that could draw any emotion from him; he was an expert at removing himself from any feelings he may have had; feelings of rage and anger that could have driven a weaker man into shoving his fists into the ugly, drunken face of the man that had helped to give him life. The brutal life that Brian had been forced to endure until he was old enough to get away, had to be paid back.

He was just about to knock on the door when he began to hear shouting coming from the kitchen at the back of the house. The foul words rang out from the open windows and although a sailor or truck driver would have barely noticed the commotion, many of the neighbors did.

It had become so common the neighbors had long ago stopped complaining and had gotten used to the constant noise and bickering. Brian decided not to knock and just go in anyway.... the door would be open and it would be fun to sneak up on the two evil beings that he had decided long ago deserved each other. As he passed through the hall to the kitchen he could smell the musky odors of the cat box that he knew never got changed until the cat refused to use it any longer, it was so full of shit and urine. Old newspapers and dishes could be seen strewn all over the living room as he passed on the way to the kitchen, which he was sure was just as filthy as it had been the day he left over twenty-five years ago.

"Fuck you, you stinking bitch, you can't do anything right. How many times do I have to tell you that chicken can't be fried in bacon-grease? It's probably rancid and you'll kill us all, you fucking moron." Brian's father could be heard shouting half way around the block, his voice booming from his large, barrel chest.

The sound of the female's voice was whinny and nasal, her words barely formed as the sound of her pronunciation was about to be slurred with the addition of just a few more drinks.

"You stay out of my kitchen you stupid old man or I'll slap you silly with this rolling pin and don't think I won't. You don't scare me and besides my sister knows just what to do if I ever go missing, so don't you forget it."

Brian stood in the doorway of the kitchen and took a good look at the two pathetic people who occupied the space around the table. His father was now fatter than ever, the idle years of little work and no exercise, along with the overuse of alcohol having taken its toll. His large head sat atop a short neck that was covered with short white fuzz that stood out on his neck, just barely covered by the long, greasy, yellowish hair that was long over-do for a cut. His face was covered by white stubble that covered a sloppy jowl, giving him a look of a tired, sick bulldog.

Brian coughed to get their attention, and they both turned at once.

"What the fuck you sneaking up on me for you little fuck brain? You tryin' to scare the hell outta me or something?" His father's words were starting to slur, but it would still be a while before he was totally incomprehensible.

"I'm still not sure why you're here? This will be twice in the past six months. You ain't sick or somethin' is ya? Shit, I still think you got somethin' up your sleeve or you'd never be here, but the wife says you're getting mellow in your old age. That true? You startin' to think your ol' man ain't so bad?" The fat, yellow-haired man almost slipped on his way over to Brian.

As the old man held out his hand, Brian found a way to move past him and ignore the gesture without allowing his father the certainty of the insult. The old family cat had just slipped into the kitty door and Brian was able to divert his attention, by giving a greeting to the cat.

"Hi there, Honeycomb, how are you doing? Getting a little stiff I see."

Brian bent over and picked up the cat, stroking its matted fur, and noting that her eyes had an untreated infection.... typical for the care it would receive in this family.

"I understand it's your birthday and seeing as I got my usual invitation, I thought it would be nice if I came to say "Happy Birthday." After all, you are the only father I've got." Brian's sarcasm was unmistakable and his father's face started to take on a dark look.

"I don't want you to start smart mouthing me boy, I can still teach you a lesson or two, so make sure your mouth doesn't start flappin' in the wind. It's not my fucking birthday."

Brian stepped a little closer to his father making sure his face was close to the older and larger man's. He could smell his father's sour breath and it almost made him want to choke. The memory of his father's face being shoved into Brian's younger one, while his father shook him and yelled bitter insults, almost made him break his resolve to stand firm and show no emotion but it would only feed his father's evil ego. The eyes of the old man said it all. They were still calculating and mistrustful. This was a man few would ever cross. There was something about him that smelled of danger and most people trusted their instincts when it came to crossing Brian's father.

"Why are you here boy? This visit is full of shit. You never cared about me before and I can see that you still don't. What brings you back here, your stepmother? Wrong again. You hate her more that you hate me, cause she took your bitch of a mother's place. You always were a baby....a momma's boy. All you ever did after that slut ran away was hide in the basement and cry. I tried to toughen you up, but you're weak. You always were and you always will be. Why don't you just get the fuck out of here and leave me alone. I've never needed you and I never will." The elder Bentham pushed his face into Brian's, daring him to get mad and to try and strike him.

Brian would have liked to drive his fist straight into the big red nose and push it up into his father's brain. He remained calm, hoping that his face showed nothing. He had spent half of his life trying to make sure no one could read his thoughts or his emotions.

"Look Dad, think what you want, but I got an invitation like I do every year. The only difference is that this year you turn seventy-five and that seemed to be a special one. So I thought, what the hell, maybe I would enjoy it. I had a good look around the last time I came and it brought back lots of memories for me. We're never too old to take a good look at the past, are we Dad? But I guess it's not your birthday, so I'll go." Brian put as much emphasis on the word "past" as he could, knowing that his father was never really sure what Brian knew of that night, many years ago.

"You can stay, but just don't fuck with me boy or you'll regret it." The old man stepped back, not wanting to test his strength against his son's.

"If you two men don't get your faces away from each other I'll shove supper up both of your asses. I swear if you were a couple of bucks you'd be locking antlers right now." She moved from the table to the stove, getting the rest of the supper ready.

"Now you two go and kill a little time, I'll only be about twenty more minutes."

"I'm going to go and take a dump. You find something to do and don't touch nothing. Are you still some kind of a clean freak?" Brian's father moved off toward the bathroom, unzipping his pants as he waddled down the hall, not waiting for the answer.

This was the chance Brian had been waiting for. He wanted to get another bag of soil. He had a plastic bag in his jacket, in hopes of having a chance to access the back yard.

He would need only a few minutes to fill the sack and put it on the other side of the fence where he would pick it up on his way out after the god-awful meal he knew he would have to endure. The soil was important. It was sacred soil. It was the soil that had anointed the head of his mother. It was symbolic of all of his killings. After all, it was because of her, that he had finally come to this. This was his way of making restitution for all of the insults that her precious body had been forced to endure as she lay in the cold, dark ground. Nothing had been sacred in her life, and nothing had been sacred in her death.

As Brian went out the back door, the cat followed,

trying to rub her tired body against his, hoping for a little love. Brian bent over, stroking the cat's orange and white fur, and noting how dirty she was....too old to keep herself clean. He remembered how another cat, just like Honeycomb, had curled up on his pillow most nights. At the time, the other cat, Misty, was all he had to love and she loved him back. He didn't cry when she died, though by then he had turned off most of his emotions. He had also been thankful that he would not have to leave her to be cared for by these cruel, selfish, lazy people.

The cat once again cried out to be picked up. Brian looked into its tired, runny eyes. He held her head in one hand and jerked back with all of his strength, making sure the kill was clean and merciful. He could not leave her here with them. Brian placed the cat at the back of the fence and pulled a bunch of dead foliage over her body, making sure no one would find the feline until the spring cleanup began. He would have to hurry; supper would be ready soon. Brian bent over the holy spot where his mother's body was now decayed under a foot of garden dirt. He would need it to symbolize the sacrifice he made. Each victim was a tribute to his mother. He would have to rush and get the job done. It would be a cold day in hell before he ate at the same table as that woman and his father.

Brian could hear his father flush the toilet. He would have to make sure he didn't suspect anything. He quickly brushed any dirt from his jeans and walked over to the patio-set that had just recently been cleaned off to accommodate sitting outside. He sat down just in time to lean back, put his hands behind his head, and looked as if he was just catching a few rays from the spring's sun.

"Here you are."

`The elder Bentham came through the back patio doors.

"You look like you're pleased with your-self. Probably think you got the world by the tail. Just remember, it has a way of jumping up and biting you in the ass when you least expect it." The old man paused and looked around as if he was noticing for the first time that something was missing.

"Where's your drink? Damn it, no one comes to my home and doesn't share a drink with me. Just wait here and I'll get us a couple of beers."

"Sure, whatever you're having is all right for me."

Brian tried to sound calm and easy-going. If he had his way, he wouldn't be staying long enough to enjoy very much of his father's hospitality.

As his father returned with a couple of open beer bottles, Brian noticed that the lines around his face were deeper than he had remembered. When he looked at his dad he could almost be fooled into thinking that he was a harmless old man, rather than the ruthless killer that he had lived with for so many painful years.

Brian was haunted by all of the memories that he had so skillfully put aside. Now, as he sat on the patio in the sunshine, a cool wind blew at the back of his neck. He felt his body start to tremble at the sound of his father's voice as the old man droned on about trivial events. It was as if Brian were surrounded by plastic bubble wrap that muffled the sounds and the real world, slowly squeezing the life out of him.

Brian tried to stay calm and not give into the panic. He had to go within, find a part of himself that was able to separate from all reality and concentrate on a low, slow hum that blocked out all of the fear. OM....OM He could hear his mantra in the back of his mind while he stared at his father and nodded in all of the appropriate places, even giving a few short answers to questions that allowed him to keep the conversation going. Soon his breathing had returned to normal and he was able to tune in again. He wished he hadn't, the conversation had taken an ominous turn.

"What the fuck you make of all those visitors getting "offed" around town? The press says they were all killed in a real strange way. They figure all of the blood was drained from the bodies and they were dumped all over town. We got some real sick fuck, running all over Chicago and the police haven't got a clue what's going on."

The old man leaned back in his chair and took a swig of beer, wiping his mouth on the arm of his shirt afterwards.

"I'll tell you what. The cops are just plain stupid, wouldn't know what's right under their nose. The killer is probably laughing all the way to the blood house; if you know what I mean. I know I probably would."

Brian tried to keep calm and not smack the look of contentment off of his father's stupid face. He was probably remembering how the cops hadn't really tried to find out what had happened to his wife when she had gone missing. It made the bile rise up in Brian's stomach. To think that his father had some pride in the killer getting away with so many murders; as if he had some hand in it, made him want to vomit. But since he was the killer, then in some sick way his father did have a hand in the killings.

"Sooner or later the police always get these serial killers and I'm sure they'll catch this guy eventually."

Brian looked his father right in the eye, seeing if he would rise to the bait. "After all, they say most mass murderers have something in their past that makes them kill. This guy will turn out to be no exception. I'm sure he's just another fucked up kid who can blame his dad."

"What kind of a "point" are you trying to make, boy? You think that all of the things people do are because of their parents. Not every "sick fuck" has a bad mother or father. Some people are just born sick and evil... Not everyone can blame their childhood."

The elder Bentham's face started to become a bright red, knowing his son was referring to his own childhood. He wanted to make sure Brian knew that he was not willing to take the blame for any of Brian's negative feelings in this regard.

Brian tried to stay calm. He could barely fight the feeling of wanting to strangle his father with his bare hands.

"You're right, Dad. Not everyone can use his family as an excuse. After all, some people are just born evil. They are able to take their hands and put them around the neck of their princess and squeeze the life out of her with no excuse at all. No one will miss her and the police are so stupid they'll just think she ran off with some "dumb fuck."

Brian held his breath. This was the closest he had ever come to telling his father that he knew what had happened to his mother that night on his birthday so many years before.

Suddenly his father exploded.

"You cock-sucking, ungrateful little twerp! You get out of my house. I know what you are thinking. You blame me because that slut of a mother ran off with that wimpy, little bastard of a hairdresser. She was nothing but a piece of filth. She never loved me. She was saving up some money so she could leave me. Well I showed her. I found the money and made sure she could never get her hands on it. Who cares what happened to her? No one would blame me for anything I did to that ungrateful piece of trash, and you're just like her. Get out. I don't have to listen to any-more of your shitty accusations."

The spit that came from the force of the statement spattered all over Brian's face. He stood up and wiped his face, only too glad to get out of the presence of the one man on earth he hated more than anyone or anything.

Brian had thought he would be able to close off all of his feelings and stay separate from the turmoil that tore at his guts. But this was the man who had taken away the most beautiful, kind, and wonderful love he had ever known. To live without his mother's love and only know hatred and brutality had made him the man he was, and now all he could think of was how nice it would feel if he could put the steel of the blade into sweaty, fat, flesh of the monster that stood before him. The man who had made him the cold, calculating killer he had become. There was nothing special about him. He would be a classic textbook case of family dynamics; a natural-born killer, just like Dad.

"What's all the commotion about? They can hear you two all over the neighborhood. She came from the kitchen, a dirty towel in her hand.

"No one will be staying for supper. This ungrateful, little fuck face is leaving this minute or I'll kick his ass out." The older Bentham stood, his fists clenched at his side.

"No need, Dad, I know the way to the door. After all, I left once and swore I'd never come back. If it weren't for some unfinished business I'm sure I could have kept that promise, but now that we're through, I'll have no need to return."

Brian stood up, looked his father in the eye, and went through the patio doors to the front door where his van was parked. He suddenly felt great. He had said things to his father that he had wanted to say for so long that the only way to stay sane was to keep everything bottled up inside. The best thing about the altercation was that he no longer had to stay and eat that shit supper. He slowed his van down at the corner of the fence, got out and picked up the bundle of soil. All in all, it had been a great evening.

Chapter Fourteen

Shelley felt elated as she put on her white lab coat. She had just finished doing an autopsy on the last two victims; an overly bleached blonde and her handsome young companion. A slow smile spread across her radiant face as she remembered her evening with Brian. As she closed the trays into the rollaway drawer and locked the small compartment door she felt a sense of relief that there was no longer any suspicion towards Brian. He now had an airtight alibi. There was no way that he could have committed the murders of these two latest victims.

With Bara's and Lexy's statements as to the time the couple had left the restaurant and Shelley's own statement of when she had picked Brian up, there was absolutely no way he would have had enough time to wine, dine, drug, murder, and dump the bodies off before meeting her. He was now officially off the hook. She had never accepted that he was the killer or she would never have gone out with him. Or would she have? He was a good-looking man and with her track record for picking the wrong kind of man, she might have let his good looks overrule her better judgment. Shelley was thankful that she would never have to find out if her instincts were off. Brian was simply not the killer and she could now go on and explore a relationship with him.

She dragged her thoughts back to her task at hand. Once again there was going to be very little new information to give Detective Kortovich. With all of the bad press with their city being dubbed the, "Mass Murder Capital of the USA" and the victims nicknamed, "The Vampire Victims," the citizens of Chicago were becoming a little hysterical. The tourism department people, as well as every other city official were turning up the heat at City Hall and Dennis was under immense pressure from the Mayor and the Superintendent, to find the killer.

The Superintendent had exhausted every avenue available to connect with other agencies to see if anything similar had happened anywhere else in North America. Nothing! These unusual killings had only taken place in Chicago. Nothing even similar had happened anywhere else. Even Interpol as well as Scotland Yard had been contacted and an exhaustive search was conducted, but to no avail. Officials with these agencies had taken the time to review the files and could offer little except to say good luck. Every expert agreed this was a tough, crazy case and only dumb luck for the police or a lack of luck for the killer would help solve and end this citywide nightmare.

Shelley had to hurry. She was due to attend a meeting with the Chief of Police as well as all of the members of the task force for the serial murders. As she hung up her lab coat and checked her pocket for her favorite tube of lipstick, she allowed herself one more dreamy thought about Brian. He was yummy and smearing a little lipstick across her lips gave her delightful thoughts about lips; his and hers.

When she arrived at the police station, several members of the team were heading towards the elevator to go to the boardroom where the rest of the team would gather. She smiled at a couple of the men, but maintained elevator etiquette and said little on the way up.

"Hey Shelley, you come up with anything new on this last set of victims?" A young, skinny man in a dark, navy suite gave her an earnest look from the side of his eye as they walked together towards the meeting.

It was Peter Clark, a new-rookie detective who was liked by everyone on the team for his earnest, open style. His ability to pick up information and learn quickly had endeared him to the rest of the team. He often asked intelligent questions and had a way of keeping the older members of the team on their toes. They were afraid he would ask an unusual question and they would be caught off guard. After all, they were the veterans and should have most of the answers.

"No, nothing, and it pisses me off that this guy is so consistent. He changes nothing from victim to victim. He's in no hurry so he keeps his head on straight and never messes up. I sure hope something changes soon, because the killing is happening at more regular intervals. He will have to get tired or make a mistake. If he has to step up the pace any faster he's bound to get something wrong. We can only hope that happens before we get another dozen or so victims."

Shelley and Peter were now at the door of the boardroom....the meeting had just started and they both found seats around the table seconds before the captain walked in.

Robert Creston had been the precinct Captain for the past decade.

He was a man of principle and intelligence with a reputation for getting the best results possible from his police force. They'd had an unusual success rate when it came to solving crime, much higher than other forces across the country. But that record was being massacred with this latest string of homicides. The reason for the captain's success was simple; Robert had a knack for knowing and understanding his key men at every level. It came from a keen sense of observation as well as a highly developed intuition in knowing how to read people and figuring out each key person's greatest strength as well as his or her weakness. When Creston teamed up people and departments he ended up with unbeatable combinations of almost perfect teams. Alone they were all right, but together each combination was unstoppable. The captain also took an unusual interest in all new recruits, often taking time to have several of them join him for lunch. This helped them to feel comfortable, boosted their morale, and had everyone giving him more than their best. When you went to his office there were hundreds of pictures of police officers who excelled at their job.

It was like a badge of honor to have your picture hung on his office wall in recognition of superior service. Robert Creston's desk was situated in the middle of the room, and dead center on the back wall was a picture of Dennis Kortovich. It was the special place of honor for officers that had excelled over the year. Dennis was the best the force had to offer. Intelligent, diligent, and well balanced, he had a way about him that inspired great teamwork. Everyone wanted to work with him and being made his partner was a special distinction.

Dennis did everything by the book and unlike Hollywood cops his even-paced, unemotional, thorough investigative style solved most of his cases. He was able to keep hundreds of pieces of information compartmentalized in his keen, analytical brain. When it came to questioning a suspect no one was better than Dennis. He never played "good cop-bad cop," he was much too clever for that.

Dennis would take several files into the interrogation room with the suspect, keeping his energy calm and non-judgmental. Much like a CEO interviewing a potential manager he stayed respectful, polite, and forthcoming. He would shoot off a few simple questions that had already been answered by the suspect, making him feel as if they were just confirming a few already-known facts. Dennis would begin slowly and over the next few hours his questioning style would become so brilliantly complex that confusion would finally set in. Once he had tripped the suspects up many times with contradictory information, they would become more flustered as time went on, and at length, give up some crucial bit of information. This would make it impossible for the suspect to do more than resort to the truth, allowing the police to tie the case up neatly. "*Gotcha*" Dennis would have them cold.

The captain knew there was no finer man to head up the special task force than Dennis and all he could do was to try to keep the political heat low, as well as calm the press down, making sure they didn't get too nasty.

Shelley mentally summed up the environment Dennis had to work in. She was glad her job was just to report the plain and simple facts; conclusions that, had been arrived at by the evidence only.

"I know that these past six months have been tough and most of you have had to work around the clock trying to follow the leads that have come in. Most of these have been dead ends, but we still have to remember that the press is going a little crazy with these killings. Even the tabloids around the country are selling papers like hot cakes, trying to get a "Hollywood Horror Movie" spin out of this."

Robert looked around the room trying to emphasize how big this case had become and that he wasn't pleased with the bad press the cops were getting.

"But we have to make sure we don't get caught off-guard and say something that will fuel the fire any further. We all know that some of the tabloids aren't above printing any kind of shit they want to, and then simply saying an "inside source" said whatever. But if I find out one man or woman has said more than a, "No Comment," I'll have their badge. Let our lead investigator Dennis, or his partner Chuck, handle all of the questions from the press. Is that understood?" The Captain looked around one more time before dismissing the team.

The meeting had drawn to a close. It had mostly been a summing up by the Captain about how to handle the press and the public in regards to the investigation. Things were getting nasty and the department didn't want to set off any fireworks in regards to rumors or fear mongering. The street talk was that it was a "gothic cult" and everyone was afraid that if the case wasn't solved soon, the public would take justice into its own hands and innocent but "freaky" people might get hurt.

As Shelley stood up she gave her spine a much-needed

stretch, raising her arms over her head. She wasn't getting any younger and the long hours of standing on hard concrete were taking their toll. It was a good thing she was a good money manager; she'd never make sixty-five at this job. Early retirement was her only hope. Once she was back at the lab she continued to work on her other cases that were getting left behind with the extra workload. It was soon well into the evening and after several interruptions she'd finally finished enough work to feel as if she could call it a day. She was just reopening one of the cold trays that held the body of one of the two sisters, which had been found a few days before, when she heard footsteps on the cold concrete floor.

"Oh, it's only you." She smiled as Dennis paused in front of their latest tragic set of victims.

"I just wanted to take one last look at this young girl before I left for the night, she reminds me of my Tiffany. I can hardly imagine what it must be like for a family to lose one member of your family, let alone two." Shelley's face displayed the horror of the thought.

Dennis paused one more time to look at the young girl on the stainless steel tray; then turned to face Shelley. Not wanting to appear overwhelmed by all of the events of the past six months, he let his face become an emotionless mask.

"Tell me you have something new.... anything." Dennis voice was deliberately void of any emotion, not wanting to lose control of himself and let any fear well up, sending him over the edge.

"This guy has to make a mistake!" He suddenly felt overwhelmed by the sheer nothingness of it all.

"Yeah, he left his driver's license, home address,

Christmas card list and underwear preference pinned to the victim's coat."

Wanting to lighten things up, Shelley laughingly answered back, knowing Dennis would feel ashamed if he lost his composure. She knew he felt a great deal of pride in his ability to stay cool and calm throughout an investigation, a quality he depended on.

Dennis looked startled for a second, not having expected any humor with his grim mood having overtaken any ability to stay impartial. He smiled back, grateful for the comic relief.

"Don't forget his personal diary giving dates, times, and names, just to tie things up neatly." he countered with a smile, feeling his dark mood lighten.

Dennis noted that Shelley's coat was in her arm and that the dress she wore was not the usual casual attire she wore to work.

"What's up, you going somewhere special?" His eyes showed his amusement and obvious approval of how great she looked.

"None of your business, but if you must know I have a date and it's your fault." Shelley countered with the same lighthearted mood, pulling Dennis back on track, and feeling like things were "business as usual." He followed Shelley out of the lab down the hallway towards the parking lot.

"You know Brian Bentham; the guy with all the wrong knives." Shelley was making more of a statement, rather than a question.

"We've been out a couple of times now and I'm really enjoying his company. It's so nice that his schedule can work well with mine."

"Be careful." Dennis suddenly felt the need to protect her.

It was more than just courteous advice, something inside felt wrong, Dennis didn't have enough solid evidence to tell Shelley why she shouldn't go out with Brian; he just felt she shouldn't. He also knew that a woman like Shelley would do what her heart and not her head told her to do and from the look on her face Dennis knew she was about to give this new guy the "thumbs up," something he felt was wrong to do.

"You still don't know that much about this guy and he's still our only link via The Beef Chateau."

Dennis's mind flashed to Chuck and how disappointed Chuck would be when he found out Shelley was dating again. There was something about Brian that Dennis felt uneasy about, but he couldn't pin down what that something was.

"You can take Brian off any likely suspect list." Shelley beamed up at Dennis. "I can tell you for sure that on the night Candy and Brock were found, Brian would have had no possible way to commit the crime and keep his date with me."

"How do you figure that?" Dennis questioned, unwilling to let go of his only lead, as weak as it was.

"First…." Shelley started becoming all business, removing any personal involvement she may have felt for Brian. "It has been established that Bara and Lexy always leave the restaurant around midnight every night. The victim's bodies were found at six the next morning, time of death four hours earlier. That meant the soonest they could have been killed would be around 1pm, If they were killed around one, Brian would have had to feed them, knock them out for a while, slit their throats, clean everything up, remove them from the site of their death and dump them, all within a half hour." Shelley stopped long enough to take a deep breath. "After all, I picked him up at one, not quite enough time to do the dastardly deed."

Shelley noted the reluctant look on Dennis's face. She knew he was finding it hard to let go of his only suspect and not a very serious one at that.

"Brian's not the kind of man who's been busy killing people over the past months. After all, this nut case has killed over twenty young people and taken the time to make sure we have nothing to go on; a very busy man indeed. I doubt a man like that would take the time out for a date." Shelley had a triumphant look on her face, feeling she had summed up the situation well enough to dismiss Brian as a suspect.

"OK, OK. I'll take him off my list of dozens." Dennis laughed as he held the door open for her. "The last thing I want is for you to be dating a serial killer. after all, you just got over your stalker." Dennis's eyes held a lighthearted twinkle, letting Shelley know that he had conceded to her logic.

"You rat!" Shelley gave him a playful smack on the back of his arm.

"You don't trust my choice in men." She was standing in front of her old blue Topaz, a car that long ago should have been retired.

Dennis's face took on a soft, but serious look. "No, it's not that I don't trust you, it's just that there's someone special just under your nose and if you just gave him a chance, things just might work out for the two of you."

Dennis's gaze held Shelley's, hoping to see a spark of hope for Chuck.

"I know you love the guy," Shelley returned Dennis's gaze with all the love and respect she could feel for a fellow colleague and friend. "But Chuck is just a friend and so far I just can't seem to feel more than that for him. Maybe I just like the unknown and Chuck is like an open book. What you see is what you get, very unromantic."

Shelley's eyes softened as her mind drifted to Brian and she mentally compared how different the two men were.

Dennis held Shelley's door open and helped her to settle in, making sure her coat was tucked in before closing the door. "Eventually you will find you like what's between the pages of a familiar book. It's like an old friend who will sit beside you and whisper the tales of your childhood softly in your ears when you go to bed at night and you feel safe and warm. The old stories are still the best."

Shelley unrolled the car window and Dennis bent over, his head level with hers. Their eyes locked and each knew that they were more than colleagues. They were genuine friends that wanted and needed nothing more from each other than an honest dialogue and warm understanding.

"I just don't want you to get hurt." Dennis stood up as she closed the car window. Knowing an answer was unnecessary. She blew him a kiss and drove off, leaving Dennis deep in thought.

Chapter Fifteen

The young couple at the table would have stood out anywhere, let alone a busy dining room like The Beef Chateau. They were simply stunning. Both of them had the kind of look that young stars on the afternoon soaps depended on for success; trendy, gorgeous, and full of energy, as well as with that distinctive look of a young couple in love.

"I can hardly believe we're here." The dark-haired beauty softly whispered to her equally handsome companion.

"We've been married for nearly twenty-four hours and it still seems like a dream." She put her shiny dark head next to his, moving closer while he planted a firm warm kiss on the top of her head.

The Maître d', André sat them in Andrew's section. Andrew enjoyed his job waiting on tables and the tips helped pay for his University and fun. As he approached the table he slowed his pace just a little. It was nice to see young couples in love. He had just recently met a very special young lady himself and he hoped it would lead to something real, much like the special magic that surrounded this couple.

"Hi, my name is Andrew and I will be your server tonight."

Andrew started his usual pitch, but found himself unable to continue as the girl lifted her head off her companion's shoulder and flashed a dazzling smile. It took his breath away and made him feel as if all of the beauty that could be summed up in the world was in this perfect woman who was staring up at him. Her energy and his entwined at this moment and he was so drawn in he lost his train of thought and stammered through his presentation.

Her skin was flawless and smooth with just a hint of honeyed tones adding to the perfection. Almost black, her brown eyes framed by thick blue-black lashes gazed intently at him making him feel as if time was slowing down as he lost his ability to concentrate on his task at hand. Her nose was set perfectly on a soft, oval face, while full, sensuous lips covered her even white teeth to complete a perfect face. Thick, shiny, dark hair with glints of auburn danced off the dining room lights. Never had Andrew seen such perfection.

"But, but ....you can call me Andrew." He wound up trying to pull his eyes away and focus on her companion.

The young man withdrew his arm from his companion's allowing him to take the menus from Andrew. Again Andrew was taken aback by the complementary image of the young man who was the partner to the young goddess, sitting next to him. They were a perfect match; flawless.

"The specials tonight are first....a delectable eight ounce Steak Neptune." Andrew found it hard to concentrate with the intense blue eyes of the young man, whose gaze never wavered from his face.

Soon Andrew fell into his friendly, warm manner and was finding the young couple to be an absolute delight. After a few visits to the table he found himself engaging in more and more of a conversation and he began to feel as if he had known them for a long time and was getting reacquainted with a couple of old friends.

"So you decided to come to Chicago for your honeymoon and eat here for your special celebration. Where are you from?" Andrew could tell they weren't big city kids. They were much too open and had innocence about them.

"We're just here for a few days from Abilene, Texas. I have to be back to work at my job as a foreman in a cattle feed lot and I don't mind staying a few days in a city as big as Chicago. Our honeymoon trip is going to have to be enough for a long time to come."

"Yes. It took everything for me to convince Ryan to come here for our honeymoon, but I wanted to see Grant Park and the statue of Abraham Lincoln as well as the Depot Museum. And then there is the DuSable Museum. I have a degree in African-American History and a passion for Lincoln. Ryan tells me I was probably a slave in a past lifetime; I can't seem to get enough. And seeing as this isn't the South, it's the best I can do for a holiday and a little history." Angela laughed up at her husband who seemed content to amuse her and share his honeymoon with whatever and whoever made her happy.

"Where we come from, it's just too small to get any real history, so a trip to the city has to satisfy me."

"If my sweetheart here had her way, we would come back every weekend, but my job won't let me so I guess we'll just have to see as much as we can until we get back." Ryan pulled Angela closer to him with obvious pride at her education and curious nature.

Andrew had just finished serving them their meal when he caught Brian coming out of the kitchen doors. With little thought, Andrew continued to survey his section, making sure all of the food was out and that the patrons' beverages were full, before seeing to the cleanup of his other empty tables. It was now past nine and things would be slowing down within the hour for a midnight close.

* * * *

Brian needed another set of victims. As he stepped out of the doors from the kitchen into the dining room, he spotted the young couple in a second. It was almost as if a spotlight shone on them, making it seem as if they were the only ones in the room; a difficult feat when one considered there were nearly three hundred tables divided into different sections in the dining room.

As Brian went from table to table to talk to the diners, making sure the food and the service were adequate, he knew he had already found his special guests for the night. The vibrant energy that the couple exuded could almost be felt halfway across the room. It was the extra-sensual energy that was being exchanged between the two of them that set them apart. Not the raw sexual energy that he often saw, like Candy and Brock. No, it was an extraordinary energy, when two very special souls connect in a way that most people only dream of.

This was the kind of couple that legends were made of. Romeo and Juliet, Cleopatra and Mark Anthony would pale by comparison to these two absolutely incredibly, beautiful, young people. Brian could almost taste them. The extra pheromones in their systems would no doubt add a new dimension to the elixir their blood would make. He would keep this batch for him-self; it would be his special brand.

His visit to the table was finished. They were perfect, from out of town, young, and eager to return tonight to find out his secret and share a late night, or should he say, "last night" toast. Brian continued to make his way around the diners, saying hello to many repeat customers while he watched Andrew finish serving his new friends. They had taken the bait. They would be back tonight. Brian had sworn them to secrecy and made sure they understood that only a few were ever invited and that even the staff didn't know the secret to the marinade.

Andrew went back to the table to present the bill to Angela and Ryan. He marveled once again at the beauty of the couple. They were funny, intelligent, and very much in love. He envied them and hoped that he could find the time to pursue his relationship with a young woman he had only met a few months ago. Watching this couple made him glad he was in love.

"Thank you again." Angela reached out to take the tab and without looking at it handed it over to Ryan. "You made our evening. Ryan and I agree we've never had such great service or good food." Angela's soft, rich voice made Andrew feel the sincerity of the words.

"We're so glad we came to Chicago for our honey-moon." Angela ended with a warm smile that made Andrew feel as if his job mattered more than it really did.

"Yes, Angela and I decided having only four days' off

won't be so bad after all. This could be one of the best times of our lives." Ryan beamed, looking like he had just caught the big one.

"We have unexpected tickets for Steppenwolf Theater Company and then a very special treat after. This is going to be a killer of an evening and Angela's blood is running hot for a good time." Ryan gave her a look that said she was good enough to eat.

They exchanged special glances. When the evening was over they would be able to have some knock-out sex and then drift off into a heavenly sleep. Only the angels would be able to hear their thankful prayers for such a great night.

When Andrew took the cash he felt a foreboding chill cross his chest. He suddenly felt cold. He wondered if maybe he was coming down with something. Strange, the chill ran deeper than that. It ran deep enough to almost make him feel a little dizzy. He stood taller, trying to pull himself to his full height and shake off this weird feeling. He needed to get some change and push away this stupid feeling of impending doom.

Angela and Ryan enjoyed their time at the theatre, but it was really their meal at The Beef Chateau and their waiter Andrew who had made the evening. Andrew gave the kind of service you rarely find. The connection between them made it seem as if an old friend was taking care of them rather than a stranger. Maybe it was because they were close to the same age; early twenties or that Andrew was confidant as well as being handsome, without any conceit or arrogance. They had found out they had much in common; music, movies, and snowboarding. Coincidentally, both Andrew and Ryan had even competed against each other at different boarding events around the country, but had somehow never connected off the hill. They exchanged phone numbers and would make sure they made arrangements one weekend during the next season to meet and snowboard in a mutually agreed-on location.

Angela commented to Ryan on how wonderful it was to be invited back to the restaurant to have a special dessert and wine. But better still they would be given the secret recipe for the marinade for their steaks. It was an honor to be given this privileged information and Brian made them promise to tell no one. They would have to sign a confidential agreement tonight, but they could dazzle their friends with the recipe when they prepared summer steaks. The evening had been cool, but calm, until just before they walked up to the double oak doors. Suddenly a cold gust of wind blew hard, making its way through Angela's heavy jacket. Ryan instinctively put his arms around her. He had the sudden feeling he should run, it was late well past midnight and the light-hearted mood they had felt only minutes ago now seemed to disappear with the cold wind, leaving a sick feeling of dread. They had no sooner knocked on the door of the restaurant than Brian stood before them, all smiles and genuine warmth. Ryan shook off the feeling of dread, dismissing it as post- wedding stress; after all, keeping up with Angela could tire a guy out. The feeling of anticipation for new things overtook his momentary feeling of doom.

"Welcome, welcome." Brian waved his hand toward the warmth of the dining room as he held the doors open for the couple to enter.

He could smell her perfume as she gracefully stepped

past him, Estee Lauder's Youth Dew. He was suddenly pulled back in time, into his mother's arms as he clung to her. Oh how he loved her. She smelled like spices and woodland flowers, a very unusual smell that mingled with her skin. Besides her soft face and beautiful eyes it was her smell that meant the most to him.

Brian's heart dropped suddenly to his stomach. He saw Angela for the first time. He really saw her. It was her smell, it had pulled at the walls that had so far kept him safe in a world that he had invented and learned to live in. Now, her smell gently pulled him into the real world. A world he had worked at forever to block out, a world where he could never feel love, but he could never be hurt either. He had built so many layers around himself, that few knew that his life was all an act.

He had learned to function in the real world, pretending that he was alive when he wasn't. He had died a long time ago. He had died the day he had found his mother's belongings hidden behind that secret panel under the crawl space, beneath the stairs. He had removed her nightgown; it smelled like her, with just a hint of perfume. As the years went by he's been able to keep it hidden away from his father. Brian went back into his mother's hidden stuff often, whenever he couldn't feel her. He would re-spray the Youth Dew on her nightie and bury his face in it and cry....

Cry for all the times she would never be there to stroke his head and whisper in her soft voice, "Soon, you'll be all right." Cry for the beatings, cruel words, and often endless insults his father hurled at him. Sometimes the insults and beatings were better than the complete nothingness; at least he got some attention.

Always he would retreat to the bottom of the stairs, pull her nightgown from its hiding place, smell deeply of its scent and remember her touch, voice, and the way she made him feel safe and loved. Then he would cry. By the time he was fifteen he had cried himself out. He put the nightgown back underneath the stairs in its secret place and vowed to never pull it out again. For every tear he'd cried he placed an invisible stone around his heart until finally there was only a pile of rocks, just so much rubble where a heart should have been. He had developed great charm and personality. Few knew it was a well-rehearsed act. He was a man who appeared to be alive, but in reality, was dead.... dead for a long, long time. Brian's eyes held Angela's for so long he was afraid she had pulled his very soul from some hidden place that even he never entered

"I'm sorry." Angela looked bewildered and a bit scared. "Are you all right? You look like you've just seen a ghost."

"No...No..." Brian stammered. "I just felt suddenly very sick." A light sweat appeared on his brow.

The sound of her voice was very warm and reassuring, and his heart suddenly began to ache. He needed to be alone.

"Maybe we could take a rain check on this evening and do this another time." Brian tried to turn his eyes away from hers. Ryan stood silently on the side, sensing that any involvement from him was not needed and would somehow be dangerous.

Angela stepped even closer to Brian, making the smell of her flesh mingle with the Youth Dew. It was the exact smell of his mother. He was nearly undone by it all. They just had to go....get out before he fell completely apart.

"You take care of yourself." Angela said in a tone that

tore once more at his heart. "We will sure to be back and we'll cash in on that rain check."

With those final words she gently held his face in her hands, looked deeply into his troubled eyes, and stroked the side of his face with her warm, soft hand.

"Don't worry, you'll be safe, you'll be all right."

Angela took Ryan's hand, opened the double oak doors, and walked calmly into the evening. Her only thought was "poor little boy." Both she and Ryan disappeared into the night.

* * * *

Brian slept a deep, dreamless sleep for the first time in more years than he could remember. He couldn't recollect what time it was when he finally pulled himself up off the meat-cutting room floor, all he knew for sure was that he had cried like he had never cried before. Tears of anger, rage, hate, love, longing, and loss….memories flooded back to the day he had finally left home, the day his father in a drunken rage had slapped him for the last time. The funny thing was he'd felt nothing. By then he had put away all of his feelings, vowing to never allow anyone to have any power over him again. Not love or hate could make him tear down the walls.

Brian couldn't remember how he got home or exactly when, but the clock at his bedside said it was now three in the afternoon, and he was late for work for the first time. He had never slept this long before and just before he was fully awake, he could smell and feel his mother again, or maybe it was Angela. He felt good….free from the hidden demons for the first time. A quick shower and he would have to get back to work. Brian sat up quickly and felt dizzy. He lay back down. Maybe just this once he would call in sick and miss work. He desperately needed to just go back to sleep. It seemed he needed to catch up on a lifetime of sleep. He called Bara and Lexy, made his excuses and drifted back into a dreamless, peaceful sleep.

Chapter Sixteen

Chuck walked to the side door of Dennis and Veronica's home. He always loved coming up the walk, the white arbor lent a quaint look to the stone walkway and the large trees along the side of the fence were well over twenty feet tall, spreading their branches out over the pine cone and wood-chip pathway that wound through their sweet branches. As he approached the back door the picturesque window box was covered in bright, colorful flowers, all of them fake. Veronica couldn't stand her window box when it was bare so she put silk flowers in to give it a cheerful welcoming look until late spring, when fresh flowers could be planted. That was how Veronica was.... bright, cheerful, and always welcoming.

It was the second Sunday of the month and over the past four years, supper at the Kortovich home had become a welcomed ritual.

Twice a month, depending on the situation at the police station, supper with the family was a dependable event. It was also wonderful because Chuck got to spend time with Shelley McPherson, who was also a welcomed guest and whom he long ago had realized he loved. She was so full of laughter, wit, keen intelligence, and an easy, accepting manner, that he wondered how he would ever find someone to love other than her. Everyone else seemed boring and lifeless next to Shelley. He knew it was hopeless; she saw him only as a friend. The only time they had spent a lot of time together was during the year that she had been stalked by that sicko. But life had a way of getting even. A human hand, guided by fate, had made sure the stalker had died of a staph-infection. It was simple. A lot of people died that way. No regrets.... things happened. He would do anything to protect her. Over the years, the only thing Chuck had been unable to protect Shelley from, was her own poor taste in men.

She always seemed to be attracted to the handsome, flashy guys who had a slight edge to them. Over the time that Chuck had been able to observe the interaction between Shelley and her dates, he had developed a theory. Shelley's adventuresome spirit and quick wit liked the danger that these losers seemed to add to her relationship. As far as Chuck could see, he had no chance at all. He was loyal, predictable, kind, even tempered, and not controlling. Being with Chuck would be much too peaceful....not enough excitement. If she ever gave him a chance, she might find out when the lights were out that he could provide a great deal of excitement.

Shelley looked up at the back door as Chuck walked in, all frowns and scowls. "What's up your ass? You look like a little boy whose bike just got stolen." Shelley shot at Chuck, catching him off-guard as he entered the family room.

"I wish it were only my bike!" Chuck responded quickly, putting a lighthearted smile on his face. "No

Shelley, my darling, it's only my heart that's been stolen and I doubt I'll ever get it back." His eyes held hers knowingly.

Shelley started to blush. She was only too aware of the fact that Chuck was referring to her. There was a part of her that loved Chuck. She just couldn't understand why she didn't start a relationship with him; after all, she knew it would be an easy, comfortable love affair and one that would be risk free. Maybe it was that very fact. Chuck was the kind of guy who would commit to her forever, and that scared the hell out of her. Maybe her shrink was right, she had a real fear of intimacy and that was the reason she picked losers. There was a part of her that knew things would end with her lovers, usually badly. That was the reason she never fell truly, deeply in love. All of the men in her life had been affairs, not real relationships.

Some had lasted longer than others, but sooner or later they all ended. In some ways Chuck was both safe and scary. Safe because he would always be there for her and would never step over the line, scary because if he ever did, she would have to face her worst fears. Fear that at some deep level she was unable to have a real relationship. A full commitment was more than she could handle, and scarier still was the thought of having anyone love her more than she was prepared to love herself. So it was simple, Chuck scared the hell out of her and her only defense was to keep it light and make sure there was always someone on the side to run interference. At this point in time, Brian looked like he had what it would take to win the race.

After a few minutes of awkward silence they both welcomed the flamboyant entrance of Veronica, with a plate of hot hors d'oeuvres.

"Hey you two what's happening? Cat got your tongues?" She glanced knowingly at Chuck and Shelley, thinking silently to herself that one day these two just might figure out they were attracted to each other. So far, though, they seemed happy to pretend they were "just friends."

"Here, try some of my stuffed mushrooms; low in fat, high in flavor." she added, placing the tray in front of Chuck. "Dennis will be right back, he's just picking up some ice. His drink won't be the same without it." She laughed, knowing how much the men loved their "rum and cokes."

Chuck loved Veronica. Her wacky personality and zest for life always made time spent at their home one of his favorite places to be. He studied her warm, beautiful face and the physical grace with which she carried herself. Chuck always admired the fact that as a larger woman she looked just as sexy as any woman half her size. He could take a page from her book and learn to accept the fact that at five feet ten inches and two hundred pounds he was never going to be the kind of guy that Shelley went for; tall and slim. No matter how hard he tried he couldn't fight genetics.

Chuck reached over for the largest mushroom on the plate that was being set before him. At last he could enjoy a good, home-cooked meal, something that he only seemed to get when he visited Dennis and Veronica.

Veronica finished placing the mushrooms in front of Shelley and Chuck, stood back, and looked around the room making sure everything was in its place and well organized. She loved having Sunday suppers with her family and friends. Her mother Pat, a realtor, and father Wayne, a former Fire Chief, were the usual supper quests along with Chuck and Shelley, whenever their schedules would allow, which was often. And of course the kids would pop in for the good food and company, especially Trina, she hated cooking and as far as Veronica knew she couldn't boil water, not that Veronica and Natasha hadn't tried to get her into the kitchen; she just had too many places to go and too many people to see. And as far as she was concerned, Steve would do all the cooking when the time came that they needed to stay home.

When Veronica came back into the family room later she found Shelley and Chuck deep in conversation about the Vampire Murders, although she would never call them that out loud, she hated the name the press had given to the string of disgusting murders.

Veronica secretly suspected that Chuck and Shelley tried to hold Sundays open so that they could make the family events. A part of her was sure it was the great food on the other hand, she knew that on some level Shelley and Chuck belonged together. Veronica knew Chuck had accepted long ago that he loved Shelley but she was still fighting the attraction not willing to give in. Maybe it went deeper.... Veronica suspected that Shelley's fear of intimacy was the very thing that kept her away from Chuck and in the arms of anyone who was bound to hurt and disappoint her. At some level that was the way she liked it even if it hurt like hell at times. After all, Chuck was always around to comfort her.

They were still exchanging information at the kitchen table when Pat and Wayne arrived. As usual Pat bought dessert and Wayne an extra bottle of rum. The kids and their partners would arrive soon, empty-handed but happy enough to dig into the hearty supper. They would then catch up on all of the week's news, laugh a lot, and soon head off to an early show or visit friends, leaving the adults to finish off the evening with a fair amount of shop talk and dishes.

"Veronica, were you able to put together some gift certificates for me?" Pat, Veronica's mother, asked right away, not wanting to forget to handle this bit of business before the evening began.

"Yes, they are by the back door, don't forget them when you leave."

Veronica's mother was a real steamroller. At seventy she was about as far away from retirement as a woman half her age. One of the best Realtors in the Chicago area, Pat had continually stayed at the top of her field for over thirty-three years. She was now selling homes to the grandchildren of her many clients and loved it as much as ever. As a top agent for one of the country's best companies, RE/Max, she was always thinking about work. Wayne, her second husband, was a good contrast to her, and his quiet, competent nature was the lifeblood of what made all the little things work in their home. He was the one who fixed up everything. Something each one counted on because they were all useless when it came to the "fix up" stuff. Pat was tall with a full head of naturally curly hair, full figured, and full of life, while Wayne was nearly bald with only a small amount of hair that fringed his head like peach fuzz. His medium build supported a small paunch, but it was his clear, nearly wrinkle-free face that belied his seventy years, making him look much younger, which was surprising when one considered he smoked two packs of cigarettes a day, a fact that was evident in his breathing.

Everyone turned to the door at once as Dennis fumbled through, trying to carry everything at once, two large bags of ice, some coke, and a large bottle of rum, almost too much for one trip, but not quite enough for two. Chuck quickly stepped forward helping Dennis with the two bags of ice.

"Good to see you looking a little less tired, you must have gotten a good sleep," Chuck offered.

Chuck noticed that for the first time in the last six months, Dennis looked like his old self again, the deep lines around his mouth were softened by a good night's sleep, his eyes clear, with little to no puffiness underneath. The white pallor that was starting to be normal seemed to have disappeared. He now had a warm golden glow and once again looked ten years younger than his fifty years.

"What happened?" Chuck whispered close to Dennis's ear. "Veronica gives you a little extra loving? You look like you might just live. Lately you've looked like you've been at death's door." Chuck tried to give his back-handed compliment.

"I really don't know." Dennis responded with a sound in his voice and a look on his face that really caught Chuck's attention. "I suddenly feel very calm; it's as if a huge burden has been lifted from my shoulders. It was like a weight that I have carried for a lifetime was suddenly gone and I slept for the first time in months. A dreamless, peaceful sleep and I somehow feel great today. I don't know why, but I'm going to enjoy it. Who knows, maybe we're about to get a break!" Dennis put his hand on Chuck's broad shoulder and gave it a brotherly squeeze.

"Okay you two, you're starting to worry me. I've heard that partners who have been together for a long time will have a bro-manse going, but you two make a strange couple." Shelley teased feeling an unfamiliar twinge of jealously at being abandoned by Chuck.

After that speech Dennis planted a big kiss on Chuck's forehead. Not to be outdone, Chuck grabbed Dennis and flung him backward in an overly romantic gesture and planted a second kiss smack on Dennis's lips.

"You're right and after supper Dennis and I will be announcing our engagement." Chuck turned his smiling face towards Veronica. "Of course we'll have to make sure you two get a proper divorce first."

"You can't have him." Veronica shot back with mock seriousness. "He's too well trained in housework and laundry for me to let him go willingly, and besides I can control his snoring. Who could ask for anything more? A man I can turn over and who will take care of me in my old age."

Veronica punched Chuck softly on the shoulder, making it look like she was taking the whole thing seriously. Chuck sat back down trying to look like the jilted victim.

"Where are the girls?" Dennis asked as he poured drinks for his guests. "The whole hungry pack is usually here by now." He finished handing Wayne his rum and coke along with Pat's diet soda.

"This week they won't be coming." Veronica answered with a genuine feeling of sadness. "The boys are working and so Tasha and Trina are going out for a special supper and then to catch a new movie.

They even came earlier; all dressed up, did their hair

real fancy, and outdid themselves with their makeup. They looked like movie stars. I never get tired of looking at their incredibly, beautiful faces." Veronica said sincerely. "I'm sure they'll turn every head in the place." She added with a mother's pride.

"Where are they going, dressed up so special?" Shelley asked, agreeing that every head would turn when the girls walked into the restaurant.

"I'm not sure? Trina has Steve's credit card and plans to do some damage, payback for his big night with the boys." Veronica offered, knowing Trina would make sure she and Tasha had the best.

The Sunday meal was great and Chuck felt he had eaten just a little too much and needed a short walk to help settle the great food. As usual, the conversation turned to the latest events and what was new for the three couples.

"What did you think of the last episode of *"Survivor"*? Veronica asked her mother, who was a fan of the show.

"I hate it when they have a food challenge and they have to eat some kind of local dish. I almost vomit every time. Did you see what they had to drink this time?" Pat screwed up her face as she asked the question.

"Yes. The milk mixed with cow's blood wasn't as bad as some of the more wiggly stuff they have had to eat from other shows. Besides, it was the best thing they could have had at the time, with all of them being so weak." Veronica's face took on "that" look. She was about to launch into some far-out story; something that had become a common occurrence over the years.

"They say that blood will digest immediately and pass through the system almost instantaneously, giving anyone who drinks it a feeling of well-being. That's why they all seemed to pick up energy after they drank the unholy mixture. Who knows Dennis; maybe whoever is killing these couples does it for the same reason as the African Tribesmen do, to feel better."

"You may be right. No one has come up with a reason to drain the blood, and drinking it to feel better is as good as reason as any, but we still don't know *who*?"

Dennis emphasized the last word to make sure everyone knew this subject needed to be left alone for the night. Suddenly everyone went silent. Veronica got up to do the dishes, whishing she hadn't brought up the recent killings. Dennis had seemed in a good mood and she now realized he had wanted a night off to forget.

"I think I'll go for a ten-minute walk before dessert or there will be no place to put it. Shelley do you want to come with me?" Chuck looked her way, his eyes hopeful.

Shelley hated that look. She knew that he just wanted some time alone with her. Part of her wanted it more than she cared to admit, but on the other hand, she didn't want to get too close. If Chuck ever pushed for a closer relationship she would have to face her feelings for him. There was a part of her that knew she would run and then regret it. Her life was full of half-missed opportunities and some regrets. It would kill her to lose Chuck; he was her anchor and the one man who could be counted on to save her, no questions asked. The look Veronica gave her made her feel as if she should go. She grabbed her coat from the front closet and joined Chuck at the side door, deep in her own thoughts.

* * * *

Suddenly Shelley went back in her mind to a time at the hospital cafeteria. She had just finished an autopsy on a man who had died from complications of a severe staph-infection; one of the more deadly ones. It was rapid and unforgiving to all treatment, a strain of the flesh-eating disease that had developed over the past decade. They suspected that a new strain may have developed and Shelley had taken two swabs that were to be tested at the lab.

On the way, she had agreed to meet Chuck around noon. She'd been worried. Roger Grant; the stalker who had been making her life a living hell for the past year, had been admitted to the hospital with a large gash in his leg. But he would continue to stalk her. He was getting better and Shelley had hoped that he would die from his wound. But now all her hope was fading, it looked like he would live and the terror would start all over again. Shelley knew how the accident had occurred; he'd been trying to keep tabs on her. He said he had tripped at his place.

When Shelley had returned home after that first night, she had found her garage torn apart and a trail of blood that lead to the driveway. She knew instinctively that it was Roger's blood and what he was trying to do.... break into her house, to do what, she did not know. The restraining order wasn't working, it never had. She'd broken down sobbing, crying that it would never be over and that she wished Roger would die. She couldn't take it any-more. Chuck had come over and held her in his arms until she could go back into the house. He'd stayed the night trying to calm her and have her get some sleep.

"It's OK Shelley, I'm here and I won't let anything

happen to you." Chuck put his arms around her. She was still holding the cell phone in her hand as she slumped on the concrete floor of her garage, beside a pool of blood that she knew was Rogers.

"It's not OK and it never will be. As long as he is alive I'll never be safe and one day it will be my blood on the floor. If he was here when I came home and wanted to kill me, who could have stopped him?" She clung to Chuck. The look in her eyes told him that she was at the end of her rope and couldn't take much more of this sick bastard's abuse.

For the past year Rogers threats had gotten worse and Shelley's experience had led her to believe one day he would follow through on his threats. When she found the pool of blood she put two and two together and understood that there was a killer in the hospital that would only need a little more time to claim the title for real. She had no idea what Roger had been trying to accomplish in the garage, but she didn't want him to get back out of the hospital for her to find out.

"I'm going to kill him Chuck, even if it means I'll go to jail. If I don't, nothing will stop him from getting to me. We've tried all the legal ways and nothing has worked. You and Dennis have even had a rough talk with him and he didn't take the hint. He has left me with no choice. If he turns up here again, I will kill him." Shelley's tear-swollen face showed all the determination of a woman who had now been cornered and must come out fighting.

Chuck pulled Shelley tighter to him and began to rock back and forth in a slow deliberate rhythm, all the while speaking softly for her to put things out of her mind for the night; they would come up with something and no-one would go to jail.

Somehow she knew Chuck meant it. Together they would find a solution and he would protect her. She drifted off to sleep and in the morning they agreed they would meet for lunch to discuss things.

The next morning Chuck sat next to Shelley, a cafeteria tray in his hands loaded with all sorts of high fat, low nutrition foods, none of which tasted very good. "What's up Shelley? You look much too happy considering how you were last night, what's changed?"

Shelley smiled brightly as if she had the world by the tail. All the while showing Chuck the two swabs she was taking to the lab, she told him she was working on a staph-infection that was fatal to anyone that came in contact with it if they had an open wound or sore. As the lunch progressed both of them steered clear of any discussion about Roger, it was as if both of them could read each other's thoughts and words were not needed. Shelley had laid the swabs beside her drink and when she stood up to go Chuck slipped one into his coat pocket. As she got up to leave, she bent over and gave Chuck a hug of true desperation while a genuine tear of fear ran down her freckled face. Her sudden change of mood was a sign of just how desperate she truly felt.

Shelley picked up the swab and looked perplexed. "Where did my swab go?"

"It was here." Chuck stood up and looked the table over and then bent down checking the floor.

"Not here, where could it have gone?" Chuck's expression was one of surprise.

"I have to find it, it is dangerous. If anyone finds it and they have an open cut they will get the infection, and it is a killer." Shelley's voice was rising in fear. "I will have to report it and let the cafeteria staff know what to look for. It must be found."

* * * *

Chuck stood over Roger Grant's bed for a few minutes. He was sound asleep, even so, you could see the twisted look in his almost handsome face; it had a grim set to it. Chuck knew Grant's resolve to continue stalking Shelley was still set firmly in his mind.

Without a minute's hesitation Chuck removed the swab from the vial. He went over to Roger's arm, the one with the intravenous drip that contained the antibiotic. He knew that there was an open area around the entrance to the wound. His veins were small and collapsed easily, the opening made it easy to access the intravenous drip; Chuck wanted to stem the flow of medication to the wound. He took the swab, put it into the open wound, and turned it gently several times, making sure every killer germ would find its way into Grant's bloodstream. Roger never even woke up. The rest was now medical history; another statistic for Staph-Infection. It was over. Chuck never said a word to Shelley, and Shelley never figured it out.

* * * *

Chuck brought himself to the present. He could smell the sweet scent of Shelley's fragrance. It made him feel good. The air was cool and spring was only days away. The lawns and the sidewalks were clear of snow, with only an occasional patch of black ice. They were talking easily about work, friends, and future plans. Knowing how Chuck felt about her and not wanting to hurt him Shelley tried to avoid any discussion about Brian, but the topic was inevitable.

"I hear you're seeing Brian Bentham," Chuck blurted out, hating himself for the need to hear it from her. He ended lamely. "I can't say I blame you, he's a good-looking guy."

"So far we're just friends." Shelley wanted to make things easy for Chuck.

"He asked me out a few days after we were at the restaurant," she continued, feeling the need to explain. "At least we can rule him out as a suspect. I was with him at an after-hours club the night of the murders of Candy and Brock." She was trying to turn the conversation toward the investigation. It was safer that way.

"Well, he was never really a strong suspect anyway, just the only common link to all the victims. They all ate at The Beef Chateau. Dennis and I thought someone from the restaurant might be stalking them and Brian was the only one without an alibi, but I guess he's lucky.... he's got one now." Chuck tried not to make it sound like sour grapes.

"Yes," Shelley reflected. "I guess he's lucky."

Chuck wanted so badly to just put his arms around her and tell her how he felt, that they belonged together. But instead he suddenly turned and headed for Dennis and Veronica's house. Shelley followed. She welcomed the chance to get back. Once they were back in the warmth of the home, the boys went off on some topic neither of the girls cared about.

Shelley and Veronica were able to discuss

culinary secrets.

"Did you buy the meat fresh from the butcher today? Shelley asked. "The steaks were wonderful and fresh."

"Heavens no!" Veronica's eyes got wide with excitement. "You'd never believe it, but the steak was over a year old. It was the freezing process called "flash freeze" Once the steaks thawed, it's like the day I bought it."

"You've got to be kidding! It was like the freshest steak I've ever had, almost as good as Beef Chateau," Shelley answered in disbelief. "I can't believe it was ever frozen."

Dennis suddenly found himself listening to the girls' conversation. It was one he would usually have found boring, but for some reason his heart started to race and all his senses became very alert. It was another gut moment, one he had experienced often. Usually something profound would happen when he felt like this

"Yes," Veronica continued, unaware that Dennis had suddenly become all ears, "It's a new process, and all of the products that this company puts out are frozen so rapidly that they lose virtually no moisture. Once they're thawed you absolutely can't tell they were ever frozen. There is no tissue damage to the meat or vegetables and they will never have freezer burn. Everything is as fresh as the day it was killed, cut, or processed." Veronica was proud of the fact that her huge freezer purchase had paid off. As the girls continued their conversation, Dennis excused himself from Chuck's presence, saying he had to go to the can.

Once inside the bathroom he sat on the edge of the tub, put his head between his hands and tried to make sense of what he had just heard. He knew he had a huge piece to the puzzle, but he needed a few quiet moments to put it all together. Suddenly his mind was back at The Beef Chateau. Everything was in slow motion; the conversations muffled, drowned out by the slowing down of time. Dennis stood next to Lexy and Bara while Chuck, Shelley, and Brian were standing on the other side of the meat-cutting room. He could see the reflection of stainless- steel, and smell the Clorox bleach used to disinfect the large, wooden cutting block. The smell of spices and wine mingled with the smell of the meat. The bleach covered up most of the smell but the odor still hung faintly in the air, if one took the time to breathe deeply. Then the words became less muffled. As Dennis strained to hear them in his mind's eye, he suddenly stood up.

"I've got you, you fucking bastard!"

He knew most of it. Why they had so few clues. Why nothing made any sense. It was simple. Every investigation works backwards from the estimated time of death, and for Dennis and his team that was usually estimated to be the last four to six hours from the time the victims were found. But what if the time was wrong? What if they were way off by a long shot from the time of death? Not by hours, but by days or perhaps weeks. Then everything they turned up would be wrong. It would all lead to a dead end and it did. Every case went nowhere, and Dennis knew why. The victims had been flash frozen. Dennis also knew where, The Beef Chateau. Bara and Lexy had a state of the art, flash-freeze system. They had briefly mentioned it when they showed him around the meat-cutting room. At the time he had been more interested in the various knives and cutting tools, so the mention of the freezer was filed in his brain and only now made its way to the surface.

Now everything made sense. He knew where the murders had taken place; The Beef Chateau. He knew how. Something with the way they hung and cut the beef then froze it. He knew whom, Brian Bentham, the only one in charge of the cutting and processing of the meat. The only one left alone after hours. He still didn't know why. Again, one thing stood out. The profiler ad said the killer hated cops. There had to be something in Brian's past that would cause him to kill dozens of people and play the deadly game with the police. And by God Dennis was going to find out. When he returned to the family room, he could tell things had wound down for the night.

It was well past ten and these past six months had taken their toll on everyone. Dennis needed more time to think things out. Tomorrow he would go back over all of the evidence and work things through from this new perspective. They would have to catch Brian cold. Forensics had very little evidence that would be more than circumstantial. Dennis would have to nail him tight if he was going to get a conviction that would hold. Suddenly he felt very tired. Tonight he would sleep well. It was almost over.

Dennis and Veronica said their good byes for the evening and went off to bed. After the last farewells had being said, Dennis said nothing to Veronica. A hot shower and some sleep; tomorrow would come soon enough.

Veronica slipped quickly under the covers, hoping she could get a little snuggle from her husband. Dennis was sound asleep, much to her surprise. Something had happened tonight. Veronica had seen it before, Dennis had somehow solved the case; she knew it. She could sleep soundly knowing it would soon be over and her family would be safe. She wouldn't wake him and tell him the girls had called, they were having supper at The Beef Chateau. They too found the steak to die for.

Veronica had invited them back for coffee and bagels in the morning; they all had Monday off. As she drifted off to sleep, her last thought was about cheesecake – cheesecake and wine.

Chapter Seventeen

Brian was out front in the dining room and as usual looking around for a fresh set of victims. He had thought that it was all over and for him it truly was. He had missed one day of work, the only time in ten years. Bara and Lexy were like the parents he never had. A cruel, heartless monster of a man had ripped his mother from him.... his father. The only thing he could ever tell anyone about his father was that he kept a nice back yard, especially his flowerbeds. They were well tended and perfect. His father never let anyone near them and each year he made sure he put fresh dirt around the edges of the lawn where the flowers were planted and guarded them with his life. Brian knew why the flowers grew well. Because his sweet mother's soul nourished the soil with her life's blood. That bastard would never be able to grow anything as wonderful as he did if it weren't for Brian dead mother, buried beneath the plants.

For years Brian had felt nothing for anyone, but now, ten years later, Bara and Lexy were his only true family. When he had returned to work he had told Bara and Lexy that he would no longer be preparing the special steaks. They took too much time and the ingredients were just too difficult to get. Bara and Lexy were shocked and adamant that the steak would stay on the menu. Brian had never seen them like this before. Usually they deferred to him on all items on the menu. Finally Brian got a confession from Lexy.

Because the steak had done so well on the menu, Lexy had agreed to"cash up front" deal on the lease of his new location. If he paid cash for the first two years, he would receive a twenty-percent rebate back on his rent over a five-year lease. It was a wonderful deal and Lexy only needed another ten thousand in cash and the deal would be done. If only they could keep the steak on the menu for at least another week, everything would be finalized, and Lexy and Bara reluctantly agreed to then fade the steak off the menu.

For Brian that meant one more set of victims. At first he felt he did not have the stomach for it. Finally he pulled all the rocks and bricks back up around his heart. He could do it one more time for Bara and Lexy. He moved around the room feeling nothing, a charming smile on his face, seeing everything in the dining room all at once. Over in the corner near the west wall, in the back booth, sat two of the most striking young woman he had ever seen. Curiosity more than anything brought him closer to their booth. As he came within hearing range he knew that they must be from Russia. He recognized the sound of the language, although he could not understand it. One of the young women was tall, with a typical Slavic look. Big green eyes, high cheekbones, porcelain white skin and a square chiseled jaw, set atop a long elegant neck. Her hair was a dark brown with flashing highlights of auburn. It was cut stylishly with soft wisps pulled around her face, framing it like a perfect picture. She was a rare beauty.

The second girl had dark hair as well, but it was worn much longer with stylish pieces of hair flipped out in a tousled carefree way. Her face was softer and much rounder. Her perfect brows matched the other girl's and her green eyes flashed brilliantly with dark, thick lashes framing her eyes beautifully. They were different, yet the same – sisters. Brian was sure of it. The younger one's features were perfect and her full mouth was set over small, even teeth, making her a parallel beauty in an entirely contrasting way from the older girl.

* * * *

Natasha and Katrina had decided to dine out at The Beef Chateau and try the new steak everyone was raving about. It was very expensive but Katrina had just received a promotion at work and had wanted to celebrate, with her husband's credit card and his blessing. One of their favorite games when they were out together was to practice their second language, Ukrainian. Natasha spoke both Russian and Ukrainian, but Katrina only Ukrainian.

It was always fun to fake a Slavic accent in English when the waiter came, and then speak Ukrainian, pretending they were from some exotic place in the Ukraine that they had only heard about in school. They had played this game as teens, mostly to keep up their skill in the Ukrainian language and partly because it was fun to see the reaction of the waiters as they spoke to them in their fake, broken English. Because of their "language difficulty' they usually had to have a little extra help from the waiter and the girls loved the extra attention. Even now that they were adults the game of being someone else was something they still enjoyed.

As Brian watched them finish their meal, he strolled leisurely through the restaurant greeting new clients and reminiscing with old, all the while honing in on the two beautiful, seemingly mysterious young women. For some reason his usual homing sense about people was off. He could tell little about the girls as he observed them from a distance.

Their waiter informed him of their accent and was unable to pin it down. Russian, Polish, something Slavic was all he could tell.

Brian figured that the break-through of the past two days was the reason his intuition was off and he was unable to come up with any advance clues about the girls. He would have to find things out first-hand.

Natasha noticed Brian first and knew instantly who he was. She had met him several times the first year Bara and Lexy had opened The Beef Chateau, but at that time she had been a gangly, thirteen-year-old with long thick hair. She knew he would never recognize her or Katrina. From young girls to exceptionally beautiful woman, the transformation was too great and with their fake accents she was in the mood for a bit of fun. She and Katrina would continue the game for a little longer. Besides, she was starting to feel very, very good, sharper than she could ever remember. From the looks on her sister's face and the sparkle in her eye, she knew both of them were ready for a lot more fun. It must be something in the food, she was sure of it. What was being said about the steak was true, it really was the best meal ever and the wine they used as a marinade was having a very unusual effect.

"Ladies, welcome to The Beef Chateau." Brian held out his hand to the tall, dark woman and flashed a brilliant smile at the younger one. "I hope our food and service is surpassing our reputation."

"Yus...et is most vonderful," Natasha replied, making her accent as pronounced as she dared, not wanting to be too dramatic. "Vee have saved our money for a long time these past months and tonight is our first night out since we have come to America." She smiled up at Brian, her green eyes flashing.

"For us, this is most special." Katrina added not wanting to be out of the fun.

"Welcome to Chicago." Brian tried to get a quick picture in his mind....definitely Slavic. The oldest looked very Russian, the younger less so. "Where are you from?"

"The Ukraine." They both responded together and laughed at their simultaneous attempt to deceive.

"Why Chicago? It's a long way to come?" Brian continued, hoping these two would fit his profile.

Young, definitely from out of town, but could he play his game and make sure they wouldn't be missed for the few days? He would need to ask a few more questions to be certain he could cover his tracks. Their blood was all he would need to get Bara and Lexy the money. Then the killing would be over.

Katrina started things off making stuff up as she went along. "Ve are students at the University, but this veek we are off, and next veek we head home to Kiev.

"Oh, I hope you found Chicago exciting and made lots of friends." Brian continued to probe.

These girls were not the usual visitors. He would have

to know a lot before he felt safe enough to invite them back after closing. If they were still seeing friends here, it would not be safe to kill them. No one must report them missing.

"No, very few." Natasha picked up a small thread of Katrina's story and continued to weave a few more twists and turns. "Ve have been very busy with our own studies, and tonight ve celebrate that they are over. This veek we are on holidays. It is nice. We have vorked....how you say....diligently." The girls were deliberately acting as though it took some thought to use English as a language.

"Now ve party!" Natasha laughed, enjoying the game. She spoke a few words to Katrina in Ukrainian, loosely translating into the phrase, "This is a lot of fun."

Katrina replied with a simple "Da." and looked playfully at Brian. Of the two girls, Katrina was the most adventurous; a definite party girl.

"Where are you staying?" Brian asked strategically. This next answer would be the deal breaker. If they were being billeted with a family or on campus, the game was over, and he would move on. If not, he would take things a step or two further.

"We were at the university but this week we are staying at the Crown Plaza," Katrina answered, wanting things to sound grown up and exciting.

For some reason, she felt this answer would be best. She could feel Brian tense up and the game suddenly took on a sharper edge. She liked the feeling of power and playfulness that always came when you were able to step out of your own world and make up a new one.

"Yus. It is our last chance to really see Chicago, before ve go home," Natasha interjected. "All study, no play.

Now ve play."

Katrina lifted her wine glass toward Brian in an attempt at a seductive playful salute.

"Then let me offer you a little more enjoyment to your final days." He said, "I have tickets to a late showing at the Kinston Mines, one of our top Jazz clubs… your choice of seats if you get there early." He pulled two tickets from his pocket as he spoke. "As well as a special invitation back here after hours, for more wine and dessert. Every night we ask an out of town guest to come back and get the secret to our marinades." Brain paused for only a moment to get a feel for a receptive response to his offer, "and after dessert, a tour of the kitchen. I'm hoping you both would be interested in returning to the Ukraine with several of our secret recipes." Brian summed up his invitation with another smile, knowing he had the girls interested, and feeling sure of their acceptance of his offer.

Katrina and Natasha both looked at each other and started to talk in Ukrainian at once.

"I feel guilty." Natasha was the first to respond.

"So do I." was Katrina's echo.

They smiled at Brian, not wanting him to know that they were alarmed at their deceit.

Brian felt their hesitation and not wanting to lose his opportunity, he felt he needed to assure them. "Don't worry. This is something we do regularly and it is a complete business write-off. We make this offer to a select few each week and I assure you, it's all above board." He put his most sincere spin on his presentation.

"Why not?" Katrina asked Natasha in Ukrainian. "If this is something he offers all regular clients, then our game isn't the reason he's asking us. It could be anyone here tonight." Her logic sounded good even to her ears.

"Maybe," Natasha answered, "but I hope we're not being asked because he's trying to be kind to foreigners." Natasha's natural instinct to always do what was right was making her feel a little guilty about lying to Brian. Especially when she knew their father and mother knew Brian personally.

"Please accept my offer, I won't take no for an answer. You will just be another two of many who will be part of our secret club." Brian's sincere look and warm tone finally won them over.

Once again they laughed openly and answered together. "Dah, it vould be our pleasure. Vill we get the secret to the steak?" They both responded at once, which only brought another round of laughter.

"I can assure you delectable young ladies that you will find the secret to the steak marinade a real killer. You have no idea just how special it and you are. "Birds of a feather," I'd say." Brian seemed to find his statements most amusing, but both girls missed his point. It was a good thing.

They were definitely going to have fun tonight, making this the best girl's night out ever. "*I've never felt so alive, it must be the steak.*" Natasha thought to herself as Brian finalized the details.

The Jazz club was wonderful. For as long as the two of them had lived in Chicago, neither of them had ever been to a jazz club. It was a style of music that they had never enjoyed before, but tonight they had decided to change their minds and the music was wonderful.

Later, back at The Beef Chateau Brian had greeted them at the door and he seemed to have mixed feelings about their being at the restaurant after hours. They hoped they hadn't misconstrued his invitation; it had seemed so sincere. They were just finishing their cheesecake, a lemon-orange specialty with a drizzle of Kiwi sauce. It went well with the light, fruity dessert wine Brian had picked for them. So far they had continued with the charade, but as the last part of the hour seemed to be bringing the evening to an end, Katrina began to sense Brian's mood change. He had asked dozens of questions. How was it they had decided on the U of C? Would they be calling home before they left? When were they expected back in the Ukraine? Would they have a farewell party? Were they going to spend some time with their friends before they left? At first they had felt special but as time wore on something clicked and Katrina felt a little guilty about all the lies. Never before had they done anything like this. Usually they only went out and faked an accent and used their language skills. Now it was just too many lies.

"I can't continue this!" It was Natasha who spoke first, using her Ukrainian again.

"No. I'm not happy about it either, and we will want to come back. We had better tell the truth." Katrina could feel herself blush as she faced what their confession would feel like, unsure of Brian's response.

Brian watched the girls as they broke into Ukrainian and sensed a strange swing in their mood. He had poured the last of the wine. The last two glasses now had a small amount of Halcion. Soon he would begin his last game. He knew this was the last time, but tonight was different. He had always been able to stand outside of life. Every day of his existence since he had put away his mother's things he had always felt as if he sat on the inside looking at the outside world, where things seemed normal, but he knew different. He had always been amazed that the world responded so well to him, and knew that his looks helped. He was bright and well-studied and always knew what people wanted to hear. Because it meant little to him, giving people what they wanted was easy, giving Brian the lifetime label of charming. Now, things were different. He could really feel these girl's energy and vital presence, and part of him wanted to take away the last of the wine. He knew the game was over. It was no longer about his hatred for his dad or his contempt of the police.

For a second, he almost felt as if he could smell his mother's Youth Dew and hear her voice whisper in his ear.

"Don't be scared, everything will be all right." Her face flashed before his eyes.

At that second Brian reached over toward the glasses filled with wine, pulling them back towards him.

"I think maybe you two girls have had enough wine. I wouldn't want you to get into trouble just before you are about to head home."

That was it. Natasha knew she had to come clean. She saw the blush on Katrina's face and hoped their confession wouldn't sound as bad as she now felt.

"Brian," She whispered, dropping her accent. "We have a confession and we hope you have a good sense of humor." She dropped her eyes for a few seconds before looking deeply into his.

She saw a deep sadness and hoped that it wasn't caused by the obvious charade. Brian must have figured out something was up with the lack of accent she now displayed. His face looked older and more worn than it had only a second ago. It was as if he had accepted defeat for some battle yet to be won.

"Katrina and I were just practicing our second language skills....something we've done for years, and we never meant our game to go this far." Natasha's beautiful eyes pleaded with Brian to understand.

"As a matter of fact you know our mom and dad, Dennis and Veronica Kortovich." Natasha's tone was very apologetic; she somehow hoped that the mention of her mother and father would help, although she didn't know how.

Brian tried not to show any emotion on his face, but he could feel the tension go from the back of his neck, and travel down his arms into his hand that held the wine. His knuckles were white from the sudden pressure he put on the stem of the glass. If he didn't let go fast, he would snap the stem. If the girls had finished the wine before their confession, they would have become his last victims. He knew he would not be able to cover up their deaths. Sweat broke out on his brow. Their father was Dennis Kortovich! Detective Dennis Kortovich! Fuck, life was a bitch.

Chapter Eighteen

Dennis awoke to the smell of gourmet coffee; a special blend made by Veronica with some vanilla, hazelnut, and chocolate beans ground fresh each day. He loved it. Dennis had had his first dreamless sleep in months. Tonight he would go out for supper and if he was lucky, catch a killer. He grabbed his jogging pants and pulled on his heavy blue housecoat. The house was cool and would take a while to warm up. After he got out of his warm bed, the cool air helped to get his brain in gear....today he would need every brain cell he had on full throttle. The pieces were almost all there. Now he just had to slide them all together and make sure they fit and would stay together. He had to put this bastard away for good. As he walked down the hall toward the kitchen, he could hear his wife's voice. At first he thought she was on the phone or talking to herself or their dog Mickey. Then the sound of Katrina's laugh and the look on Natasha's face as he rounded the corner, confirmed that once again the girls had just happened to drop by at mealtime. They always knew where their bread was buttered, but somehow it was always his bread. He laughed inside. It was true....

kids never really leave home.

"Hey girls, you both sound in good spirits." He noted that although their mood seemed light, they both looked like they could use more sleep.

"You both look like you could use a little more shut eye. Why are you here at this early hour?"

Dennis looked at the clock on the stove, noting that it was nearly ten a.m. and although it was a Monday, he had slept late, something he seldom did. But due to the fact that it was a public holiday, he didn't have to be on duty early today.

"We don't usually see you two before noon." Dennis observed, noting that today was already starting off on an unusual note.

"Look who's talking." Trina replied with a teasing tone. "Mom said you slept like a dead man and just got going now. What happened? You start using some of those drugs you have down at the station?"

Katrina's face showed just how much she loved her dad and enjoyed catching him not being perfect; an unusual event for the normally disciplined Dennis.

Dennis smiled back at his youngest daughter. For him she had always been a challenge. Her spirit and mischievous personality always gave him something to think about. Usually she was just a little undisciplined, but always fun. She had come out of the womb with her hands on her hips, and the mantra she would use as she grew up was, "You can't be the boss of me!"

"Look you." He pretended to be stern. "Just remember that's my coffee and food you're enjoying, so show me a little respect." His eyes twinkled as he pretended to cuff her across her pretty head.

He felt good. He knew he had things figured out. He just needed to go downtown to the boardroom and put all the pieces together. Then he could figure out his next move.

"Why don't you two grow up?" Veronica got in on the fun, pretending to find their usual banter annoying.

"Now sit down and stay away from each other!"

"She started it." Dennis wanted to keep things going for a while.

"Did not!" Trina retorted.

"Did too!" Dennis shot back, grabbing for the coffee and bagel that were already sitting in front of his usual kitchen chair.

Natasha just rolled her eyes at her mother as if to say. *"They'll never grow up so just let them have their way."*

"So tell me. Why are you here this early, looking tired and a little on edge?" Dennis knew something was up just by the fact that both girls were here this early on a holiday Monday. He turned his attention to Natasha, knowing she would get to the point first.

"We went out last night for supper and maybe we went a little overboard and it might cause you a little embarrassment." Natasha had jumped right in, but things still weren't very clear.

"What did you girls do? Get drunk and dance on a few tables, or did you stiff some waiter?" He made light of the confession, knowing that whatever it was, it would be a lot less serious to him than it would be to the girls. So far all they had ever done was make him proud.

"No Dad, be serious, we really did do something bad. We were very deceitful." Natasha tried to get her dad back into a more serious mood. He really must have slept well;

she hadn't seen him this relaxed for months, ever since the murders started last November.

Natasha started back into her confession. "We told a lot of lies to Brian Bentham, at The Beef Chateau, last night, and this morning we both feel real bad. We know you eat there a lot and know everyone so we figured that we might have stepped over the line of fun and now you'll be mad. We were just having a good time and got carried away."

Natasha looked down for a few seconds. When she looked back up at her dad's face she got scared. She had never seen him look like that before. It sent a chill down her spine and she almost couldn't comprehend the sudden change, no matter what the confession.

Dennis froze when he heard Brian's name. The pit of his stomach suddenly felt as if he had been kicked by a mule, and he was winded by the sudden blow. It took a few seconds before he realized that he had actually stopped breathing and was still holding his breath. He let the air out of his lungs slowly and took a few short breaths. He felt his head go light and the room seemed to spin for a few seconds.

He pulled all of his cop's training from the depth of his toes and tried to refocus on the girls, keeping his face blank. The second that Natasha had mentioned Brian's name, Dennis knew that both girls had been in a great deal of danger. He had to make sure he separated his fear as a father from his fear as cop. Either way, he had to pull himself together.

"Dad, are you okay? We really didn't kill anyone." Katrina had never seen her dad like this and she suddenly felt an unreasonable fear, given the severity of their crime.

After all they had just been having fun. They hadn't meant their lies to go so far, but heck it wasn't that bad. She thought her dad was almost going to have a heart attack the way he tried to catch his breath and held on to his coffee cup.

"It's okay girls." Dennis tried to reassure his daughters. "I think it must be all the tension of the past six months." He gave the girls a weak, reassuring smile.

Veronica stood back from it all, watching her husband and two daughters banter. Something huge had just happened and from experience she knew that Dennis's reaction meant more than he was telling. When the girls left, she would get to the bottom of things.

"So tell me, what crime it is you've both committed." He tried to put back the lighthearted feel into the conversation.

This time Katrina picked up the conversation. "Dad, you always said when Natasha and I are together we should practice our Ukrainian. Use it or lose it. That's what you've always said. Well, last night we were using it and when Brian came over to see how things were going, he thought we were from the Ukraine and he invited us back after hours for wine and cheesecake. But we think he did because we told a few lies and we felt really bad." Katrina hardly took a breath from this running monolog. "We did come clean and confess, and Mr. Bentham was really great about it and said not to worry, but somehow we got the feeling from him that he was really very, very upset. Especially when we told him you were our dad." The confession sounded very sincere. Dennis reached over and put his hand over his youngest daughter's. Katrina thought it was touching to see a tear in her dad's eye, but golly he was acting so strange. What they did had been wrong, but it seemed to be causing their dad so much pain and fear. You would have thought with all that their dad had seen over the years, this would not have been such a big deal, but he was acting like someone had died. It was really very unlike him. He was always Mr. Cal.... Mr. Perfect.

* * * *

Dennis sat alone in the boardroom at the police station. It had been well over an hour of staring at the white board that had all the information on the crimes. All of it was useless. They had no real suspect because the killer had been more clever and more brilliant than anyone could have imagined. Because of it, Dennis had almost lost the most important thing in the world to him; his daughters. They didn't know it, but he was sure that without their confession to Brian they would be dead by now. He could feel his heart rate increase every time he allowed his mind to play back the story that the girls had given to him. He had made them go over every detail. He knew they thought he had gone crazy, but he had to know step by step, all that had happened from the time Brian had approached them, to the last few minutes before he let them out of the front door of the restaurant. He knew only too well how most of the special guests had left the Beef Chateau over the past six months; dead, frozen, and bloodless.

The faces of all the victims passed before his eyes and at the end of his visual list, the lifeless faces of his daughters flashed brilliantly, slowing down long enough to allow a sweat to break out on his face, making his palms wet and tacky, and his stomach hurt. The breakfast confession had been too much to face. He had been unable to even think about eating once he'd realized what had almost happened to the girls. Veronica knew better than to press him to eat the beautiful breakfast she and the girls enjoyed. She had developed a keen instinct to know when to ask questions and when just to let things go. He loved her for it. It showed the level of trust they had developed over the years.

At this moment, sitting at the boardroom table, he almost felt as if he could just fall apart, but his ability to handle details and his keen mind gave him the strength to know when and how to detach himself from the crime. Most cops developed this quality, making it possible to be up to your knees in blood and guts and not lose your lunch. Over the years homicide detectives all over the country had been witness to some horrific, gruesome scenes. It was this one quality of detachment that was an absolute necessity when it came to solving crimes. The other ingredient was the need to know all the answers. The best cops never let go, and Dennis was simply the best.

He pushed his chair away from the boardroom table, stood up slowly, and started to breath in a deliberate, rhythmic pattern. He needed to center himself. He breathed deeply, closed his eyes for a few seconds, and mentally closed the door on the imaginary scene of what almost happened to his girls. He needed to finish the puzzle that would enable him to put Brian Bentham behind bars and he couldn't afford to be distracted by the awful vision of his girls under the knife of the killer.

Chapter Nineteen

Brian woke up early Monday morning, knowing that it was a public holiday. A holiday was usually a day of rest for most people, but for him, it was just another workday. This Monday would be different. After last night he knew there would be a good chance that his game would be over. Either way, for him the killing would end. It had served its purpose. He had figured out early, after only a couple of killings, that he had spent most of his life waiting to prove to himself that he was better than his father. That was what all of the books, tapes, shows, and classes had been about, "how to get away with murder?" He knew that the police and his father had been his greatest adversaries. The cops were stupid, while his father was an evil bastard, but somehow Brian had sensed that Dennis Kortovich was different.

He had met Dennis over a decade earlier, just a few days after Lexy and Bara had opened The Beef Chateau. Dennis had often shared stories with him about already solved public cases. He never became cocky or bragged about how he had solved the crimes; instead he credited his partners and team, always sharing the glory. Over the years, Dennis's calm, easy manner and total lack of personal ego had made Brian feel less antagonistic towards the police. More importantly, Bara and Lexy liked Dennis, and Brian loved and respected the two people who had hired him and treated him like a son.

Brian had gone to work for Bara and Lexy after many years of unsettled and unhappy employment. With them he had found the parents he felt he had never known. With his mother taken from him it had made him sick emotionally and he had formed no attachments to anyone over the years. His hatred for his father had spilled over into most of his former places of employment. It usually only took a few months or so at a job or in friendships before anyone who held power or authority over him would be made to pay the price for Brian's hurtful youth. He seldom showed his adversaries his true nature. He was far too clever for that. Instead he would bide his time until he had figured out their weaknesses. Then he would lie awake at night, and devise elaborate plans on how to utterly destroy them.

One time, when Brian was employed at a local dining room and dance club, his revenge was simple. He set up a scenario where betrayal and suicide would be the only outcome. Then the fun began and he only had to watch the drama unfold. His boss's greatest love was his wife, Monique. She was a slut who knew what side her bread was buttered on. She had always been very careful not to let her husband ever suspect that she was anything but a loving, devoted wife. Meanwhile, behind his back, she had slept with at least half of the male staff and almost all of the male clientele. Everyone knew not to tell. Jake was a maniac who would have destroyed whoever came near what he thought was his. He turned out to be a cocky little dictator. After Brian had enough of him, he did the one thing that would hurt him the most. Brian secretly taped one of Jake's wife's many sexual trysts. The tape was graphic in sound and detail. Not only were there the sounds of basic, animal sex, but she also confessed to her lover what a lousy lay Jake was and that she had only stayed for the money. She told her love of a plan to take most of what Jake had built up in personal assets, when she felt they were large enough to make it worth her while.

Brian had slipped the tape into the cassette player in Jake's car. That night, on Jake's way home he listened to more than a sad love song. Obviously what he heard caused him a great deal of pain. Jake was so distraught, he took a curve on the highway at almost eighty mph. The speed was too fast for the sharp bend in the road and he never made the dangerous curve. His car was found wrapped around an old tree that had seen a few other bumpers over the years. The best part of the whole revenge thing was that Jake had never made a new will after he had married, which was something of which Brian was aware. Jake's mother, Rose Marie, a domineering but bright woman was left everything. Monique never stood a chance against her.

Brain had stayed on at the restaurant for another two years, watching the wife slowly go mad over the loss of Jake's fortune. The mother proved to be an artful and delightful lover. All in all, Brian figured things had worked out well.

The pattern had stayed the same until he had started working for Lexy and Bara. Never in the years that followed could Brian ever remember a time when the couple was anything but fair and loving. They listened to their staff, making everyone feel valued and appreciated. Finally Brian had come to trust them. Now he loved them more than he cared to admit. Other than his mother, he had loved no one else and to this day there was no one he respected or admired except Lexy and Bara. No one except maybe Dennis Kortovich, and Brian found it surprising that very early after meeting Dennis, he felt drawn towards him in some unexplained way. Now he knew why.... it was fate. Brian was sure that it was always going to be Dennis who would finally bring him home. Home to a place in his head and heart where he would let go of the past.

Brian showered and took a little extra time and effort to dress. He knew time was running out. He needed to enjoy each moment he had left. Soon many things would be different. He took out a new uniform; one designed as an authentic, sixteenth-century costume of a French chef. It was the whitest of white and made of special cotton and a linen blend. The doublet was full and crisp. He looked every bit the part of a fine European gentleman and chef, one who could serve only the best of epicurean delights. He knew he had dared to serve what few cooks anywhere in the world had ever dreamed of. Now there was many a citizen of Chicago who had dined on his one-of-a-kind beef and tonight he could still delight a few more. There were just enough steaks to finish the night off and then it would be over. Brian hoped tonight's clients would enjoy his final effort.

* * * *

After spending several hours at headquarters and going over all of the details, Dennis felt he had a pretty good idea of how things had transpired before and after the murders. First, Brian had found his victim's patrons of the restaurant who were drawn to the location by its world famous reputation. For someone like Brian it would not be difficult to find out-of-town victims who would fit the profile he needed. Their waitress or waiter could give him information. All he would need to do is go to every second table and half of the people would be from somewhere other than Chicago.

After making first contact he would invite them back after hours. Dennis now knew exactly how that happened. After questioning Natasha and Katrina, he found out they were offered tickets to another event that evening, a show at a jazz club. This always made the police come to the conclusion that once the victims left The Beef Chateau they went on to another place, alive and well. The police however had no idea that the victims would return. Brian would then kill and freeze his victims, thus preventing the police from thinking the restaurant was the last place they would have been before their deaths. Dennis now knew they were invited back for cheesecake and wine and a few of The Beef Chateau's special recipes. He couldn't help but feel the terror that the young people must have felt moments before their deaths; disbelief and a sense of terror that had left their endocrine system in full throttle.

Thank God his girls had confessed their youthful prank and been spared the intimate but deadly secret. Dennis broke out in a sweat just thinking about it. He continued to guess what went on next. He knew for certain that the victims were strung up like hinds of beef, their throats cut, and the blood drained. For what reason he still did not know, nor could he guess. Maybe Brian drank it in some bizarre ritual. Even though the profiler from Atlanta did not think so, Dennis knew it had to have some symbolic meaning to Brian. He would find out soon enough. Next, the victims were frozen and put somewhere else until they were thawed and dumped in an area where there was enough early morning traffic to obscure the killer's tire tracks. Finally he would rake his footprints, leaving very little circumstantial evidence to tie him to the killings if the police ever suspected him. He would also plant a bag full of ordinary dirt on the victims at the dumpsite. Dennis still had no clue as to why he did this. Was it a part of the ritual and if so, what was the message the dirt was to convey?

So far there was nothing that made any sense. Just being crazy was all he could come up with. Brian must have had a lot of excitement and fun covering up his crime; especially leading the cops on a wild goose chase, and trying to keep up the perception that each of the victims was still alive for a few days before they were dumped. This all took time, talent, and imagination and Brian had them all. The victim's beds looked slept in and the shower had been used, while daily newspapers were always found in the room, complete with fingerprints of the victims. The cops found chocolate bar wrappers, tickets to other events, and trays with half-eaten food in the rooms. The smallest details were covered. Even the toilet paper roll had been used. Finally, a last meal was ordered up to the room. It was the same meal eaten by all of the victims before they were killed. Those meals had been eaten at The Beef Chateau and were served by innocent waiters, while dessert and wine were served later by a madman, Brian Bentham.

The last meals had been made to look like they were ordered and eaten at the hotels. When room service arrived, they would find the door slightly ajar, and the guest would call from the bathroom to just leave the food and take the cash. The waiter always assumed it was one of the guests and thought nothing more of it. Dennis had no doubt that the person behind the door was Brian. Dennis doubted Brian ate any of the food, considering the time the meals were ordered to the room.

Dennis now knew Brian would have to leave The Beef Chateau undetected, get into the hotel room, remove the food, set the trays back in the hall, and return quickly enough not to be missed before he was needed in one of his many capacities as the head chef of The Beef Chateau. This took timing, and he likely brought the food back with him and dumped it with the other scraps from the restaurant. Once the police found the bodies, everything had been put in place at the hotels to look like the murders had been committed only hours before. No wonder the detectives had nothing. They had been chasing the wrong fox on a trail that went nowhere. Now Dennis was sitting in the fox's den and all he had to do was sit back, watch, and wait. Sooner or later Brian would say or do something that would give Dennis reason to obtain a warrant to search his home. He was sure he would find the kind of evidence needed to arrest Brian.

Dennis figured Brian wouldn't attempt another murder tonight. He had to suspect that the girls might alert their father and Brian was smart enough to lay low. Dennis had been told by forensics that he would have to nail the killer cold and that he would have to find something that would link the victims directly to the killer. He was sure that in Brains home he would find items belonging to the victims, which had not yet been missed. It was very unusual for a serial killer not to take some trophy item. But so far Brian had proved to be an admirable adversary in a 'blood game" that Dennis was only now beginning to understand.

* * * *

Dennis drove to The Beef Chateau. Chuck was not going to join him until later. He would have to find something that proved beyond a doubt that Brian was involved in the killings, in order to get a warrant to search Brian's house. For now he would watch and wait to see if he could come up with any excuse to confront Brian. Dennis was halfway through his steak when Lexy came over to his table. Lexy looked round and happy, almost like Humpty Dumpty. Dennis always found it surprising that any human being could be so round. It wasn't that Lexy was fat. He was just round.

"Dennis, my friend!" Lexy held out his hand as he moved closer to Dennis. "I didn't know you were here. Why didn't you ask for me?" Lexy scolded Dennis in a light and friendly manner. "I'll make sure your steak is on the house. Your money's no good to me." Lexy punctuated his statement with his famous laugh.

"That's why I didn't let you know." Dennis countered. "You never let me pay, and I don't come here for a free meal. I come here because you make the best steaks in the whole world." Dennis knew Lexy loved being told how wonderful his steaks were.

Lexy's rosy cheeks took on an even deeper hue of pink, a telltale sign that he was pleased by the comment.

"I know, I know, and that is why you don't get to pay." He made sure Dennis understood his decision was final.

"Okay, Okay." Dennis smiled back at Lexy. "But I'll tell you what. I promise not to pull out my credit card if you tell me what is in the marinade of your special steak. It's wonderful and the kick you get from it makes it all worthwhile letting you pay."

Lexy took the seat next to Dennis. His round eyes beneath his rounder glasses got even wider and rounder as he lowered his voice and moved a little closer to Dennis. He looked about making sure no one was near.

"Well!" he started, taking a second look around the dining room. "I can't tell you much about this recipe because it's Brian's, not mine." Lexy took one more precautionary glance. "Even I don't know what's in this one. But I can tell you that all of the marinades have one thing in common." He lowered his voice even more, making Dennis close the final small distance that separated them.

Lexy leaned next to Dennis's ear and whispered. "It's in the blood."

Dennis froze for a second. He wasn't sure he'd heard what he knew he had heard... "Pardon!" he said, turning his face in full view of Lexy. "What did you say?"

Lexy put his finger to his lips and a quiet shush... shush... came from his round mouth. "My secret," he whispered, "the one that has made me famous, is blood; the basic ingredient for all the marinades."

He looked behind himself, making sure no one was standing near-by, especially Bara. They had sworn Brian to secrecy and so far only Bara, Brian, and Lexy knew that beef blood was the base for all the marinades, but now he was telling Dennis .It was something he felt compelled to do.

"Blood!" Lexy repeated. "Beef blood is the secret. It always makes the steak tender. Forty-eight hours marinating, along with different wines and spices for each cut. That's it. It's always in the blood."

Dennis's head felt light. For a second he almost felt as if he was going to faint as the enormity of what Lexy was saying sunk into his brain. He looked down at this plate and suddenly knew not what, but whom he was eating. The killer was using the blood, but rather than him drinking it, half the town was eating the evidence and Dennis too had consumed his fair share.

"You'll have to excuse me for a second!" Dennis said. "I have to use the bathroom, I'll be right back." Dennis barely made it into the bathroom. He stumbled in his haste as he found his way into the stall. Once he was over the bowl heaving the unholy meat that sat in the bottom of his stomach, he thought he would tear his guts out as he continued to heave several more times. He hadn't thrown up since his early twenties when he and Veronica had gone out for an evening of drinking and fun. It had been the early 'seventies when drinking and dining went hand in hand. Dennis had downed a bottle of rum over several hours, although it had been the lemon meringue pie that finally did him in. But this was a far different cry from too much booze and an overly sweet lemon pie. This was gut-wrenching puke.

This was perhaps one of the worst taboos left over from primitive man's ascent out of the jungle to a civilized world. We simply did not eat each other! This barbaric meal was a little harder to throw-up than the rum and lemon pie. The thought of who had contributed to the meal made it all the more difficult to face the chunks that lay at the bottom of the toilet. There was a part of him that wished he could pass out, wake up later, and find out it had all been a bad, nasty dream.

Dennis stood up slowly, feeling much older than his fifty years. His shoulders were slumped forward as he walked toward the sink to splash cold water on his face.

He could feel the cold sweat on his forehead and upper lip as a shiver ran down his spine. His knees felt weak and his stomach hurt from the upchucking. He thanked God no one was in the washroom at the moment. He really couldn't face anyone right now. He looked in the mirror at the red-rimmed eyes that now seemed lifeless and dull. The slow ache that started at the back of his neck was about to explode into one hell of a headache. Soon his head would be pounding and he really needed to keep his wits about him. The next few minutes would matter more than even he could imagine. Now he had most of the pieces of this crime, but it was almost too gruesome to even comprehend. It was no ritual killing.

Dennis felt emotionally sick, even he couldn't understand what would make someone use the blood of human beings just to soak steaks in and serve it to unsuspecting strangers. Every face of every victim now seemed to sink into his very soul as he realized that some of the victims really were now a part of him.

"Stay calm," Dennis told himself. Out there sitting on a plate was the evidence that would convict Brian stone cold, he just had to bag it and get it into the lab. He could prove that the only one who had access to the steaks directly was Brian. Soon he could nail this case shut and God save everyone from the mayhem that would unfold if the public got wind of what the steaks were soaked in. Bara and Lexy would be ruined and the whole of Chicago would wear the stigma that would follow.

Chapter Twenty

Mike Wilson was at work in the lab when Dennis walked in with a bag in his hand that held a half-eaten steak. After Mike ran a test on the blood as well as going over the DNA of all of the victims, even he had to sit down and put his head between his legs to prevent himself from being sick or fainting on the spot. Mike was only in his thirties but at this point he'd had ten years with the department and he felt he had seen or heard everything. But this! No way! Human blood! The fucking beef was soaked in human blood and now he knew whose blood it was. It was the blonde's, Candy Cook. The DNA was a perfect match. He was very glad at this moment he hadn't eaten at The Beef Chateau for a very long time but he was sure many a member of the cities finest would find that their stomachs would be turning when the news got out, and a secret like this would be impossible to keep.

Dennis had stayed at the lab waiting for the results. Now he had the report in his hand. He had known ahead of time what the report would be. But even now he found it hard to believe. Why? Why would anyone do such a thing? Dennis knew he would soon find out. He had two squad cars sitting out front and back of the restaurant. They just had to wait for him to arrive. Dennis wouldn't miss this moment for the world. He owed it to every victim to make sure that Brian was held accountable and that justice was done for the dead as well as the living.

* * * *

Brian was ready when they came. He was glad that he dressed for the occasion. It was finally over and he knew he looked good. He looked like and felt like a new man. The uniform was crisp and everything went exactly as he had envisioned it would. When Brian walked into work that afternoon as he always did, Bara had put her hand on his chest, looked into his eyes, and said something that would make him love her for-ever. It showed him how much she had really gotten to know him over the years, to be able to be so astute that she could pick up the change in his face even though he felt he looked the same as ever.

"Brian. What's different about you? You look peaceful for the first time. I have never seen you like this."

Bara reached up and pulled Brian's face a little closer to hers, looking him in the eyes. She paused and gave him a long and lingering look that made him feel as if she were trying to see something deep inside of him.

"I have always felt that you were the son Lexy and I never had. I have also known that you have had a deep secret that you have kept to yourself over the years, and lately you have been so distracted that I often wanted to take you in my arms and tell you not to worry about whatever was going on in your life. But today you are different. You are at peace. What is it? What has changed?"

At that moment Brian knew he loved her more than ever. His mother was a memory that he had clung to all of his life since her death. All he had ever thought about was avenging her death and getting even with his father and the cops who he felt had betrayed him. It was now over, but he also knew that the disclosure of what he had done would not only break Bara and Lexy's heart but would also ruin their reputation and business.

"Bara, I want you to know how much I love you two and that I would never hurt you or Lexy intentionally. Whatever happens in the future I want you to know that I am sorry, I have now come to terms with my past, but I have had to travel to hell and back first. If along the way I brought the devil home with me, I never intended to cause you any harm. Whatever happens today, I'm sorry!"

Brian put his arms around the woman he felt was almost like a mother, bent his head to smell the clean fresh scent of her and let her draw him close to her full motherly chest.

* * * *

Chuck met Dennis in the restaurant. He couldn't believe how pale Dennis looked. The usual high color that made Dennis look healthy was diminished by the ashen look to his skin and the grim determined look on his face.

Dennis pushed a file toward Chuck. As Chuck read the top lines, he realized he was reading a report from the lab on s test performed on a steak that had been brought in by Dennis. As he read further he froze, reading the line itemizing the ingredients of the steak marinade, soya sauce, brown sugar, red wine, and blood.... human blood!

The DNA was 99.99% positive that it belonged to Candy Cook. Chuck reread the ingredient list once more, trying to wrap his head around the meaning of the list. When he looked up at Dennis's face he knew he understood the list all too well. The steaks were soaked in human blood and he had eaten not one, but many of them that had soaked in this grotesque sauce.

"Holy fuck, I think I'm going to be sick. I can't believe this. Why would anyone do such a thing? How did you figure it out? When did you get the steak to the lab?" Chuck placed his elbows on the table and put his head in his hands, hoping to calm his nerves and his stomach.

"I figured it out when Veronica said the steaks she served us yesterday were flash frozen, as well as her comments about the last episode of *"Survivor"* although they only made sense after I figured everything out. At first all I knew was that the murders had been committed on another day than when the bodies were found." Dennis flipped the report shut and turned toward Chuck. "But it was when the girls went out last night and ate here that I got all of the pieces to the puzzle. Shit Chuck, the girls almost became the victims of this bastard and I should have acted on my hunch last night. If they hadn't confessed at the last moment that they were my daughters, he would have strung them up like so much livestock and drained the life from them."

Chuck could see that the look on Dennis's face was the fear any father would feel when he knew his children had just missed a brush with death. The only difference was, that it was up to Chuck and Dennis and the rest of the police force to protect the public from a friend like Brian, and Dennis's hunch the night before might have come too late.

“So what do we do next?”

“We wait until the end of the evening and we arrest Brian. I don’t want the public or the press to get wind of anything until I have him safely behind bars. I also don’t want Bara and Lexy to see me arrest him, that’s why I have unmarked cars out front and back. If Brian tries anything funny I have backup.”

“Well it’s close to closing time so we’ll have to let Brian know that we’re here.”

“I have asked Lexy to tell Brian that I want to talk to him when he’s finished, so we just have to wait.”

Chapter Twenty-one

The bright lights made Brian feel a little like a prize on display. He knew the mirror was one-sided viewing and he could only guess at how many people were watching him. Dennis sat across the table taping him while Brian gave the details of the murders over the past six months. The terror was finally over. Brian could let go of the past even if he was behind bars. He knew he was free in his soul, freer than he had ever been. Brain loved Bara and Lexy and he knew he had to find a way to protect them from the scandal that would follow if word got out about the steaks, so he cut a deal with the prosecution. He would plead guilty and give all the details of each murder, if the police and prosecution would keep his secret. Everyone had agreed and Brian had it in writing. They would try to keep Bara and Lexy out of this. It was the only way he could repay them for their love and kindness.

There would be no trial. Only a few days of headlines and soon he would be yesterday's news. He would have his fifteen minutes of fame and hopefully a lifetime of peace. He could keep his secret forever. His lifetime of anger and personal separation from all other emotions of trust and love were now over. He could let go of the past. He was now ready to talk.

Dennis looked at Brian's face while he put the tape recorder in position to record his confession. Brian's face was peaceful. A resigned calm registered on his face, making him appear as if he were preparing for a job interview, rather than a death-row confession. There was one question Dennis had to ask before allowing Brian to talk freely. It was important that he didn't lead the confession – everything had to come freely from Brian. But this one question needed an answer now!

"Brian I need an answer to one question before we start." Dennis sounded calm even to himself, a feeling that was far from true at the moment.

"What was the soil about? We just can't figure that one out." He saw Brian's mood shift a little.

"I'll tell you what!" Brian felt a hot rush of blood going to his head. He had rehearsed this answer a hundred times in his head over the past few months. "Just remember that family skeletons aren't always hidden in a closet, sometime they're buried in the back yard. I trust you Dennis. You'll know what to do."

Dennis had it all on tape, every gruesome detail. Brian was truly brilliant. The attention to detail was spectacular. This confession was one for the books. Dennis was still stumped on the statement Brian had made about a crime that tied the soil into Brian's murder spree. In order to close this case, Dennis had to have the answer to the puzzle.

But where would he begin? Chicago had more crime than even Dennis cared to admit. Why couldn't Brian just tell him? But he knew for a killer like Brian, not telling was the whole point. The murders were his way of telling the cops something and he had devised this diabolical crime spree as a way of getting their attention. It would be up to Dennis to find the final pieces and put Brian and this case to rest. He had to go back to the boardroom and debrief the rest of the team and have them all type up their final reports, then he could see what he could do to unravel the mystery of the soil.

The team stood and started to clap as Dennis entered the room. Chuck was standing off to the side, a big grin spread across his face. Dennis loved the guy. He never got his ego in a knot and always seemed comfortable whenever Dennis seemed to get the attention, even though they were a team.

"Thanks guys, but I couldn't have done it without your professional determination." Dennis raised his voice above the loud clapping and hoots from his colleagues. He indicated that they should sit, as he directed Chuck to take over and sum up the case.

"This case is over and we have a full confession from the killer," Dennis said, motioning to Chuck to take over.

Chuck looked around at the faces of the detectives and special forensic team that had been involved in the case.

"There are a few details to clear up and we still don't know what the soil is all about, but Dennis and I will finish up this case and let you guys get back to the backup files that haven't had the attention they deserve. Does anyone have any further information that we may need to wind this case up?"

Detective Ferine O'Donnell spoke up first, indicating to the group that Detective Patrick Getty was also a part of what he was about to share.

"I think that my partner and I may have found something that will help close this case. It's about another case that we have been working on at the same time as this one. As some of you may know we were also assigned to the investigation into the death of Margaret Mendoza. We won't go into the details, but another wise cop told us that when you're at a standstill all you have to do is stick to the weakest link. Our weakest link was a doctor by the name of Clarence Fielding. We checked into his background so we could learn all that we could about him, discover his weakness, and maybe find a way to get him to crack." O'Donnell indicated to Getty that he should pick up the next observation.

Getty stood up from behind the table to stretch his long legs. At six foot two inches, he hated to sit and standing would make what he has to say all the more impactful.

"We discovered that Dr. Fielding's father; who was divorced from his mother for several years, went missing nearly twenty-six years ago. His father was a hairdresser by the name of Max Fielding and it was rumored that he'd had an affair with one of his clients and ran off with her. He was never seen or heard of again. The hairdresser's boss suspected foul play and called the cops. The department did an investigation but it appeared to be a case of a runaway wife and her lover. Anyway, the case was dropped and nothing more was done about it until this morning when my partner and I heard the name of the suspect, Brian Bentham. You see the name of the missing woman was Mrs. Bentham. She was Brian's mother." Ferine looked over at Dennis and could tell he had hit a home run, leaving Dennis out in an emotional left field.

"By the way, the advice turned out to be good because

we did finally crack the case. With the evidence we had, the good doctor confessed to having been hired by the husband to "take care" of his wife. He got drunk and told some hooker that was on our payroll. As usual it was the killers' big mouth that got in the way. He lured Mrs. Mendoza to his office on a pretense that he was treating her husband. When she got there he told her that her husband had a rare virus and that she would have to be checked as well. He took some blood and said that he would get back to her. Later, he went to her home on the pretext of having to give her a transfusion. The only problem was that the blood was the wrong type. Two hours later she was dead; blood clot to the lungs. It was cold-blooded murder for money, but we couldn't prove it until he slipped up."

Dennis went cold and seemed to shift out of his body, going back in his mind to the interrogation room where he had sat with Brian that morning. Brian's words echoed in his head, skeleton, closet, back yard. He had it! Bingo!

Dennis stood up and grabbed his coat, flinging it over his shoulders while he went over to Ferine and grabbed the file he had in his hand. As a shocked room of detectives watched, Dennis devoured the details in the file. He could feel his gut respond to the information like a pigeon finding a "home nest". The final piece of the puzzle rested on what was in this file and Dennis intended to hang on to the manila folder like his life depended on it. Before he could act upon the information, he still had one more detail to attend to. It was now early afternoon and he would have to wait until late evening when most of the world was asleep. That was the way he liked it. He was going to have to do a little trespassing and at a later hour he would have a better chance of not being discovered. If he were right, he would be able to solve another crime. One that few, except maybe a little boy, ever knew existed and if Dennis could, he would be able to right a wrong, freeing that little boy's spirit, which was now trapped in the body of a very mentally ill man.

****

It was now six a.m. and the late evening excursion having proved fruitful, Dennis was once again in the lab. Mike Wilson had been just about to clock out when Dennis came over to the locker room to find him before he left. Dennis trusted Mike. The slim young man reminded him of himself when he was handling information in a case. He always took that extra step when it really counted and Dennis couldn't afford any mistakes. For this analysis he needed Mike.

"I've got two samples of dirt here Mike, and all I need is for you to tell me if they come from the same area. I need it to be accurate. If it is the same soil I'll need to get a judge to give me a warrant to search the area I got this sample from, and for that I need a one hundred percent match.

Dennis decided what he needed was a coffee. It was now Tuesday and soon the press and the world would be at his doorstep. He would need to tie up every detail before that happened. Chuck would meet with him soon and he needed this last detail to go without a hitch. It was another hunch that he knew was right. He just needed to have it confirmed in writing.

Mike found Dennis at the coffee machine. Handing him the computer print-out, he knew that the information about the soil would confirm some suspicion Dennis had made on the case of the Vampire Killings. The grin on Mike's face told Dennis the answer long before he read it from the printout. They were from the same place!

"You've got him, Dennis." Mike punched his shoulder. "It's a perfect match."

Dennis gave a huge sigh of relief. Until that moment he'd had no idea that he had been holding his breath. It wasn't until he saw Mike's face and heard Mike's excited voice giving him the important answer that Dennis felt free to breathe. He grabbed his coat and hurried out the back door of the police station. He would see the judge in person. This warrant was going to be tough, but Dennis knew he could convince Judge Switzer to give him one. The judge was noted for his accessibility and fairness. As Dennis walked toward his car, he felt a calm and clarity that always came at the end of every case. He was about to nail this one shut and a lost soul turned brutal killer was about to have some long-awaited closure. It didn't make what happened right, but fate has a way of making a "fucking mess" at times and this case was certainly that. Once the case was over Dennis knew he would have the usual feeling of somehow coming down off a high. When you've spent this long living with the ghosts of the dead, you begin to feel comfortable with their company. It was time to set free the victims and everyone else that was involved in this case.

* * * *

Dennis and several officers sat outside the small, modest home along Bungalow Belt, which had been built in the early twenties. The house was at least ninety years old and looked as though it had seen a much better day. While most of the houses along the street had been upgraded with new siding and windows, this house was tired and worn looking. It seemed to say "fuck you," to all of the other homes while it thumbed its metaphorical nose at the obvious need to be upgraded. Dennis was sure that the owner would prove to be as shabby as the home.

The man who answered the door was well into his seventies and there was a look of surprise on his face as his mind registered the cops sitting outside his door. It took him a few seconds to get angry. The sounds and words that followed were of pure hatred and evil.

"You bastards get off my property," was the best he could do. "Who do you think you are?" he spat at Dennis.

"I'm the man who's going to put your ass behind bars," Dennis answered calmly. "Mr. Bentham, this is a warrant to search your back yard and these police officers are here to make sure you co-operate."

Dennis pushed the paper into Bentham's hand and turned and pointed to an officer who stood at the bottom of the stairs, holding on to a leash that held a beautiful German shepherd at the other end.

"That dog held by Officer Grant is Lucy. She is going to help us nail your ugly carcass to the wall, so I suggest you get dressed and be ready to go downtown." Dennis nodded to Officer Grant to enter through the back gate with the dog.

"You can't go back there. Get off of my fucking property, you have no right." The elder Bentham sputtered at Dennis as the shock of what was happening registered on his face.

"No Mr. Bentham, you go back inside and get ready to face what you should have thirty years ago." Dennis pushed the elderly man back inside and handed him the warrant for the search just as a woman rounded the corner.

"What's happening?" The woman noted the uniformed police officers standing behind Dennis. Her face went pale and the look on her face told him that she knew why he was here. "You get out of my house. You have no right."

"I suggest you call a lawyer and pack a few personal belongings of your husband's because I'm sure you won't be seeing him back home for a long time."

Dennis told the officers to make sure that the elderly couples was prevented from leaving the house as he joined the other officers in the back yard, including Chuck who was leading the team. The action in the back yard was sure and steady as the officers followed the dog, whose tail was wagging in anticipation of completing her job.

Lucy did one full tour of the yard before she returned to the south side, along the back fence. The yard was also facing south and Dennis was grateful, it would make things easier to dig. It was the middle of April and the ground would still be half-frozen. Lucy turned around several times over a dirt-filled section of the yard, whining softly as she wagged her tail in response to her handler, police officer, Max Grant.

Lucy was at her best when working alongside her partner, and by the way she was acting it was a sure thing a body would turn up soon. She stopped suddenly at the far end of the yard where a large section of the ground was ready for spring and summer flowers. From the look of the mound, the dirt had been maintained and well attended, a stark contrast to the condition of the home and the rest of the yard. Dennis was sure that this was the spot where he would find the final resting place of Brian's missing mother….a woman that the police had assumed had simply run off and left her husband and son.

A boy had grown up hating the cops and feeling betrayed by their lack of interest in solving the case, and in a final, desperate attempt had been driven to unforgivable ends to have a "just and final" ending to the disappearance of his mother. The young boy was now a man and serial killer, Brian Bentham.

"Dig here, boys!" Dennis directed four young officers with shovels in their hands.

The digging didn't take very long and the grave, even with the fresh dirt, was still very shallow. The first thing they saw was the decomposing edges of a yellow blanket. When they finally uncovered the full area of the grave, they pulled on both ends of the blanket, trying to dislodge its frozen edges. When they unrolled the blanket they were shocked to find not one, but two bodies wrapped in the blanket. Were they really lovers? If they weren't in life, they certainly were in death. It was difficult to untangle the bones that clung to one-another.

Dennis could tell from the position of the decomposed bodies that they had been forced to lie together just before their deaths, when two small-caliber bullets had been put through the front of their heads. It was over. The woman that had been the mother of one of the city's worst serial killers could be laid to rest. Dennis couldn't help but wonder if the police had done a better investigation three decades ago, if today's cops wouldn't have had to face the bloody accumulation of so many innocent victims. It was a calling card sent by a madman who had found a unique way to get the attention and justice his mother deserved.

"Mr. Bentham had better be sitting down when we read him his rights. I wouldn't want the bastard to keel over from shock. After all, it's been nearly three decades since he's had to face anyone about this crime"

* * * *

On the drive back, Dennis tried to put all the details together. Chuck sat beside him, and both were silent trying to tally up the details in their minds.

"So what do you think we have come up with so far?" Dennis turned to Chuck as he maneuvered through the late mid-afternoon traffic.

"Brian's father killed his mother. Not in a rage, but deliberately and willfully. While Brian was in school, his father shot his wife and her lover to death. He had obviously tricked Max Fielding into coming over, in order to kill them both at once. He then drove over to Fielding's home, and packed up Max's personal belongings to make it look like he had left town. The police had to follow up on the call from his boss, saying that he was missing. It was just what the old man wanted, to make it look like his wife and Max Fielding had run off together. The result was that the cops figured it was a missing persons cases rather than a murder. The killing was easy."

Chuck knew that Dennis had all of the answers, but it helped to clarify the facts for both of them if they did a narration of the case between the two of them. They were like a Sherlock Holmes and Watson.

"Then the elder Bentham wrapped his wife and Max up in a blanket and buried them in the back yard. He packed up the hairdresser's personal belongings and brought them back to the house."

A thorough search of the house had uncovered the secret hiding place under the stairs where Brian's mother's belongings had been kept hidden all of these years.

Chuck continued. "He had laid his wife and Max side by side. Max's belongings went with them. He then covered the couple up with dirt, laying a fresh layer of potting soil over their bodies. He planted flowers for the next thirty years, not in a tribute but to make sure the dirt was deep enough so that no one would discover the bodies. He made sure he planted flowers early enough that no one would disturb the flowerbed." Chuck turned the conjecture over to Dennis with a nod of his head.

"Brian must have known of his mother's murder all along. Whether he knew of Max or not, we can't be sure. But the painful years with his father, compounded by the murder of his beloved mother somehow created a serious shift in Brian's thinking. Brian's hatred of the cops for not solving his mother's disappearance, as well as the brutality of his father, finally drove him over the edge. It's ironic that the actions of one man affected two young boys who never met and the results were that both men grew up to be killers....all from the actions of one man." Dennis stroked his mustache in a familiar move.

"This is one for the shrinks to figure out and I for one am grateful it's over. For Brian it was a game, and win or lose, he figured out a way to win at all costs." Dennis was only thankful the price hadn't been paid with his daughter's lives, after all, blood is everything and family blood was the most sacred of all.

Epilogue

The sound of the organ was solemn, but full of promise as the wedding march was played and Shelley McPherson walked down the aisle to her beaming groom. The day was warm and the few guests that would witness the event were glad it was a casual wedding. Dennis stood next to Chuck who beamed beyond control, his smile stretched so far across his chubby face that Dennis was sure it would have made the rubber man proud. Dennis's wife Veronica was the only bridesmaid, and Dennis was Chuck's best man. Later they would gather for a summer barbecue in Dennis and Veronica's beautiful back yard. A few family and friends were all that were in attendance.

The spring and summer had been a time of renewal as the city of Chicago and the special police task force began to recover from the gruesome months that had proceeded.

Lexy and Bara sat in the front row of the church. The past few months had been especially hard on them. Everyone had worked very hard at keeping silent about the gruesome details of the crime. The use of the blood from the victims was known by only a few and they had vowed to keep it a secret till the end. They had circulated a rumor that the blood had been used for a satanic ritual. Brian had been adamant that his co-operation depended upon everyone protecting the loving, caring couple. To this day, Lexy and Bara never knew what the blood had been used for.

Although they found it unforgivable for Brian to do what he had done, once they found out what had happened to him as a child, they decide to stand behind him and were frequent visitors at the prison, bringing him what they could to make the rest of his life bearable. They found it hard to believe that he was at peace and that the conviction of his father and the vindication of his mother had in some way set him free, even though he would spend the rest of his life behind bars.

Shelley had been devastated by the news that Brian was the killer and finally sought some counseling. Chuck had stayed at her side throughout the ordeal and without a lot of convincing, finally let Shelley see that many of the problems with her romances were deliberate. She was avoiding a good and loving man based on an unreasonable fear. From the look on her lovely, heart-shaped face and the soft gleam in her eye, Dennis was sure Shelley had worked her problems out. Today was a positive step towards a future full of love and promise.

Shelley's daughter, Tiffany stood at her side. She would be giving her mother away today and the wink she gave Chuck along with the big grin was a sure sign that a happy family unit was now being forged.

Dennis stood tall. All in all it was a fine day. He looked forward to the barbecue that was to take place after the wedding. They had all decided to keep the menu simple. The usual trimmings, and of course they would love the marinade.....for the chicken.

THE END

ASHES
THE BIBLE KILLINGS
Coming in the fall of 2015

ROOKIES REVENGE
Coming the winter of 2016

POETIC JUSTICE
Coming in the spring of 2016

E*njoy the "Chicago Heat" series, featuring Detective Dennis Kortovich* E*njoy the first two chapters of Ashes, now released.*

ASHES
Chapter One

Jade pulled back the faded floral curtain of her second-story bedroom window and took one final look through the dreary, rain spattered day, at the official scene below. Her head was still pounding from the torrent of warm tears she had shed during the police investigation that morning. Until now she had been unable to find even a second to absorb the full repercussions of what happened. She thought of her mother's body, cold and lifeless at the bottom of the basement steps. Her mother was gone for good, and however bad things may have been before the accident, Jade knew they were about to become worse.

She heard the wail of the ambulance sirens as they took her mother away. Even the closed window couldn't muffle the sounds of the official voices as people on the driveway below discussed the tragic events. Jade could see several of the police officers shaking their heads as they continued to make notes. Neighbors stood on the sidewalk hoping for a snippet of information they could share with one another.

"Jade, what will we do now? I'm scared," Crystal whispered as she looked to Jade for comfort. "This is the worst thing that could have happened to us. How will we cope without Mother? He might be passed out in his chair now, but what will happen when he wakes up? You have to do something!" said Crystal, her voice becoming louder with a hint of hysteria.

"Don't worry Crystal, I'll think of something," Jade promised, trying to keep her voice even, not wanting to alarm her youngest sister Amber, who lay rocking on the other side of the bed with her legs curled under her tiny body.

Jade thought again of their mother's body at the bottom of the basement steps and turned away from the window. The sun was just beginning to pierce through the heavy, gray clouds, a beam of light shining through the window encircled Crystal and Amber, giving them both an angelic look. As if from nowhere, a song her mother used to sing came to her mind.

"Don't worry, be happy!"

Her mother Jewell had loved that song from the first moment she had heard it in the 'eighties. It had become Jewell's theme song, like a lifeline through the hellish days of her life with Sam. Amber, the youngest, held her baby blanket tightly in her small hand while she stroked her face with the other. She rocked back and forth in her usual way. It was at times like this that Jade was glad Amber was so different. Amber seemed untouched by the outside world; her inability to attach herself to anything real sheltered her from its harsh realities. Amber continued to rock while Jade and Crystal talked in hushed tones.

"I wish I could just be like Amber and not have to

think about anything!" Crystal moaned, moving closer to Amber, shaping her body into her younger sister's small form, finding comfort from her rocking motion.

Jade knew Amber would never be able to cry over their mother's death, a fact few children could comprehend. But Amber would be able to sense the mood of her two older sisters, and today's events would only make her draw further into herself. Jade always marveled at how a human being that looked so perfect on the outside could be so mis-wired on the inside. If it wasn't for Amber's remarkable talent you would believe there was very little going on inside her blank, but pretty head. Jade could never remember Amber making as much as a sound, even as a baby. Amber's eyes could fixate on an object while she rocked and stared for hours, an action that often made her father go ballistic. Jade loved her sister as she was.

Their father treated Amber like a freak. Even her musical gift didn't soften his hatred of his youngest daughter. However, when Amber played the piano the heavens would open up and wonderful music could be heard. Jade thought that if anyone was listening they would be transported to a place they could only dream of. This was when Jade knew her sister was perfect and that even in a moment of despair, there is hope. Jade walked over to the bed where Crystal made room for her, turning slightly so that she could face Jade while still gaining comfort from the rocking motion of Amber, who wiggled her bottom so that she would still have a connection to Crystal. Once Jade was curled up beside Crystal's warm body, they both pulled the worn old comforter up around their slim necks, making sure Amber was covered in the process. The room was warm with the window closed, but as was often the case, the comforter was more for emotional reassurance than real warmth. It also helped to soothe the gripping chill deep in the pits of their stomachs, as the two girls faced the future.

Crystal finally said what Jade was afraid to say. "You know with Mom gone we will never be able to live with Dad and survive."

To live with Sam you needed all the skill and guts you could muster. It was always Crystal, the realistic one, who would meet the challenge head on. The years spent with their brutal father made her the one sister most likely to survive. They say middle children are like that and Crystal certainly fit the mold. Once she got a hold of something, she seldom let go or backed down.

"I don't see how we can make it without Mom. She was the only one that could handle Dad and without her, we will suffer a lot more than we already have," Crystal said, a shutter running through her body at the thought of what her father was capable of.

She didn't say more. She didn't have to. It was the nightmare that Jade had been living since she had gone through puberty. It was bad enough that Jade always had to be careful never to be alone with her father, but she also worried about the possibility of future abuse when Crystal started to develop and blossom into a pretty young woman, and then there was Amber. Jade knew Crystal sensed the danger their dad posed and had done everything to be as unattractive as possible. It was her way of hiding the fact that she was maturing. Crystal would soon turn nineteen, but she looked no older than thirteen or fourteen. Sensing her father's sick looks made Jade shudder and she knew Crystal would fall prey to his evil taunts and touches that were unbearable.

"I know, but don't worry. I promise I won't let anything happen to you or Amber." Jade reached over and squeezed her sister's hand. Trying to calm her own fears, she hoped it would never come to this, but now she knew that Crystal was right. They would have to deal with their father, but how? Jade put her trembling hand under her head and rested on her elbow. She looked over Crystal's body to Amber, who continued to rock, unaware of what was happening.

"Try and get some sleep because we need all of our strength," Jade said, pushing back her tears.

Jade knew Crystal needed reassuring. In a different environment Crystal would have been an outgoing, demanding child, but with Samuel Walker as a father, she was sullen and angry. The way she dressed said it all; black, black, and blacker.

Lips, eyes, even strands of her soft copper hair were covered in a washable black dye. Jade wasn't sure if it was just a disguise or a "Goth" stage, or if Crystal was deliberately trying to look as glum and dark as she felt. So far it seemed to have worked. Sam simply scowled at Crystal and moved away from her as much as possible. He was always afraid of the things he didn't understand. Jade turned back toward Crystal, cuddling into her small warm body, and the fresh, baby powder scent of Crystal's odor filled her nostrils. Jade liked the rocking motion. Both girls often found they slept better if they let Amber rock them both to sleep.

After a while Jade moved away from Crystal who was now motionless, having finally fallen asleep. She pulled the comforter further up under her chin. She loved the smooth feeling of the worn old comforter. It smelled clean and fresh the way laundry did for the first few hours after a wash. It was one of the last things her mother had touched before the accident and Jade was sure she could smell her mother's clean, floral scent on the comforter. Her thoughts of her mother brought a fresh rush of warm tears to her face. Her dear, sweet mother, Jade had never heard Jewell speak a harsh word toward anyone, not even Sam.

Jewell had stopped loving Sam years ago, but she bore the burden of Sam with silence. She had tried to leave once, and the imprint of the violence she bore was still visible on her hand when she died. Leaving wasn't an option; Sam took no prisoners. Jewell had learned to squeeze what joy she could out of each day and the love she had for her children. Jade knew it was Jewell's fear of what Sam would do to the girls if she were to step out of line that kept her with him. Now Jewell was gone and Jade would make a decision about her sisters' and her futures. She was the oldest and the care of her sisters would be her burden.

Jade tried to hold back the stream of tears that ran down the side of her face into her ear, while a few drops found their way to her pillow, which would soon be soaked. *Oh well, these tears won't be the last,* she thought. They would join the thousands of other tears she had cried during her brutal years with her father. What was she going to do? She had to find a way to protect her sisters and get away from her father. Samuel Walker was supposed to protect and care for Jade and her sisters. Instead Sam was a monster who kept an iron hand on his family, and only the soft, protective touch of Jewell had prevented their father from doing the unforgivable.

It had been Jewell's job to keep her daughters safe, at least as much as possible. It had taken all of her wit and cunning to keep Sam's attention on anything but the girls. Now, without Jewell, it would be impossible for Jade to continue. Jewell had done all she could to protect them. In the end even she didn't survive. Jade knew she and her sisters were not safe. She took one final ragged breath and hoped that the evening would bring her some peace, at least as long as Sam was passed out. Memories of the day's events tumbled through her brain, and thoughts of Detective Dennis Kortovich kept flashing before her mind's eye. Thank God Dennis had arrived first. It had made what had happened to Jewell and the horror of the moment so much easier.

Chapter Two

Detective Dennis Kortovich sat back in his old, but comfortable swivel chair, behind a large, functional desk. He had spent the last few hours updating several files. Dennis was noted for his attention to detail. At a crime scene his ability to note even the smallest detail was a marvel, even to the other successful detectives. Dennis's ability to recall statistical data in forensics, as well as places, names, and dates, even several years after a case was closed made him valuable to his colleagues. The motto, "When in doubt, ask Kortovich," made his partners over the years feel privileged. If you were lucky enough to get on a team with Dennis, your work would be noticed by the brass.

Dennis looked at the pictures above his desk, a slow smile crossing his face as he remembered when they had been taken. Dressed in full uniform, he and another man were shaking hands with the mayor; big Cheshire grins were spread on their faces. Dennis and his partner, Chuck O'Brien, had been given their first award together. Many more had followed, but this had been their first case and the beginning of a great friendship. Chuck, with his off-the-wall sense of humor had made the past several years more enjoyable.

Hearing someone approach, Dennis turned around. He knew who it was even before the man appeared in the doorway of his office. Partnerships were like marriages; after a while you got used to each other and once in a while you became so in tune you could finish each other's sentences. Dennis knew the lumbering footsteps could only belong to one person, his partner, Chuck O'Brien.

"What's up?" Chuck asked as he sat down across from Dennis trying unsuccessfully to cross his short, chubby legs. Dennis noticed he had a donut in one hand and a coffee in the other.

"We've been given an immediate assignment; it's Judge Switzer's daughter. She's gone missing." Dennis indicated a file that sat in front of Chuck. "He has asked for us. The superintendent agreed to assign us to this case at the judge's request. We're to be at his home in less than an hour." Dennis grabbed his jacket from the back of his chair while he continued to fill Chuck in on the details of the case.

Chuck and Dennis were usually involved in homicide cases known as heaters; the kind of cases that caused the press or the higher-ups to put unusual pressure on the police department. The latest case had involved a serial killer, and there had been more slayings within six months, other than in drug-wars, than at any other time. But when the request came from the superintendent, you didn't argue.

Judge Switzer was one of the most respected judges on the bench. Most of the police force loved having him preside over their cases. For those lucky enough to have him rule on the case, they were assured fair and impartial treatment.

"Judge Switzer's kid can't be more than fourteen or fifteen. He's nuts about her," Chuck said.

Dennis remembered meeting the judge's daughter at a birthday party the judge had thrown for his wife's fiftieth birthday. She was the youngest of four children, the only daughter. All of the boys were at least twenty and Mandy, his only girl, was the apple of her daddy's eye.

"How long has she been missing?" Chuck began to gulp down his coffee and make short work of his donut.

"Just overnight, but the family is beside themselves," Dennis responded.

"Whatever happened to the twenty-four hour policy before we become involved?" Chuck stood, throwing his empty cup into the wastebasket beside Dennis's desk.

"Policy is like an old pair of shorts, it gets changed whenever things get too uncomfortable or start to stink. In this city you know almost everything is done on the 'I'll scratch your back, if you scratch mine bullshit.' That may not seem fair, but that's the way things are sometimes. The rich and the powerful make great media. If the judge's daughter doesn't show up in the next twenty-four hours, her disappearance will make headlines and all hell will break loose. Let's hope she just has a boyfriend somewhere and spent the night out gazing at the stars." Dennis ran his hand over his moustache as he finished his summation.

He looked up at the clock on his office wall, a gift from his daughters for his fiftieth birthday. The face of the clock had a picture of Dick Tracy, the famous cartoon detective. Dennis felt a shiver run down his spine at the thought of anything happening to one of his daughters. He knew that the Switzer family would be going crazy at the thought of anything happening to Mandy.

"You know if anything goes wrong with this case it will be our asses on the line," Chuck stated. "I hate anything political, and this has all the signs of a suicide mission."

Dennis gave Chuck a nod of agreement as he wiped the crumbs from his desk; the remnants of Chuck's donut.

"This is what happens when you're good." Dennis smiled.

Chuck lacked the same faith in their ability to navigate murky waters, but he knew his partner was right. This would be a tricky case. The Superintendent of Police wanted to talk to Dennis and Chuck first. It would be embarrassing if a regular team of detectives took the case and the press found out. Dennis and Chuck were used to the media and they would be able to side-step any questions until there were more answers. A phone conference had been set up. They would leave soon after the call had been made. Seconds after the first ring, Dennis picked up the phone. It was the superintendent.

"I'm at the judge's home now. I think you two had better handle things as if it's well past the twenty-four hour rule. I'll take any flack if the press finds out," the superintendent stated.

"Is there anything you need us to know before we get there?"

"Only that you need to get this solved before the press find out. I'm counting on you to get the job done."

After a few more instructions Dennis hung up the phone, a look of angst on his face. He hated the politics of the job, and being told he had to solve a case on a short timeline made him feel a tightening in his chest. All a man could do was his best. Would his best be good enough? A young girl's life counted on it.

"If she is out drinking and having a little fling and then turns up all starry-eyed, the press will have a field day. Then again, if she turns up dead, the superintendent will demand our heads." Dennis gave one last look around his office as he continued his summation. "The superintendent believes the judge, who says his daughter would never stay out all night. Most parents think that they know their kids. I hope the judge is right."

The drive to the Switzer home gave both men a chance to mull the case over. The judge lived in an upscale suburb called Oak Park; the home was on North Oak Park Blvd. Frank Lloyd Wright had designed many of the homes and the area had become a tourist destination for many would-be architects.

As one of America's most famous architects, Lloyd Wright had spent over twenty years making this area a landmark of quality home design at the turn of the century. It was still a great place to go for a Sunday drive. Dennis maneuvered his car through the elegant entrance of the estates. This was a wealthy area and most of the homes were situated on a full acre of well-manicured lawn. The judge lived in the largest house in the historic landmark section; an example of Wright's classic Prairie style. Powerful limestone windowsills and overhanging roof lines, along with the horizontal layout exemplified Wright's quest to reflect America's Midwest.

The circular driveway wound past an impressive entrance. The flair and style of a Latin inscription had been carved into the door by a finely skilled craftsman, reminiscent of old money. Dennis knew the inscription translated into "Truth and Honor" a befitting motto for the judge who was known to live by those two simple words.

Chuck was the first one to reach the front door, Dennis arriving at his side. A tall, thin woman, well past seventy greeted them with a soft smile. She was obviously once a great beauty and carried herself with regal bearing. Her expensive Chanel Suit was a soft, pearl white, with contrasting gold and black braid running along its edge. Her slim legs were in nylons, and considering how hot the day was, her attire was very formal. But they both knew that this breed of woman wouldn't be caught dead with bare legs, no matter how hot the day. The family was definitely old money, which demanded refinement and good manners.

"Detective Kortovich and Detective O'Brien." She held out her well-manicured hand as she spoke. "Come in, we've been expecting you."

Dennis and Chuck were ushered into a large, elegant entranceway. Deep oak paneling encompassed the foyer, and a circular staircase led up to a second floor that was paneled in an off-white oak with deep oak wainscoting adding to the richness of the wood. The décor matched the nature of the owner; warm and tasteful. The tall woman slowed before she ushered them into the judge's study.

"I'm Marsha Phillip, Lena Switzer's mother. I came over as soon as I heard Mandy was missing." Marsha lowered her voice and turned her beautiful eyes towards the detectives. "We're all beside ourselves with worry. I've heard from the superintendent that you two are the best.

Please help us. Mandy is our world and she would never stay out all night."

She turned and opened the door to the library once she finished her plea for help. Superintendent Tom Holland greeted Dennis and Chuck. He was a tall man in his late fifties. His thick head of dark, wavy hair framed an intelligent face that showed little of what he felt or thought. There had been a time that both Dennis and Chuck had respected Tom Holland, but lately it seemed he was more a politician than a cop. Most of the other officers felt he was no longer watching their backs. Maybe that was the way it was when you got to the top. You forgot where you came from and how you got there. Dennis was aware that some of the more senior officers were suffering from a bad taste in their mouths from the sour grapes they kept feeding on. It had become a divisive issue in the department, but Dennis and Chuck preferred to keep their opinions to themselves.

Tom Holland was an old friend of the judge's, so when Mandy hadn't come home the night before, Judge Switzer had called him, knowing that he could be trusted to keep things quiet and to bring in the very best to find Mandy.

As soon as Chuck and Dennis were seated Dennis asked, "Judge, can you give us some of the details?"

Judge Switzer spoke with a cool detachment, but Dennis could tell from the pain on his face and the fear in his eyes that it was taking all he had to give the coolly delivered report. "Mandy spent the early part of the evening at a rave with several friends. The rave was just off of Clark Street, a part of town you wouldn't expect to find a proper young woman, but we trusted Mandy's judgment. At well after six a.m. when we still hadn't heard from her, we began calling her friends. No one had seen her since about two a.m. One of her friends, a young man, said he thought she had gone out of the club alone to get some fresh air. He hasn't seen her since. I'm afraid I have few other details at this point. We thought it was best to call in expert help before we let too much time pass." Judge Switzer's voice remained steady. "I apologize for the political maneuvering, but I'm sure you understand why I want you two, and the superintendent to handle this situation."

A familiar hand was thrust forward giving a warm and thankful handshake to both men, a forgotten nicety, in the rush to report the events. Judge Switzer was a tall elegant man who wore his wealth and position with a simple acceptance of his position. Dennis had always thought Phillip Switzer looked like the James Bond type, minus the English accent. He was tall, slim, and dark. Phillip Switzer's bright blue eyes seemed to see all of life, finding what he saw most amusing. His colleagues were both his detractors and advocates. The judge was known to be obsessed with finding the truth, and relating the facts to the law.

His obsession could drive a legal mind crazy, especially if a lawyer ever decided to argue a case with Judge Switzer, without doing a ton of research first. Switzer was a detail guy and it could send you raving and ranting after spending any time arguing with him. He had a way of tying his opponent into a mental knot, but you had to respect his mind and his search for the truth.

Judge Switzer stood to introduce his wife Lena, who had been sitting by the window in a large, winged-back chair. She obviously got her looks from her mother. Tall, at least five foot eleven inches, fashionably thin, and graceful, her fine-featured face was surrounded by an abundance of rich, shiny, auburn hair. Her dark, piercing blue eyes, framed by dark lashes, were red rimmed from crying. Her worry over Mandy's disappearance was obvious on her face.

Dennis and Chuck sat back down after the formal introduction on the big, leather chairs that were drawn up in front of a large, unlit fireplace. The day was hot, a summer storm on the horizon. She gave a brief smile and pushed a list towards Dennis. "You will need this," she whispered softly, as she gave Dennis a list of all of Mandy's friends as well as a recent photo.

"We drove Mandy to the rave at midnight. I know that seems late to be letting a fifteen-year-old out, but Mandy is very responsible and the raves are alcohol free. Mandy is aware of many of the drugs that are available and the troubles they can cause. She was even open to us searching her room at any time and if need be, she would allow us to do drug testing," Lena stated, her eyes pleading. "I hope you can understand what it's like to be the wife of a judge and have a teenage daughter. I hear so much about crime and drug abuse, my first instinct is to just lock my daughter up in her room and not let her out until she's twenty-one. But that wouldn't teach her how to handle the choices she will have to make in the kind of world we live in." Lena's deep, but now shaky voice reflected her fears.

"I have two daughters, they're now in their twenties, but it was hard for me too," Dennis reassured her. "Go on."

"We were to pick her up at six this morning but she

wasn't there. She has a cell phone if she wants to go sooner and she knew we would be only too willing to pick her up if she wanted to leave at any time. When we didn't get a call from her, we went to the prearranged spot – she wasn't there. However often we tried her cell, there was no answer. I asked whoever was lingering behind if they had seen her. There was only one boy who remembered seeing her somewhere around two a.m. After that he says he never saw her again. His name is Jackson Page. I took his cell number and home address. He said he would ask around and see if anyone could remember seeing Mandy after that time," Lena said, handing a piece of paper over to Chuck who seemed to be uncomfortable in the deep, leather chair.

"I've made a list of all of Mandy's friends, both in school and out. We belong to the Shore-Side Country Club and I've also made a list of everyone she knows there too." Lena gave Chuck a second list and handed Dennis a picture.

Dennis looked down at the 8x10 picture of Mandy. The girl in the picture was a pretty, young woman with bright, blue eyes and a sweet smile. Long, soft copper curls surrounded an oval face that held the same intelligent look of her father and the beauty of her mother.

"I've put her height and weight, as well as what she was wearing on the back of this photo," Lena Switzer said, as she indicated the information. "She takes after my maternal grandmother when it comes to stature, not me," Lena noted wistfully. "She's not very tall, something she bemoans regularly. She is five feet, two inches and weighs about one hundred ten pounds. She was wearing 'hip hugger' jeans and a tank top with spaghetti straps, in coral and green. She wore sandals. I know it sounds like she is dressed scantily, but it's the way girls dress nowadays." Lena looked sheepish.

"I assure you she hasn't any tattoos or piercings. We say no to most things. But going to the raves, meeting up with her friends, and dancing all night is the one thing we relented on. She loves to dance. Now I feel like it's my fault." Lena suddenly started to cry.

Judge Switzer was standing next to Lena when she started to weep; tears welling up in his eyes as well. "Don't say that sweetheart. Mandy is a responsible girl. We can't protect her from the world. She has to have a chance to be with her friends. We can't blame ourselves," he said as he put his arms around his wife.

Dennis looked at the way the family seemed to be handling the situation. He dreaded having to ask the next questions. And although he believed the judge about how responsible Mandy was, it was still his duty to ask all of the questions; even the tough ones. "Is there any way Mandy would have met up with a special young man and have been talked into leaving?" Dennis asked, looking the judge in the eye.

The judge responded, "I know you must hear this all of the time, but Mandy knows that all of her privileges depend on her doing what she says she will do. She would never take off with a boy. The only thing that concerns Lena and me is that maybe someone slipped something into her Coke. We told her to never leave her drink unattended because of the date-rape drugs. She promised that she would drink a fresh Coke if she felt someone else might have access to it."

"Is Mandy happy at home?" Dennis asked; knowing it

was a question that had to be asked.

"I can understand you having to ask these kinds of questions," Phillip Switzer said as he stood, his wife standing up along with him. "Let us take you to Mandy's room. She has a diary. I've never read it, but at times like this, we need you to see what kind of girl she is. If there is anything that you have to know about our family and Mandy's feeling about us, it will be there."

Lena Switzer led Dennis up the stairs to Mandy's room; Phillip Switzer following close behind. Chuck stayed with the superintendent to go over the procedures he would like Dennis and Chuck to follow.

"This is her room. Look through anything you like. Mandy keeps her diary in the top drawer of the desk. She also has a bunch of letters and notes from her friends in that small trunk at the foot of her bed. I'll leave you alone. It's hard for me to be here, not knowing what has happened to my daughter," Lena said, choking back a second round of tears.

Judge Switzer kissed his wife tenderly as she passed. Lena gave him a tearful hug and quickly left the men standing in Mandy's room.

"My wife is a strong and intelligent woman. She knows what happens when young girls go missing. It's hard for her not to tap into her worst fears." Judge Switzer went over to the south wall of Mandy's room where a series of pictures hung in expensive frames. He took one from the wall, holding it tenderly in his hands. "She is very special. Our lives would be intolerable without her. Find her for us." Judge Switzer replaced the picture on the wall and turned on his heels, leaving the room without another word. Dennis knew it was all beginning to be too much for the judge.

Mandy's room was tastefully decorated in yellow and mauve, playful, but not too young. In the center of the room a queen-size bed with a grape-colored canopy dominated the space. Three-tiered bed tables reaching midway up the wall flanked either side of the bed. Matching lamps sat on the top of each table with a clock radio on one side and a gilded framed picture on the other. The picture was of the family; Lena, Phillip, Mandy, and three strapping young men, her brothers. They looked like a happy, well-adjusted family. But as Dennis knew, a good investigator must consider all family members as potential suspects. Mandy's diary would give him a better impression, one way or the other. He pulled the white, leather-bound book from the desk drawer.

As he read through it, he began to laugh. Many of the entries reminded him of his youngest daughter Katrina. Katrina was the spunky, quick-tempered one in his family. She had an opinion on everything, as only the young can, but as his wife was finding out, Trina was very wise and deep beyond her years. The problem between his wife and his daughter was that they both wanted control.

Mandy seemed to be cut from the same cloth. – So and so is stupid – This one thinks too much of herself – That teacher is an ass – This boy is a jerk…another might be all right if he "dressed differently and had better shoes," and so on and so on. Mandy had a few crushes; she liked to keep her options open. Most of the entries about her parents seemed to be nothing more than the usual notations about them not being hip enough. Mandy felt it was the "square, moneyed world" her parents lived in. She felt that if her mother were to ever wear jeans or a

T-shirt, like some of the other mothers, she would faint.

Dennis thought if the only complaint a teenager had about her parents was the way they dressed, that wouldn't be motive to run away. He put away the diary. It didn't reveal any conflict or discontent. Not among her family, friends, or even teachers. He decided he would start with the list her parents had given him. Good old-fashioned detective work. Today being Saturday, the school was closed. He and Chuck would start with the friends that had seen her at the rave and would hope for a lead from there. He came down the stairs just as Marsha Phillip; Lena's mother was coming up.

"I was just coming to find you, Detective," she said. "We are just having some coffee and warm croissants and wondered if you would like to join us."

"No thank you, I'll wait until lunch."

As Dennis returned to the library, Chuck was gulping down the last of his coffee, a half-eaten croissant still in his chubby hand. Chuck had a sheepish look on his round face. Dennis knew he had enjoyed a donut for breakfast and that the croissant would only add to Chuck's weight problem. He gave his partner a big smile. Chuck didn't see it as a problem, but Shelley, Chuck's wife would give him hell if she found out.

As Chuck stood, wiping whipped cream from the corner of his mouth, he held out his hand for one last farewell. Dennis joined in the hand-shaking, letting Chuck close out the meeting.

"We will be on this case with as much discretion as we can, but if we need to we may have to put a task force together. If we do, we won't be able to keep it from the press. So we will handle this list first, and see what we come up with. Depending on the time that Mandy has gone missing, every hour that passes puts more pressure on the case. That is when we can make a decision about other detectives helping on the case. We may even have to appeal to the public," Chuck said softly, wanting the family and judge to know the steps that would be taken to get Mandy back.

After providing assurances and promises, Dennis and Chuck made their way to the car. From the front window, Lena Switzer stared out at the detectives. The strained look on her face told Dennis of the pain that would come if Mandy weren't found soon.

CPSIA information can be obtained
at www.ICGtesting.com
Printed in the USA
LVHW021917270119
605446LV00011B/40/P

9 781460 264065